The Bad Mothers' Bookclub

To all the Bad Mothers
And to Rhian, Catherine and Nikki who are not bad at all.

The Bad Mothers' Bookclub

Keris Stainton

First published in Great Britain in 2019 by Trapeze,
This paperback edition published in 2020 by Trapeze,
an imprint of The Orion Publishing Group Ltd
Carmelite House, 50 Victoria Embankment,
London EC4Y 0DZ

An Hachette UK company

1 3 5 7 9 10 8 6 4 2

A CIP catalogue record for this book is
available from the British Library.

ISBN (mass market paperback) 978 1 4091 7586 5

Typeset by Born Group

Printed and bound in Great Britain by Clays Ltd, Elcograf S.p.A.

www.orionbooks.co.uk

Prologue

'Please leave,' Jools said, pink patches appearing high on her cheeks. 'Now.'

'Seriously?' Emma asked.

'This really isn't working out,' Jools said, wincing as she bent down to pick up one of her small daughters, who was standing in the doorway.

'Right,' Emma said. She couldn't bear to look at the other women, all of whom had gone silent since Jools had first spoken. She stood up, the backs of her thighs making a ripping noise as she peeled them off the leather sofa. She turned back for her coat – catching Maggie's widened eyes – before remembering she hadn't brought one, and then followed Jools down the hall to the front door.

'I'll see you at school, I guess—' Emma said, as she stepped outside, and then jumped as the door slammed behind her.

It was only when she reached the main road that Emma realised she'd left this month's book behind.

Chapter One

Three months earlier

'Have you got my wallet?' Paul asked, as he opened one of the kitchen drawers. And then a cupboard. And then flicked the kettle on.

'Why would I have your wallet?' Emma replied, rummaging through a cupboard for a clean Tupperware box for Ruby's sandwiches.

'I don't know. Maybe you took it to pay the milkman or something,' Paul said. He took his chrome travel mug off the draining board and dropped a teabag in.

'We've never even had a milkman,' Emma said. 'Ever.' She pulled out a box, causing an array of melamine plates, novelty eggcups and – inexplicably – a pair of gardening gloves, to fall onto the floor at her feet. No lid for the box though.

'God, I don't know! Window cleaner then. Can you look for it at least? I haven't got time. If I don't hit the tunnel by—'

'Eight thirty, I know,' Emma said. They'd had this conversation pretty much every morning for the past month, since they'd moved to West Kirby, and Paul had transferred to the Liverpool office of the sports agency he worked for. If he didn't get to the tunnel by eight thirty, he'd get stuck behind the buses on the A59 and well . . . Emma had no idea what would happen, since Paul never bothered with travel updates when he got home from work in the evenings, preferring to fall asleep in front of the TV instead. Today's commute would be even worse because the schools were going back after the summer holidays. But Emma was far more concerned about Ruby and Sam starting at their new school for the first time than Paul finding his wallet and hitting the tunnel before the traffic.

She yanked a lid out from behind a set of kitchen scales. If it didn't fit, Ruby was going to have to have her sandwiches in foil and like it.

'I'll go and look now,' she told Paul. 'Keep your knickers on.'

'Daddy's got *knickers* on?!' Sam said, from the hallway.

'Sam!' Emma said, seeing him sitting in the middle of the stripy runner in his pyjamas, tiny legs spread out in a V with what looked like a hundred quid's worth of Lego piled up between them. 'What the f—' She walked over to him, kicking a pair of trainers out of the way. 'I mean, what are you doing?! I left you getting dressed! You had one leg in your school trousers! We don't want to be late on your first day, do we?'

Sam looked up at her, his blue eyes wide.

Emma crouched down, her knees cracking. 'What happened, man?'

'I just thought . . .' Sam said, placing a red brick on top of a tower of other red bricks. 'I thought maybe I could stay here? I need to finish this tower. For my job.'

'For your job,' Emma said. 'What job's that?'

'Lego tower builder,' Sam replied.

Emma hooked her hands under his arms and hoiked him to his feet as he squealed with indignation. 'Go and get dressed, right now.'

'If I do, will you buy me more Lego today?'

'If you don't, you might find all your Lego in the bin when you get home.'

'You wouldn't do that,' Sam said, stopping on the bottom step and turning back to grin at her.

'Try me,' Emma said. But they both knew she wouldn't. Her kids had learned pretty early on that all her threats were empty. She wasn't proud.

'I'm dressed already!' Eight-year-old Ruby called from the front room.

'I know you are, darling,' Emma said. 'Well done.'

Ruby had actually been looking forward to starting a new school and making new friends. Emma got it. She had hoped that they'd meet people over the summer when they arrived in West Kirby, but it just hadn't happened. Both she and Ruby had made good friends at the school gates back in London, so she was keeping her fingers crossed for the same happening here.

'Em?' Paul yelled from the kitchen, the scent of burned toast drifting down the hall. 'Wallet?'

Emma had wanted her bedroom (it was Paul's too of course, but she preferred to think of it as hers) to be an oasis of calm and romance, maybe sexiness on a Friday night, if they weren't too tired (or drunk), but the raspberry carpet was covered in Lego and tiny cars, a row of teddies and dolls lined the wide window ledge blocking the view of the marina, and Sam had drawn – in permanent marker – a series of increasingly large and detailed penises across the top of the chest of drawers. Emma quite liked them if she was honest – they were oddly cheery. Unlike Paul's lately . . .

Kicking detritus out of the way, and briefly catching her foot in the strap of one of her bras – she really needed to tidy up once she'd dropped the kids off – Emma rounded the bed to Paul's bedside table, which was, as always, piled high with magazines and books and half-drunk cups of tea. Her husband almost always put his wallet on his bedside table, it almost always fell down the back, and for some reason, he was almost always utterly incapable of remembering this.

Kneeling at the side of the bed, Emma reached underneath the bedside table, her fingers immediately brushing against the leather wallet, before her knuckles knocked against something else, something plastic. She slid the wallet out, then reached back for the plastic thing. It was a small pump dispenser. Unmarked. The liquid inside was clear. Emma held it in the palm of her hand and frowned at it in confusion until she suddenly realised: lube. It was lube. Her husband had lube on his side of the bed. And he wasn't using it with her. She stared at it for a couple of seconds, blinking. She didn't have time for this now – they had to get going or they'd be late. She'd have to think about it later.

'Oh good,' Paul said when Emma got back downstairs. He was waiting for her by the front door, his jacket on, the battered leather satchel he used as a briefcase in his hand. Emma was always a little disappointed on a Monday morning when Paul was clean-shaven, his hair neat. She thought he looked hotter when he was a little rougher at the weekends.

He reached out for the wallet, but Emma jerked her arm back before he could take it.

'Emma,' Paul said, almost rolling his eyes but stopping himself just in time. 'I'm already late.'

'And I just went upstairs and found your wallet in the same place you always lose it,' Emma said.

Alongside your lube, she wanted to add, but didn't. Emma had kicked it back under the bed.

Out of sight, out of mind.

In theory.

She was definitely going to think about it later.

'I'm very grateful,' Paul said, holding his hand out again.

'What else do you say?' Emma said. She knew she should just give it to him, knew she was being annoying, but she'd let it go too far now and she wasn't going to back down until he thanked her.

'For fuck's sake,' Paul said. He had that little line between his eyebrows that Emma used to stroke with her finger to make him smile. Now she kind of wanted to poke it. Maybe with a fork.

'Nope. Not that.'

'I need to go!' He threw his satchel over his shoulder, straightening his suit jacket underneath, his shoulders rolling back.

Emma stared at him. The morning light slanting through the glass at the top of the front door shone on his face. He looked weary and the fight went out of Emma as quickly as it had appeared.

'Then go.' Emma said, handing him the wallet.

'Thank you,' Paul said, shortly. 'OK? Happy now?'

Emma shrugged. 'Not really.'

Paul opened the door, both of them wincing as the wood squealed against the Victorian tile.

'I might be late,' Paul said, pausing with his hand on the door.

'OK.' Emma took a couple of steps down the hall, before stopping and turning back. 'Paul?'

He turned, 'Hmm?'

Emma stepped up to him and curled a hand around his neck, before pushing herself up on tiptoes to kiss him on the mouth. 'Have a good day.'

Paul smiled, licking his bottom lip, eyes crinkling at the corners. 'Thanks. You too.'

*

'Wow,' Matt said when his wife Jools walked into the kitchen. 'You look hot as hell.'

'Shut up,' she said, grinning at him, and stopping to press a kiss to his temple.

He wrapped his arms around her waist and kissed her neck. 'I mean it – those trousers! Are you doing the school run or going on a hot date?'

'It's a new year! There'll be new people. I have to look good.' She untangled his arms and crossed the kitchen to pour herself a coffee from the pot the nanny, Sofia, put on each morning before Jools got up.

'You look pretty, Mummy,' Jools and Matt's eight-year-old daughter, Violet, said, looking up from the porridge she was poking around her bowl. 'I like your lipstick.'

'Thank you, baby,' Jools said, taking her coffee over to the table and sitting next to Matt.

'Want something to eat?' Matt asked her. 'I can make more porridge. Or toast?'

'I'm fine, thanks,' Jools said. 'I'll just have some fruit in a bit.'

'You should eat,' Matt said, his voice low.

Jools smiled brightly at him. 'I will. Later. I just want coffee now. Don't worry.' She turned to her two oldest daughters. 'Are you excited about school?'

Both girls looked at her with equally unimpressed expressions and she and Matt laughed.

'You know you'll love it when you get there,' Jools said, pushing her chair back and standing. 'Have you got everything you need?'

'Sofia's looking for my reading book,' Violet said.

Jools glanced up at the clock above the French doors. 'Too late for that now. We need to go. Come on! Shoes and coats on.'

'Can I come?' their youngest, Eden, asked.

'I thought you were going to stay here with me,' Matt said. 'Keep me company before I have to go to training.'

Eden nodded, curling her hair around her finger. 'You said I could have an ice lolly.'

Matt groaned. 'That was meant to be a secret!'

Eden giggled and her two sisters rolled their eyes. They both knew there was no way either of them would be allowed an ice lolly before school anyway.

'Ready?' Jools called from the hall, where she was checking her make-up and running her fingers through her long blonde hair. She was going to miss having the girls at home, but she couldn't say she wasn't ready for them to go back. She had things she needed to do that would be much easier without them around.

'Ready,' the girls said, joining her at the door.

'I can't find Puppy,' Amy said from the kitchen doorway.

Maggie was standing next to the kettle, the radio playing quietly in the background, a mug of tea cradled in her hands.

'There's one in the conservatory,' Maggie said, gesturing across the dining room to the extension they'd added after Amy was born.

'I don't want that one. I want the one we took to Whitby.'

Maggie sighed. 'Love. They're all the same. And we need to go.'

Amy had been almost permanently attached to a soft puppy toy since she was a toddler. Once they thought they'd lost it so Maggie had bought another. And then Amy had asked for another and now, somehow, she had about thirty.

'I'm not going without Puppy.' Amy folded her arms, staring at her mum across the kitchen.

'Fine.' Maggie poured her tea down the sink, turned off the radio, and headed up the stairs to Amy's room to hold up various puppies until Amy told her which one was the right one. She wasn't that keen about going to school anyway. She'd enjoyed the summer with her daughter. Jim, her husband, had been working on a school redevelopment and had barely been around, so she and Amy had eaten pizza on the beach, visited various Liverpool museums, and watched films in bed together with a bowl of popcorn.

'That one!' Amy shouted, reaching over and pulling the dog out of her mum's hands.

Now Jim's contract was done, Amy was going back to school, and everything was going back to normal.

Maggie was dreading it.

Chapter Two

By the time Emma had got Sam dressed and found his book bag (she'd been certain she'd put it by the front door the night before) and then his shoes and his coat, and Ruby's coat, and her own, it had been too late to walk. The school was only about ten minutes away, along the prom and up the side of the park, but Emma really didn't want to be late on their first day and so she'd ushered the kids into the car and turned up onto the main road, thinking – incorrectly, as it turned out – that it would be less busy.

'Oh for fuck's sake,' she muttered as the car in front let someone else out of a side street. 'You let out one person and then you move along. Everyone knows that.'

'Are we going to be late?' Ruby asked.

Emma glanced in the rear-view mirror. Her daughter was staring out of the window, but Emma could tell by the set of her jaw that she was starting to get anxious. Ruby hated being late for anything, but she really hated being late for school.

'No, darling,' Emma said. 'It'll be fine. They probably won't go in straight away on the first day anyway.'

'So we *are* going to be late!'

'We shouldn't be,' Emma said, adding, 'As long as this absolute tool stops letting every bastard out in front of us,' under her breath.

Right on cue, the car in front pulled forward and even though Emma knew it was theoretically her turn to let someone out, she pulled forward too. It was every woman for herself on the school run, that was just a fact.

Turning onto the road that the school was on, Emma spotted a parking space right up near the gate. God only knew how, because the rest of the road was crammed. She reversed into the space and turned between the seats to smile at Ruby and Sam. 'See! Plenty of time.'

She jumped as someone knocked on the window. Buddy the dog, who had been curled up in the passenger footwell, barked.

'Hi,' Emma said, rolling down her window and smiling at the nervous-looking woman standing there. She had a baby strapped to her chest and Emma could see something that looked like rusk crusted behind its right ear.

'You can't park here,' the woman said.

Emma looked past her for a sign she'd missed. There hadn't been anything painted on the road, she was almost sure.

'No?' Emma asked. 'Why not?'

The woman straightened up and arched backwards, both hands pressing into the small of her back. A child – presumably her child – stared at Emma, unsmiling.

'Sorry,' the woman said, leaning down again to look at Emma. 'It's reserved.'

'Oh! Sorry. God. I didn't see the sign.' The woman stepped back as Emma opened the door.

'Oh no, there isn't one. Everyone just knows.'

'Right,' Emma said, opening Ruby's door. 'OK. Thanks for letting me know. I won't park here again. It's our first day, so we didn't—'

'You need to move,' the woman said. 'You can park out on the main road.'

'Sorry,' Emma said, as Ruby clambered out of the car. 'Why do I have to move? Who is it actually reserved for?'

The woman's eyes flickered down the hill, up to the school, and then back to Emma. 'It's not . . . It's not an official thing, it's just that we all keep it free.'

'OK,' Emma said. 'Yeah, I'm not going to move. But I won't park here again.' She made eye contact with the woman way past the point of comfort for, she was sure, both of them. The woman's cheeks flamed and eventually she gave in.

'OK,' the woman said. 'Right. Well, we'd better go and . . .' She gestured towards the school and then she and her child turned towards the gate, the baby letting out a screech and slapping its mum on the side of the neck.

'Right,' Emma said again. She was really glad she didn't have to deal with babies any more, on top of everything else. 'Thanks. Bye.'

'*So much for making mum friends*,' she muttered to herself. Unless the woman was incredibly shy and that was her way of starting a conversation. Maybe she'd add a little bit more the following day and they might have worked up to full sentences by the end of the week. For a second, Emma wondered if maybe she *should* move the car. But there wasn't a sign, so she couldn't see any reason not to park there. Maybe the nervous woman had wanted the space for herself? Weird, anyway.

'Can I go on my own?' Ruby asked, looking past Emma towards the school.

'On your first day? No way! I need to come and kiss and cuddle you until you're weeping with embarrassment.' Emma grinned.

Ruby smiled back and then said. 'Not really, right?'

'Right.'

Emma opened Sam's door to find him staring straight ahead, his bottom lip quivering, but with a determined set to his jaw.

'I know it's scary,' Emma said.

'I'm not going,' Sam said.

'Ruby,' Emma said over her shoulder. 'Could you get Buddy out please? He's got his lead on already. Just keep hold so he doesn't run off.'

'You have to go, sweetheart,' Emma told Sam. 'You'll have Ruby there, so it won't be too scary.'

'She said she won't talk to me,' Sam said.

Emma rolled her eyes. 'She will. Of course she will. Won't you Ruby?'

'He's embarrassing,' Ruby said.

Emma glanced over her shoulder and gave her daughter a hard stare.

'Come on,' she told Sam. 'I'm coming in with you this morning. We'll find out who your teacher is and what your classroom's like and where you hang your coat.'

'I want to go home,' Sam said, tears pooling in his eyes. 'I want to stay with you.'

Emma actually kind of wanted that too. She had no idea what she was going to do at home, alone, now that both kids were at school, but still. She reached across and unbuckled Sam's seatbelt, but he grabbed it with both hands, his knuckles whitening.

'Come on!' Ruby said. 'Everyone's going in.'

Emma straightened up and looked over at the school. The playground was still full of parents and children, milling about.

'We're fine,' she told Ruby. 'Sam. Come on. You have to get out of the car.'

Sam shook his head, his lips compressed into a straight line. Emma turned around and leaned back against the car, looking over at Ruby.

'Can I just go?' Ruby asked.

Emma looked at the school again, and then down the hill where a few more mums – she couldn't see any dads – and children were approaching. If she knew any of them she could ask them to take Ruby in, but she didn't know anyone; all the mums she knew were back in London. She couldn't ask a stranger to take her daughter to her first day at a new school.

She leaned back into the car and whispered to Sam, 'If you get out now, I'll get you a Lego set, whichever one you want.'

'Mighty Dinosaurs?' Sam asked.

'Yeah,' Emma said. 'Whatever.'

Sam let go of his seatbelt and clambered out of the car.

'You have to get me something too,' Ruby said, as they approached the gate. 'Or it's not fair.'

'I know,' Emma said.

Sam's grip tightened on Emma's hand when the whistle blew to let the children know it was time to go in. Emma had seen this when she'd come to check out the school earlier in the year, but she marvelled again at how the children stood dead still on the first whistle and sorted themselves into lines on the second.

'Are you OK to go and line up, Rubes?' Emma asked.

Ruby nodded, already heading towards the playground. She stopped and turned back, giving Emma a shy smile, before joining the back of the Year Three line.

'I don't want to,' Sam said, his voice tiny.

'I can come with you,' Emma said. She knew she probably shouldn't take Buddy onto the playground, but it was the first day of the new year, presumably no one would be that bothered. She lined up with Sam and all the other new Reception class kids. At least Sam's class were all new together; Ruby was joining a class where friendships were already established. But Emma knew her daughter was resilient, and determined enough to have a new best friend by the end of the day.

None of the other parents had lined up with their children, even in Reception. Emma towered over everyone else in the line. She felt like Buddy the Elf. Sam's teacher, Miss McCarry, who Emma had also met earlier in the year, stood at the head of the line. She was tiny too. She didn't look much older than the Year Six class.

Miss McCarry turned towards the school, and the class – and Emma – followed her inside. It was only when they got to the door that the teacher stopped and said, 'I'm sorry, you can't bring the dog in.'

Emma nodded. 'Sorry. I shouldn't have brought him. I didn't realise.'

She leaned down and kissed Sam on his forehead. 'Have a good day, OK? I'll see you later.'

'I don't want to!' Sam said, his face crumbling again.

'I know, baby. But it'll be fun! And it'll go really fast and then I'll be picking you up and I'll have your Lego dinosaur thing.'

Sam nodded sadly and followed Miss McCarry into the classroom, turning once to look back at Emma, his face a picture of heartbreak.

'God,' Emma said, her stomach clenching with anxiety. She hoped he'd be OK. He seemed really little to be starting school already. Buddy tugged at his lead and reminded Emma that he needed a walk. The playground was already almost empty, a few mums had gathered near the gate, but everyone else had left.

She started walking back to the car, wondering if it would be easier to leave it parked outside the school while she walked Buddy, or to drive down to the beach and find somewhere to park on the prom, or take it home and—

'Excuse me!' a woman called from the gate. 'I don't know if anyone's told you that dogs aren't allowed in the playground.'

Bloody hell, Emma thought, first the parking space and now this. And was the woman wearing leather leggings? For the school run?

'Oh, sorry,' Emma said, glancing down at Buddy, 'I thought it was OK if they were on a lead?'

The woman shook her head, her glossy blonde hair swinging like a curtain. 'Actually, no. No dogs at all. Sorry.'

She didn't look sorry. She wasn't even smiling.

'Right,' Emma said. 'Thanks for telling me. I won't bring him again.'

'Also, I think Flic told you about the parking space?'

Flic? Emma hadn't even noticed that she was there but she saw the nervous woman now. She had the grace to look a little sheepish.

At that moment, a black and white cat darted across the road and Buddy yanked on his lead, pulling Emma's arm from her shoulder. She pulled the lead back, but Buddy ducked his head out of his collar and ran after the cat.

'Shit!' Emma said. 'Buddy!'

The cat had been heading across the green, but realising a dog was giving chase, it turned and streaked towards the road and under a white Range Rover parked further down the hill. Buddy kept running, smack into the side of the front door.

'Oh for fuck's sake,' Emma mumbled, heading towards the car, shouting her dog's name as she went. He ignored her, as he always did, and disappeared under the car.

'Buddy,' Emma said, crouching down. 'Come out, you little shit.'

She glanced back towards the school. The woman, Flic and another woman – almost as glamorous as Leather Trousers with high-heeled boots and a blunt bob – were heading towards her. Great.

'Buddy! I swear to god. No walks on the beach if you don't come out. You can just run around the garden and like it. And I'll buy the own-brand dog biscuits you hate.'

'Is he under my car?' the woman in the leather trousers said, stopping next to Emma.

It was her car. Of course it was.

'I think he hit the door,' she said, stroking the door with one well-manicured finger.

There wasn't even a mark on it. He was a small dog. It was a big car. Jesus.

'Yeah, sorry about that,' Emma said, smiling up at the woman.

'Buddy!' she hissed. Buddy's backside appeared, wiggling out from under the car. As soon as his head appeared, Emma tried to grab his collar, but he danced out of the way, barking. The baby – Flic's baby – started to howl and Emma thought about lying down and just rolling under the car. Instead she said 'Buddy!' in her strictest voice. He stopped barking and looked up at her, his mouth hanging open, tongue flopped out to one side.

'I'm sorry,' Emma said to Flic, who was shielding her baby's head with both of her hands.

Emma slid Buddy's collar back over his head, tugging him towards her with the lead, but he didn't budge. Instead, he cocked his leg against the car.

'Oh for god's sake,' Emma said.

'Jools, sorry, I need to go,' Flic said. The baby was still crying, the sound making Emma feel panicky even though it wasn't her child.

'Oh yes, just a second,' Jools said. She opened the car door and pulled out a plastic bag before handing a book to Flic and the other woman. They immediately turned them over and started reading the back cover. Buddy had finally stopped peeing and allowed Emma to tug him away from the car.

'Is that *Wuthering Heights*?' Emma asked, spotting the front cover. She immediately felt a pang of guilt about how little she'd managed to read lately. She used to read at least a book a week.

'Yes,' the woman in the leather trousers, who was apparently called Jools, said.

'Oh, I love it,' Emma said. 'I've been wanting to re-read it actually, but I just never seem to have time.'

'That's why we started a book club,' the other woman said, turning her copy over in her hands.

'You're in a book club?' Emma said, looking down at Buddy, who'd flopped to the ground at her feet and was chewing on something, she couldn't tell what. 'I used to be in one in London.'

A book club would actually be a great way to make friends, Emma thought. Though probably not this particular book club with these particular women.

'Where did you live in London?' the woman with the bob asked.

'Ealing,' Emma said. 'Mostly.'

This was progress. This was a conversation. Even though it was slightly awkward – the other women were just standing there, books in hand, but since all Emma had done so far was apologise for various misdemeanours, it seemed like a step up.

'When did you move up here?' Jools asked. She was looking down at her phone rather than at Emma, but still.

'During the summer holidays,' Emma said. 'So we've been here just over a month.'

'What made you move?' the other woman asked.

'My husband's job mostly,' Emma said. 'He works for—'

'I need to go actually,' Jools said. 'I've got an appointment. Eve, I'll see you later.'

'Sorry again,' Emma said. 'About Buddy.' She looked down to see that he was no longer chewing on something, but was squatting, a shifty expression on his flat face.

'Shit,' Emma said.

Jools walked the other way round to the driver's side of her car. 'And *this* is why dogs aren't allowed,' she said.

But apparently bitches are, thought Emma.

Chapter Three

Jools drove home, took off her make-up, had a long, hot shower, reapplied her make-up and then walked down to the beach. The older girls were back at school and Sofia had taken Eden to a playgroup. Jools could do whatever she wanted. But there was nothing she wanted to do. She had appointments later in the week, but the day was her own.

She stood on the beach and let the wind blow her hair around her face. She looked out at Hilbre Island, the small archipelago a couple of miles out into the Dee, and wondered how long it had been since she'd walked out there. She'd meant to take the girls over the summer – Matt really wanted to go – but they just hadn't got around to it. She should take them. Or maybe suggest it to the school and they could make it a school trip. Jools had gone every year when she was a kid. Her dad had loved it out there, had loved guiding everyone out there even more.

When Jools's eyes started to tear up from the breeze, she bought herself a coffee from the cabin on the corner and set out to walk around the marina. Maybe she should start every day with a walk on the beach. It could give her time to think; clear her head. Although the marina walk was quite far and maybe she wouldn't want to—

Jools's thought process was interrupted as she saw Maggie walking along the prom. She was glad she was on the narrow causeway that circled the marina; if she'd still been on the beach, she'd have had to talk to Maggie and they hadn't talked to each other alone for months now. Jools couldn't. And she couldn't tell Maggie why.

Maggie spotted her and waved from the prom. Jools waved back and wondered if there was any way to fix things. Maybe they could do something together at school. Maggie could help arrange the Hilbre trip, if the school went for it. And they probably would. Particularly if Jools suggested it.

A young couple were walking towards her on the jetty and she spotted the exact moment they recognised her. It was odd being recognised when she wasn't the famous one; she hadn't done anything apart from marry a talented man and be photographed for magazines, but people knew her and were sometimes really excited to meet her. She hadn't been out in Liverpool for ages because drunk women were forever running up to her to scream about how lucky she was and how much they'd like to shag Matt.

This couple today just said hi and asked for a selfie. Jools was really glad she'd put her make-up back on.

Maggie walked along the beach looking for pebbles. She liked the smooth white oval ones. They were the best for the bodies in the pebble portraits she'd started making. But she needed some round ones too, for the heads.

If she hadn't been late for school, she probably would have been on the beach at the same time as Jools, she realised. Would it have been awkward? Or would it have been nice to be just the two of them again?

The first time Maggie met Jools, she'd been crying in her car. She'd taken Amy to a Baby Rhythm class at the leisure centre, but Amy had filled her nappy so explosively that it was coming out of the back of the neck of her onesie.

Maggie had put a lot of effort into getting the two of them up and fed and dressed and out of the house for the eleven a.m. class and the fact that they'd now have to go straight back home was just too much. So she'd put on the Baby Classical CD Amy loved, rested her head on the steering wheel, and let herself cry.

She'd been interrupted by a knock on the window. Jools. Her bottom lip an exaggerated pout, a packet of tissues in her hand.

Maggie had wound down the window and accepted them, mopping her face and turning down the CD to talk to her.

'It gets better,' Jools had said, after introducing herself and baby Violet. 'This part's really hard because of the sleep deprivation and everything, but I promise you it gets better.'

Maggie had nodded.

'This,' Jools had said, gesturing at baby Amy fast asleep in the back, the car filled with the stench of her nappy. 'Is a fucking shitty time.'

Maggie had let out a bark of laughter then and stopped worrying about how awful she must look to this beautiful, glamorous, together woman.

'Come and get a coffee,' Jools had said. 'And cake.'

'But the class . . .' Maggie had assumed Jools had been heading there too.

Jools wafted her hand. 'Violet always falls asleep and god knows it bores the arse off me. Let's go and get a coffee. Fortify yourself to take this one home and shower the shit off her.'

'I should go and wipe her—' Maggie started.

'She's asleep,' Jools said. 'If she was uncomfortable, she'd wake up. Trust me.'

Maggie had laughed again. If she'd been alone, she would never have considered taking the pungent Amy into a café. But she wasn't alone. She was with Jools. And if Jools said it was OK, Maggie wasn't going to argue.

The following week they'd met up in the coffee shop instead of at Baby Rhythm, and Jools had made Maggie feel better about absolutely everything. Maggie was exhausted because Jim not only didn't get up with the baby, he complained when Maggie did. Jools suggested he go and sleep in what would be Amy's room, leaving Maggie to take care of Amy without guilt and allowing him to have a full night's sleep before work. Maggie hadn't been sure Jim would go for it, but he was delighted. If a little peeved not to have thought of it himself. Within a couple of days, he'd turned the baby's room into a tiny bachelor pad with magazines and a radio, crisp packets and dirty underpants piling up in the corner. But Maggie didn't care. Because she could wake up, feed Amy, and go back to sleep without having to think about him at all.

Jools had suggestions for everything. She helped Maggie with feeding Amy, she brought some nipple shields when Maggie cried about her cracked nipples, she'd even taken Amy out for walks to let Maggie get some sleep. Maggie couldn't have done any of it without her.

And then a few months earlier, Jools had stopped calling and didn't even really talk to Maggie at school. Maggie didn't think she'd done anything to upset her – she thought Jools would have told her if she had – but she'd definitely pulled away. And Maggie had no idea why.

Chapter Four

Emma was early for pick up. She'd walked and made sure to set off in plenty of time; she really didn't want a repeat of the morning's chaos. She'd taken Buddy for such a long run that morning that he'd spent the entire afternoon asleep on the sofa in the kitchen.

'Left the troublemaker at home then?' one of the other mums said.

Emma had noticed her that morning – she'd been walking up the road when Emma had been looking for someone to take Ruby in – and was now leaning on the handles of a double buggy, the two small boys inside it fast asleep.

Emma laughed weakly. 'Yeah, I won't be bringing him again.'

'I know you're probably not ready to hear this,' the woman said. 'But it was dead funny to watch.'

Emma shook her head. She could imagine. And she thought it might make a funny story at some point in the future. But she wasn't there yet.

'Sorry. I've just got an evil sense of humour. I'm Beth.'

'Emma,' Emma said, smiling finally.

'When he peed against the car,' Beth said. 'I nearly peed too.'

Emma snorted. 'Who is that woman . . .?' She glanced around to make sure she wasn't behind her. 'The one in the leather leggings? Jools?'

'Ah,' Beth said. 'Jools Jackson. Her husband's a footballer, so she thinks she's it.'

'Matt Jackson? Is she married to Matt Jackson?' Now that Emma thought about it, she remembered seeing an article about them in the local magazine. Matt was really handsome so she'd focused more on him than his wife.

'Yeah,' Beth said. 'How long have you been here? I would've thought you'd have seen them already. They're our top local celebrities.' She rolled her eyes.

'We've only been here just over a month,' Emma said. 'But I think I did see them in a magazine. I didn't realise it was her.'

'Oh god, yeah,' Beth said. '*Northern Life*? Everyone talked about it for days, like she was a Kardashian or something. I expected her to start offering to sign everyone's copies.'

'And the other women?' Emma asked, looking back over her shoulder again, just in case.

'Eve, Flic and Maggie. They're all right if you get them on their own. Well, Eve can be a bit of a cow, but, yeah, as long as you separate them from the herd.'

'It was just Eve and Flic, I think. No Maggie.' She tried to remember if there'd been another woman with them at any point, but if there had been, Emma hadn't noticed her. 'They mentioned they've got a book club . . .' she told Beth.

'Oh god,' Beth groaned. 'The fucking book club. It's exclusive. Invitation only. They were on some TV show once – something like *This Morning*, but not that – the author of the book they were reading came out to meet them and they had cocktails. The way everyone was going on about it, you'd think it'd been the queen.'

'Who was it?'

'Can't remember. Not someone I'd ever heard of.'

'They're reading *Wuthering Heights* now. They'd struggle to get Emily Brontë here.'

'Is she not local?' Beth said, and then grinned so Emma knew she was joking. 'Fucking hell though. Why would you read that if you don't have to?'

'I love it actually,' Emma said. The door to Miss McCarry's classroom opened. 'I've been thinking about re-reading it for a while.'

'What's stopping you?' Beth asked.

'I haven't finished a book since we moved up here.' Emma shook her head. 'I always fall asleep.'

'It's the sea air,' Beth said. 'But maybe start with something more fun than *Wuthering Heights* then. There's a whole shelf of *Fifty Shades* in the charity shop.'

'I'll suggest that for next month,' Emma joked.

'It's all very *Big Little Lies* – did you watch it?' Beth said, her voice low again. 'The book club. Like they're all friends but they hate each other. It'd be hilarious if it wasn't so sad.'

A few children burst through the doors of the classroom, but Sam wasn't one of them. Emma hoped he'd had an OK day. She hoped he hadn't hated it.

'Slow down!' Miss McCarry called, trying to hold some of the children back before they caused a bottleneck in the doorway.

And then Sam burst through, his hair sticking up in clumps, his red school sweatshirt covered in paint. He ran over to Emma, hugged her around her thighs and said, 'Can we go to the beach?' against her jeans.

'Course,' Emma said, leaning down to kiss the top of his head. He smelled like wet dog. 'How was your day?'

'Did you get my Lego?'

'Yeah,' Emma said, glancing over at Beth who smiled back at her. 'Let's go find your sister.'

Chapter Five

'Sam, come on!' Emma said as they walked along the prom to school a couple of weeks later and Sam stopped for what felt like the fiftieth time. 'For god's sake! We're going to be late.' They were about five minutes from school with – Emma estimated – about two minutes before the whistle.

The walk was bracing and picturesque but there were way too many distractions for a curious five-year-old. In the first two weeks of school they'd already been late three times and Emma knew that if they were late again she'd actually get called in for a meeting with the head to explain herself. And she had no explanation beyond 'it's hard to get everyone out of the house in the morning.' She wanted to avoid that meeting, if at all possible.

'Did you see the ant?' Sam was already starting to crouch down behind a bench, as Ruby tutted with impatience, wrapping Buddy's lead around her wrist as he tried to tug her across the road towards the marine lake.

Emma tugged on Sam's hand. 'No. I'll look for it on the way home.'

'Don't step on it!'

'I won't step on it. I'll be really careful.'

'You know how many ants probably get stepped on every day, Sam?' Ruby, said.

'Shut up, Ruby,' Emma said. Ruby was smart, but she suffered from a lack of empathy where her brother was concerned.

'Miss McCarry says "shut up" is a bad word,' Sam said.

'It is,' Ruby agreed. 'You should say "be quiet." Or really you shouldn't say that either because you should listen to your children and not try to stifle their creativity.'

'Oh my god,' Emma said.

'And that's blasphemy,' Ruby said.

'Was that the whistle?' Emma asked. 'Come on.'

'That wasn't the whistle,' Ruby said. She'd stepped out of her shoe and stopped to fasten it back on. 'You know at half term?' she asked, looking up at Emma.

'Yes. It's not for a while yet though. Get on with your shoe.'

'Can we go back to London? I want to see Isabelle. Or she could come up here. She says she's never been to a beach.'

'They go to the South of France every summer,' Emma said, reaching down and helping Ruby with her shoe. 'But maybe we could go down for the weekend, yes.'

'Good,' Ruby said. 'I think she's probably missing me.' Shoe back on, the three of them set off walking again. 'Look, Mummy,' Ruby said, as they turned the corner towards the school. 'Flora's going to be late too.'

Emma glanced over at the green that separated the prom from Hillcrest School to see Beth – who she'd started thinking of as her almost-friend since she was the only other mum who'd spoken to her so far – doing a shuffling half-run along the path, with Flora lagging behind and her twin boys in front in the buggy. She waved and Beth nodded back.

'We're not going to be late,' Emma said. 'It was first whistle. We'll be fine.'

*

They reached the gate at the same time as Beth, and headed into the playground. Sam's teacher Miss McCarry was just opening the door as they joined the small crowd of parents and children, milling around, waiting.

'Go line up, sweetie,' Emma told Ruby, who kissed her, grabbed Flora's hand, and ran to join the class line.

'Have your two had chickenpox?' Beth asked, leaning down and pulling a pack of baby wipes out of the basket under the buggy, her dark hair fastened in two plaits swinging forward.

Emma nodded, although she wasn't sure Ruby actually had. She'd had a few spots, but it never really developed and she'd often wondered if it would come back.

'Our Sid's got a pock on the back of his head,' Beth said, in her strong Liverpool accent that Emma loved. She stepped round to the front of the buggy and wiped the twins' faces. 'But it's under his hair so I'm not really sure.'

Emma felt Sam curling himself around her leg, as he did every morning. They'd talked about it over the weekend and he'd promised he was going to try a bit harder to be a little bit braver, but apparently they'd be having the same conversation next weekend too.

'Sam, love,' Emma said, stroking his blond hair back from his pale face. 'You like it when you get inside, you know you do.'

'I don't,' Sam whispered. 'I hate it. Can I come home with you? Please?'

Emma bit her lip. She wanted to say, yeah, fuck it, why not? They could go home, get their wellies on and go down to the beach, splash in the puddles from last night's rain. Instead she carefully untangled his arms and crouched down to cuddle him.

'Sorry, love. You're going to have to be brave. Like we talked about, remember?'

Sam nodded.

'Sam?' Miss McCarry called. 'Are you coming in?'

'No,' Sam said.

'Yes,' Emma said, giving him a little shove towards his teacher. He got halfway to the door and turned back to look at Emma, his face a picture of tragedy. Emma had to dig her nails into her palms to stop herself running after him.

'He'll be OK once they get going,' Beth said.

Emma nodded. She really hoped so.

'It's a lot to get used to,' Beth said. 'A new town and a new school. And making friends isn't easy.'

'No,' Emma said. 'Actually, would you like to get a coffee some time? Maybe after we drop them off one morning?'

'I'd love that,' Beth said.

Maggie opened the door. Her brother Nick was standing there, a bright purple suitcase on the path next to him.

'Hi,' he said. 'I've left Simon.'

'Oh my god,' Maggie said. 'Come in.'

It was only once they were in the hall, the door closed behind them, that Maggie wrapped her arms around her younger brother and squeezed. 'Are you OK?'

'Yeah.'

She took a step back, her hands still on his shoulders. He looked pale with dark smudges under his eyes. 'What happened?'

'You know we went away?'

'Yeah, Marrakesh, right?' Maggie said, letting go of him and turning into the hall. 'Come through to the kitchen. You want a tea?'

'Course.' Nick followed her to the kitchen.

'Bloody hell, Mags,' Nick said, as Maggie filled the kettle. 'Did Mum decorate for you?'

Maggie glanced around. 'What?'

'It looks just like Mum's house in here.'

'It does not. Anyway, you've seen it before.'

'I haven't,' he said. 'Last time I was here everything was magnolia. And it really does. I think she's got the same wallpaper.'

Maggie shook her head. She wasn't a massive fan of the wallpaper herself – it was cream with tiny red flowers – but it had been on offer and they'd needed a lot.

'This room would look great with the splash back shocking pink and maybe dark blue on that wall. There's so much light from that window that you don't need to go light on the walls.'

'I don't remember commissioning you to redo my kitchen,' Maggie said, leaning back against the cupboards. 'Thanks though.'

'I could, if you wanted me to.'

'Thanks, but I like it.'

'You mean Jim likes it. Then again, I can't imagine him being comfortable with the flowers, however tiny.'

'I like it,' Maggie said. 'Don't start. Tell me about Simon.'

'I wasn't starting. But you're right, we should talk about my problems.'

They took their teas through to the conservatory.

'This is so Mum too, by the way,' Nick said, lifting a puppy off the chair and dropping it on the floor. 'Entertaining guests in the conservatory.'

'Amy would kill you,' Maggie said, picking the dog up and sitting it on the sofa next to her.'

'She's not here though, is she. Little weirdo.' He picked up and sipped his tea. 'So.'

'Marrakesh.'

'Marrakesh. Yeah. It was fine. We didn't fight or anything. We just didn't really . . . I don't know. It's hard to explain. I looked at him one day and I couldn't remember why I was with him. It was like being there with a stranger. Like I'd met him at the airport. Or we were on a blind date. I was like "how did this happen? Who even are you?"'

'So the usual then?'

Nick pulled a face. 'It's not the usual.'

'It really is. You always do this. It gets too serious and you . . . flee.'

'I didn't flee.'

'You're here, aren't you.'

'Yeah, but I didn't flee. I was very mature; I told him I didn't think we were making each other happy. And he agreed, but he thought maybe we should try a bit harder, go out more as a couple, make a bit more of an effort, you know? But I said I didn't really want to do that and then I left.'

'You fleed,' Maggie said, pulling her feet up underneath her. 'Flew? Fled.'

'I reasonably and maturely after a reasonable and mature break up, came up here to see my sister and niece, who I haven't seen for ages.'

'Fair enough,' Maggie said. 'But are you OK? Really?'

Nick shrugged. 'I think so? Who's to say. I feel fine. It feels smart. Like I couldn't imagine growing old with him so why was I wasting my time, you know? And his time. So it was the smart thing to do.'

'Still hard though.'

'I'm not. It's just these trousers.' He grinned.

'I am your sister,' Maggie said, smiling into her tea.

'So how're things with you?' Nick asked. 'Anything exciting to report?'

Maggie shrugged. 'Not really. I'm very boring.'

'You're not. Well, you didn't used to be.'

'I take Amy to school. I go for a run. I make pebble pictures. I go to book club once a month. That's about it.'

'Mum told me about the pebble pictures. Are you having a breakdown?'

'Shut up, they're good! I made the first one for Amy and people kept asking about it so I made some more. People like them.'

Nick leaned back in his chair and stared at her. 'You're turning into Mum. It's creepy. Have you started following the reduced sticker woman round Asda?'

'We haven't got an Asda,' Maggie said. 'And I'm not turning into Mum.'

Maggie actually felt her throat getting tight. How embarrassing.

'Don't get upset.' Nick leaned forward and tapped her on her knee. 'I'm just taking the piss. It's just . . . is this what you imagined for yourself?'

Maggie drank more tea. It actually was what she'd imagined for herself. Growing up, she'd pictured adulthood as a house and a car and a family that looked exactly like this – almost exactly, there would actually be two kids – and she hadn't really thought beyond that. And that's what she had. She had exactly what she'd wanted.

'I'm fine,' she told Nick.

'That wasn't what I asked.' He raised one eyebrow.

Maggie ignored it. 'Are you hungry? Have you eaten?'

Nick rolled his eyes. 'Way to change the subject. Actually I am hungry. What have you got?'

'Not much, we'll have to go out. And then we can go and get Amy. She'll be so excited to see you.'

'Me too. I've missed her. FaceTime's not the same.'

Maggie finished her tea. 'I'll take you up to your room and then we can go.'

They both stood and Nick pulled her into a hug. 'I've missed you too, Sis.'

She squeezed him. She'd missed him more than she was willing to admit.

Jools lay back and stared up at the smooth, white ceiling. There was a cushion with a buddha on it under her shoulders and, she knew, a view of Liverpool's Georgian Quarter out of the original sash windows to her right, but she stared up at the smooth plaster and told herself to breathe.

The beautician, April, had told her it wasn't going to hurt much, but she'd heard that before. She'd heard that when she'd had a smear test, had blood taken, started breastfeeding, even when she'd had her babies. And every time it had been a lie. All of those things had hurt like hell. But they'd been worth it. And this would be too. She hoped.

'Are you ready?' April asked. 'I'm just going to brush and trim your brows first. Are you wearing make-up now? On your brows?'

'Yes,' Jools said, closing her eyes. She hadn't left the house without her eyebrows drawn on for as long as she could remember. She felt April smoothing a cool cream across her brows and then wiping it off again.

'Now I'm going to draw them on,' April said. 'What I think will look good, which is pretty close to what you had when you came in. I can give you a mirror to watch me do it or do you want to wait 'til it's done? Obviously I can redo them if they don't work for you.'

'I'll wait 'til it's done,' Jools said. The less she had to see of the whole procedure the better. She'd watched dozens of YouTube videos before booking this appointment. Some of them had been fine. Some of them were so horrific that she'd had to click away. And she'd avoided the 'my microblading nightmare' videos altogether. It had to be done. It was as simple as that.

Once Jools had approved the drawn-on brows, April applied numbing cream and told Jools the first pass was going to feel similar to plucking or threading. Jools had only had her eyebrows threaded once and tears had streamed down her face the entire time, so it wasn't the most reassuring thing she'd ever heard. Her friend Eve saying 'Beauty is pain' popped into her head and she almost laughed. Thank god for Eve.

She winced, digging her nails into her thighs. This was definitely more painful than plucking and threading. Her toes curled in her shoes as she told herself to breathe and focus on the outcome. This would all be worth it. Although knowing that this was only the first eyebrow and she had to go through all of this again wasn't really helping.

'So for most people this side is a bit more sensitive . . .' April said and Jools thought about getting up and going home. She could draw the other eyebrow on, it would be fine, one was enough. April started work and Jools started counting in her head. And then she tried something she'd been taught for insomnia – naming a piece of fruit for every letter of the alphabet. Apple. Banana. Jesus fucking Christ, this was painful. Cantaloupe. She felt a tear roll down the side of her face and pool in her ear and then April dabbing at her skin with cotton wool.

'Almost done,' she said.

'Good,' Jools whispered. Dragon Fruit. E. What was a fruit beginning with E?

'The arch is usually a little more painful,' April said and Jools wanted to stab her in the throat with her stupid tiny blade. Who the fuck had invented this? It was torture. And she couldn't think of a fruit beginning with E. Fig. Grapes.

'I just need to wipe the pigment off now,' April said.

Jools couldn't think of a fruit beginning with H. Or I. Or J. This was a stupid game.

'Are you OK to sit up?' April asked.

Jools felt April's fingers on her arm and she opened her eyes. April helped her up to sitting position and held out the same small hand mirror she'd used before.

In Jools's mind, her brows were bloody, swollen and terrifying, so she was amazed to see that they looked incredible. She'd never done such a perfect job herself, and even when she'd had her brows tinted in the past, they hadn't looked anywhere near as good as this.

'This is amazing.'

'You'll need to bathe them with warm water three times a day for the next week,' April said. 'And I'll give you a cream to apply. And as long as you don't feel faint or sick, you're good to go.'

'Thank you,' Jools said. 'They're even better than I expected.'

Jools swung her legs to one side and lowered herself off the bed. She felt wobbly, but she'd be fine once she had some water. She pulled the bottle she'd brought with her out of her bag and gulped some down.

'You're OK?' April asked.

Nodding, Jools followed her over to the desk to pay, handing her card over and taking her phone out to check that Matt hadn't been in touch. Or the nanny about the girls. She only had one text and it was from Eve asking how it had gone.

'Can I ask you a question?' April said, as Jools tapped her PIN into the machine.

Jools knew what it was going to be and wanted to say no. Instead she said, 'Of course.'

'Is Matt going to Liverpool? I know you probably can't tell me, but if I didn't ask, my boyfriend would never forgive me.'

Jools forced her face into a smile. 'I'm sorry. I really can't say.'

April's cheeks flushed. 'That's OK. He'll be excited you were here anyway. We saw you in *Northern Life*. Your house is so gorgeous.'

'Thank you,' Jools said, her hand was shaking, she noticed as she put her card back in her purse. 'That was a fun shoot.'

'It looked like it.'

'I think I might need to sit down a minute,' Jools said. There were spots floating in front of her eyes and everything suddenly seemed far away.

'Oh my god,' she heard April say. 'Are you—'

And then everything went black.

Chapter Six

'You scared the shit out of me,' Matt said, brushing Jools's hair back from her forehead.

'Sorry,' Jools whispered. She was lying back against a huge pile of pillows. Matt had closed the curtains against the early evening sun, but she could still see the watery light peeking around the edges. She wanted to ask him to open them again, wanted to tell him she was keen to absorb as much sunlight as possible, but she also didn't want him to move from the bed.

He was holding her hand, stroking over her palm with his thumb.

'What were you thinking? Why didn't you take Eve with you? Or Maggie?'

Jools smiled at the little frown line between his eyes. 'Because I'm not ill. Because it was just brows. Because Maggie doesn't know yet. And because I didn't expect to faint. Obviously.'

'Obviously,' Matt repeated, a smile tugging the corner of his mouth. 'You did though.'

Jools smiled. 'I know. Mortifying.'

'That place'll put up a blue plaque: Jools Jackson fainted here. I looked back as we left and they were drawing a chalk line on the floor.'

'Shut up,' Jools said, laughing. 'They won't want to promote the fact that they took me out.'

Matt leaned forward and was about to press his forehead to Jools's when he jerked back. 'Is it sore?'

'Bit,' Jools said.

He brushed his lips over her temple instead.

'How do they look?' Jools asked.

Matt laughed against her hair. 'Are you really asking me that?'

'Listen, you knew I was vain when you met me. This shouldn't be a surprise.'

He sat up and looked at her face, his forehead furrowed in concentration. She felt a flutter behind her ribs and reached out and grabbed his wrist, pressing her thumb against his pulse point.

'I love you,' she said, forcefully.

'They look great,' he said, his gaze drifting down from her brows to her eyes. 'You're beautiful. You're always beautiful.'

'I wouldn't be beautiful with no eyebrows.' She walked her fingers up his forearm, brushing the dark hair in the wrong direction.

He pulled his arm away, laughing. She'd always loved how ticklish he was.

'You would. No eyebrows, no eyelashes, no hair. Still beautiful.'

'Bollocks,' Jools said, but she knew he actually meant it. She couldn't believe it, but he did.

He dipped his head and kissed her nose, her mouth, her chin. 'I mean it. I know none of this stuff is for me, but I promise you I don't need it.'

'It's not *not* for you,' Jools said. 'But it's mostly for me. Also so I don't scare the kids.' They could hear the kids downstairs with Sofia, laughing and shouting. Jools loved how much they loved Sofia. It meant she didn't have to worry about them when she wasn't with them. And Matt was a fantastic dad, of course. They'd be fine if . . . They'd be fine.

'Have you thought more about when we're going to tell them?' Matt asked, his mouth close to her ear.

Jools's eyes filled, as they always did when she thought about having to say those words to her girls. Telling her mum and her sister had been hard, so had telling Eve, but her daughters? They were so small and she knew they wouldn't really understand, but she still couldn't bear the thought of it.

Matt had been with her when she got the diagnosis, even though she'd tried to tell him he didn't need to come. She had been so sure it was nothing. A blocked milk duct, an absess, a tumour maybe, but a benign one. She hadn't really properly expected the doctor to say cancer. Not in real life. But she had. And then she'd told them how they were going to deal with it while Matt squeezed Jools's hand and they both stared straight ahead, trying to take it all in.

They hadn't talked about Jools dying. Jools wondered if they should. If it would be sensible, mature, to have a plan in case the worst – the very fucking, almost unimaginable, worst – happened. But Jools was a planner. She always felt more in control if she had a plan in place, but she absolutely couldn't bring herself to plan for her own death.

'Before chemo,' Jools said, swallowing down the lump in her throat. 'Or do you think we should wait and see what happens? I don't want to tell them too soon, but if my hair starts falling out—'

'Why don't we wait,' Matt said. 'They don't need to know, do they? Maybe we should only tell them when it becomes unavoidable.'

Jools nodded. Her head felt suddenly heavy, her forehead tender. She rested her head on Matt's shoulder and he immediately shifted to put his arm around her, pull her against him. She snuggled into his side.

'I hope I didn't pull you away from anything important,' Jools said, closing her eyes and breathing in the scent of his skin. Everything in their lives had changed over the past ten years, but Matt always, always smelled the same. Like rain. Or maybe the ocean. She'd never been quite sure.

'Nah. I had a meeting with the player liaison guy, but it's not important. And he seems cool. I can reschedule. But you know even if I'd been playing I would've come straight to you.' She felt him smiling. He'd joked about that for as long as she'd known him. She'd never had to test him on it though. Not yet.

'I know, you always say that,' Jools said, laughing against his chest. 'Can't see it happening in reality though.'

'I would,' Matt said, running his hand down his wife's arm. 'I'd say "try me" but I really don't want you to.'

'I won't,' Jools said. 'I promise.'

'You can't promise that. But promise me no more cosmetic procedures without a friend.'

'I can get my nails done.'

'Take Eve with you.'

Jools had been starting to doze, but she tipped her head back to look at her husband. 'I can get my nails done on my own, oh my god!'

'Can't you get someone to come to the house?'

Jools dropped her head back against his chest. 'Yes, actually.'

'Do that then.'

'OK.'

'OK.'

Jools was just starting to drift off when she heard Matt say, his voice soft, 'You scared the shit out of me today, babe.'

She tried to tell him she was sorry, but she was already asleep.

Chapter Seven

'Mrs Chance?' Miss McCarry called from the classroom door at pick-up time on Friday. 'Could I have a word?'

'Cockwomble,' Sam murmured, curled around Emma's legs. 'That's a word.'

'That's a bad word, sweetheart,' Emma said, glancing at Beth who was looking at her with wide eyes, trying not to laugh.

'Of course,' Emma told Miss McCarry. 'I just need to wait for Ruby.'

Seconds later, Ruby was heading towards her, talking and laughing with Flora. She looked just as neat as she had when they'd gone in that morning. Flora was in an almost Sam-like level of disarray.

'God, look at the state of her,' Beth said, shaking her head. 'I don't know how she gets everything so bloody filthy.'

'Bloody filthy,' Sam repeated, from where he was sitting on the ground, half on Emma's feet.

'Mrs Roshni?' Miss McCarry called out. The only Asian mum at the school – at least the only one Emma had seen so far – half held her hand up in acknowledgement.

'I need to have a quick word with you too, if you don't mind waiting?' Miss McCarry said.

Emma looked over at Mrs Roshni in solidarity. She nodded at Miss McCarry, gave Emma a quick smile, and walked over to sit on one of the picnic tables at the edge of the playground, parking an empty buggy alongside. Her toddler son looked up at her and then took off across the playground, laughing.

Once the last of the children had left the classroom, Ruby and Sam followed Emma into the bright room. It smelled like paint and glue and farts, Emma thought, and made a mental note to tell Sam that later; she knew it would make him laugh.

'If you can take a seat,' Miss McCarry said, gesturing at one of the tiny chairs, next to the tiny tables. 'And Ruby, could you just take Sam to the hall? I think Mr Leyland wanted some help tidying away the musical instruments.'

'Oh wow!' Ruby said, actually clapping her hands. She loved to tidy. Emma would probably question whether Ruby was really her daughter if she hadn't seen her emerge from her vagina.

'Come on, Sam,' Ruby said, and tugged him out of the room.

'Thank you for taking the time to see me,' Miss McCarry said, sitting on another tiny chair. 'I know you're busy.'

'Yes, no problem,' Emma said, even though she'd had a two hour nap and then spent the rest of the afternoon lying on the sofa watching repeats of *A Place in the Sun*, while feeling horribly guilty about the state of the bathroom. And the kitchen. And all the other rooms. Paul had been working late most nights, which meant Emma had reverted to an almost feral existence. Once the children were in bed, she spent her evenings slumped in front of Netflix. It wasn't even as if she was mainlining box sets – often by the time she'd chosen something to watch, she was already mostly asleep.

'We have some . . . concerns about Sam. And how he's settling in. Or rather, how he's not settling in.'

'Right,' Emma said. She tried to cross her legs, but banged her knee on the underside of the table. A tube of blue paint fell over and started to roll towards them. Miss McCarry stopped it with her hand without even turning her head.

'Does he talk much? At home?'

'Sam?' Emma frowned. 'He never stops.'

'Interesting,' Miss McCarry said. 'Because he really doesn't speak at school at all.'

'Seriously? Sam?'

Miss McCarry nodded. 'Obviously at first we thought he was shy and that things would improve once he gained some confidence. But if anything, he's getting worse.'

'Worse how?'

'Has Sam told you about Golden Time?'

Emma shook her head.

'Right, so it's when we have fun activities at the end of the day. It's mostly used as a reward for good behaviour.'

'But Sam wouldn't join in. In fact, he hid under a table. And when I tried to talk to him, to get him to come out, he meowed.'

Before she could stop herself, Emma snorted with laughter. She covered her mouth with her hand. 'Sorry.' She blinked up at the sign while she composed herself. 'He meowed?'

Miss McCarry gave her a tight-lipped smile. 'I know it's early days, but the head was saying if this continues we should consider referring Sam to speech therapy, although if he talks at home—'

'He does. He never stops talking.'

'Then that's a different issue. I'll have a word with Mrs Walker about it and get back to you.'

'Right,' Emma said. 'Thank you. It's probably just a settling in thing, do you think?'

'Probably,' the teacher agreed.

The two of them stood and Emma looked around the room. The room in which her son spent the best part of every day and she really had no idea what he was getting up to.

'There is just one other thing,' Miss McCarry said. 'And I'm not sure I should even mention it, but if I don't . . .'

'OK . . .'

'One of the other children said Sam called him a name. And obviously I'm not entirely convinced because, like I said, Sam doesn't talk.'

'What was the name?' Emma asked, already wincing internally.

'Butt-puffin,' the other woman said.

Emma bit the inside of her cheek to stop herself from laughing. 'I'll have a word with him. Thanks for telling me.'

'Miss McCarry said you meowed today,' Emma said, as she, Sam, and Ruby walked down the hill towards the prom.

'Yes!' Sam said, jumping off the edge of the kerb and back on again. 'Can I go and run?'

'In a minute, yeah,' Emma said. 'Just tell me first . . . The meowing. Why?'

'I was being a cat.' He stopped hopping long enough to rub his hand over his face in what Emma had to admit was a pretty impressive impersonation of a cat.

'Right,' Emma said. 'Obviously. She's a bit concerned. Because you don't talk.'

'I do talk!' Sam said, shucking his coat off and letting it drop to the ground at his feet.

'He talks in the playground,' Ruby said, as Emma bent to pick up Sam's coat. 'He talks to his friends.'

'Do you?' Emma asked Sam.

'Course. We were playing vets today. So I was a cat and Louis was a fox and Thomas was a tiger, but then he ate the fox and got sick and the vets got closed down.'

'But Thomas didn't carry on being a tiger after playtime, did he? And Louis stopped being a fox.'

Sam looked up at her, his forehead furrowed in confusion. 'Louis was *dead*. Thomas *ate* him.'

'Right,' Emma said. 'What I mean is, they stopped playing at the end of break. But you were still a cat in class.'

Sam shrugged. 'I like being a cat.'

'Fair enough,' Emma said. 'And there's something else. She said you called someone a "butt-puffin"?'

'I didn't!' Sam said, outrage written all over his face.

'I didn't think so,' Emma said, reaching out to stroke his hair back from his face.

'It was fuck-puffin,' Sam said.

Emma's mouth dropped open. 'Where have you heard that?'

'Daddy said it when he was watching the football.'

'Right,' Emma said. Yeah, that sounded legit. 'OK, well that's a bad word and you mustn't use it, 'K?'

'OK,' Sam said, his small face serious. 'You should tell Daddy that too. Can I go and run now?'

'Knock yourself out.'

Emma watched her son and daughter dart across the green, swerving into each other and hooting with laughter. She thought about texting Paul to tell him what Miss McCarry had said, but she knew he either wouldn't reply or he'd say something dismissive or defensive and she couldn't face that. Instead, she just watched Sam and Ruby and thought about how that was why they'd moved up to the Wirral, out of London. For the big sky and the bigger house, the beach and the sea air, the shorter commute and smaller school. It was worth it, she knew. It would be worth it.

'What were you in for?' Emma heard someone say. She tore her eyes away from her kids and smiled at Mrs Roshni, who was walking down the hill towards her.

'Can I go and—' her son asked her.

She waved him off and he ran straight after Sam and Ruby.

'Sorry,' Mrs Roshni said. 'Is that too nosy?'

Emma shook her head. 'I don't mind. 'They're concerned because Sam doesn't talk. Apparently he meows.'

'Wow,' the other woman said. 'That's pretty cool.'

Emma sighed. 'I'm telling myself it's the sign of a brilliant imagination.'

'Well it is,' the other woman said. 'And as long as he doesn't start licking his own genitals, I'm sure it's fine.'

Emma let out a bark of surprised laughter.

'I'm Hanan,' Mrs Roshni said.

Emma smiled at her. 'Emma. My two are Sam and Ruby. What were you in for?'

'Yahya apparently walked through a puddle while everyone else walked round it.'

'That's not what she just called you in about,' Emma said, shocked. She looked over at Hanan's son, who was riding a fallen tree branch like a horse, while Sam howled with laughter.

Hanan nodded. 'Yup. I assume she thinks it shows a rebellious streak and she wants to nip it in the bud. She said I should ask him why he walked through the puddle.'

'Because walking through puddles is fun?' Emma suggested.

'That's exactly what he said. I mean, I know it's easier for them if all the kids conform, but . . .' She shrugged. 'That's not something I'm going to worry about. I think it's pretty cool that he walked through even though everyone else walked round.'

'I was just thinking that,' Emma said. 'I assume that means Sam walked round. I'm a bit disappointed.'

'Ah, but at least he was meowing as he did it,' Hanan said.

Emma laughed. 'True.'

They chatted while the older children played and Hanan's younger son dozed in his buggy. Eventually Yahya, Ruby and Sam ran back over.

'Can we get an ice cream?' Ruby asked.

'Or a lolly?' Sam added.

'We've got lollies at home,' Emma said, as she always did.

'Can we go home then?' Sam asked. 'Can Yahya come?'

'Are you busy?' Emma asked Hanan. 'Do you want to come back to mine for a coffee? Or a lolly?'

Hanan laughed. 'I'd love that.'

Chapter Eight

'So where are you from?' Emma asked Hanan, as she filled the kettle with water and reached up into the cupboard for mugs.

'Wakefield,' Hanan said, from the French doors, where she was watching Ruby, Sam and Yahya in the garden. 'Oh hang on. Did you mean—'

'Oh god!' Emma said, turning round. 'No! I meant cos of your accent!'

Hanan laughed. 'I know. Sorry. I was just winding you up.'

'Jesus,' Emma said, crossing the kitchen to get the milk out of the fridge. 'Don't.'

Hanan grinned. 'My parents are from Pakistan. No, I don't get back as often as I'd like. Yes, I've been to Hajj. Once. And . . . I think that's all the questions I'm usually asked about "my culture".'

'Bloody hell,' Emma said. 'I was just going to ask if you take milk and sugar.'

A loud laugh burst out of Hanan, then she knocked on the window and wagged her finger.

'Yahya,' she told Emma. 'Picking up a stick. He's bloody obsessed with sticks. Looks like bonfire night in our front garden all year round. Milk, no sugar. Ta.'

Once Emma had made the tea, emptied a packet of biscuits onto a plate, and poured three glasses of juice for the kids, she and Hanan both sat down at the dining table.

'Do people really ask you that stuff?' Emma said, wondering if she should go and tell the children about the juice or just let them come in when they were ready.

'Yeah,' Hanan said, reaching for a biscuit. 'I don't mind really. It just gets a bit repetitive. Occasionally someone'll ask about this too.' She pointed at her headscarf. 'But that's about it.'

Emma chewed on her bottom lip.

'You want to ask me about it now, don't you,' Hanan said.

Emma laughed. 'I do! I'm sorry!'

'It's fine. I can take it off actually.'

Hanan reached back and tugged, the hijab came off and her hair fell around her face. She shook her head and grinned.

'Your husband's not due home yet, right?'

'Paul?' Emma glanced up at the clock above the cooker. 'No, not for a while yet.'

'What does he do?'

'He works for a sports agency. He's been working in the London office, but they wanted someone in Liverpool and he's been keen to move back – he grew up here – so . . .'

'Ah,' Hanan said. 'And is he happy there?'

'I think so? He hasn't really said. I know he's been busy cos we've hardly seen him.'

Emma had found that the hardest thing about moving to West Kirby. While Paul went off to work each day and had colleagues, if not yet friends, to talk to, Emma was stuck at home with Sam, Ruby and Buddy, trying to keep themselves entertained and sort the house out. She'd known it would be hard. It was just a little harder than she'd expected.

'So is it a particular sport he deals with or . . . I don't know how it works.'

'Mostly football. So obviously this is the place to be.'

Hanan smiled. 'Someone's introduced you to Jools Jackson, I assume?'

Emma shook her head. 'She sort of introduced herself when my dog ran away, straight into her car. And then peed on it.'

'I bet that went down well.'

'Oh and apparently I parked in her parking space.' Emma had noticed that the space was indeed always left for Jools, who more often than not, arrived at school just before first whistle. It was ridiculous.

Hanan rolled her eyes. 'She used to get to school early each morning and afternoon to get that space. Someone parked in it once and she told them it was her space and since then people have just . . . respected it. I don't understand it myself.'

'That is nuts,' Emma said. She thought back to London, to how she and Paul had lived close enough to walk to Ruby's school, but how the actual road was a free for all, with people double and triple parked. But it worked somehow. And no one had ever demanded their own parking space.

Hanan laughed. 'People really suck up to them cos they're our best local celebrities. But don't call her a WAG unless you want to be ostracised for ever.'

'Really?' Emma had been assuming Jools would have totally leaned in to the WAG thing.

Hanan shrugged. 'Yeah. She hates it. But obviously she still uses it when it suits her. It's all too much like school for me, though. Having a queen bee, you know? So I steer clear of her. And her friends.'

'Sounds smart,' Emma said.

Hanan stirred her tea and then blew over the top of it. 'So what about you? What do you do?'

'Hmm?' Emma glanced out into the garden. Yahya was standing on top of the slide, holding a stick in the air like a sword. 'Is he . . .?'

Hanan glanced over and rolled her eyes. 'He's fine. You just told me about your husband and your kids, but not you. Do you work? Did you want to move here? Is it better for you? Where are you from originally?'

Emma sighed and then laughed. 'God. That's . . . a lot.'

'Sorry,' Hanan said. 'I'm so nosy. Just tell me to shut up. Have a biscuit.'

'No, it's fine. I can tell you where I grew up: Richmond, outside London. Only child. My dad died a month after Sam was born, Mum remarried last year and I don't see her much any more.'

'That must be hard.'

'I was close to my dad,' Emma said. 'Not my mum so much. She turns up every few months with presents for the kids and tells me everything I'm doing wrong. It's great. She was all for us moving here actually. She thought it would mean I'd have to finally become what she thinks of as a proper housewife. Home with the kids, dinner on the table, no life of my own, you know? Like her when I was a kid.'

Hanan nodded.

'But that's not what I want. I—' Emma was mortified to find her eyes filling with tears. She's swiped at them with the backs of her hands. 'Fuck. This is embarrassing. Sorry.'

Hanan smiled gently at her. 'It's fine. Crying's good. Get it all out, I say.'

Emma stood up and crossed the kitchen, yanking a few sheets of kitchen towel off the roll. She wiped her face, then ran her hands under the cold tap and held her palms over her eyes.

'Sorry,' she said, her back still to Hanan.

'Stop apologising. You're fine.'

Emma turned, leaning back against the cabinets. 'You know what the awful thing is? Until you asked me that, I hadn't even thought about it. How is that possible? I knew Paul wanted it. I knew it would be good for the kids. I'd thought about stuff like running on the beach and being close to Liverpool if I wanted to go shopping or to see a show or something, but it literally never crossed my mind to ask myself if this was something I wanted.'

Hanan dunked a biscuit in her tea. 'It's normal, you know? Thinking about everyone else and forgetting yourself. That's why I asked.'

Emma laughed. 'What are you, like the bored housewife whisperer or something?'

Hanan laughed. 'Let's say I identify.'

'Yeah? What does your husband do?'

'Hashim? He's got his own furniture company. Well, him and his brothers. His brothers are still in Leeds. We moved over here so he could open a Liverpool store. I worked there too before I had these two.' She gestured at her smaller boy, who was fast asleep in his buggy. 'I still do a bit of book-keeping for them sometimes.'

'I was a graphic designer. In London. Before kids. I planned to freelance but there just isn't the work. Everyone's doing everything in-house. And I haven't got time anyway.' She shook her head. 'I keep telling people that, but I spend most days watching shitty daytime TV or napping. It just goes by really fast.'

Hanan smiled. 'I miss *Homes Under the Hammer* so much. It's all CBeebies all the time in our house now.' She pointed at her toddler again.

There was a scream from outside and they both looked up to see Ruby, wide-eyed at the window. Emma and Hanan both jumped up and ran to the French doors.

'Look what they did!' Ruby shrieked.

Emma yanked the door open and found Sam and Yahya standing on the patio, soaking wet. Water dripped from Sam's hair, his nose, and the garden hose he held in his left hand.

'It was a accident!' he said, his lower lip already wobbling.

Emma opened her mouth and closed it again. 'Give me the hose, Sam.'

Sam handed over the hose and Emma held it away from her body so the water didn't trickle on her shoes.

'You boys look like you're having fun,' Hanan said. 'You didn't want to join in?' she asked Ruby.

Emma turned to look at her and Hanan raised one eyebrow.

Ruby was frowning, but her eyes were bright. So Emma turned the hose on her.

All the children had ended up drenched and Yahya and baby Mo, who'd been woken by everyone's screaming and laughter, had gone home in borrowed clothes. Emma had cobbled together what Ruby and Sam called a 'monkey grab' – random bits of food eaten in front of the TV – before putting them in the bath, and they were now cuddled up together in Emma and Paul's bed.

'Today was a good day,' Ruby said, rubbing her forehead against Emma's arm, the way she'd done since she was a baby.

'Yahya is nice!' Sam said. 'And the baby is so cute!'

'You were naughty to turn the hose on though,' Ruby said, for possibly the fiftieth time since she'd snitched in the first place.

'I know!' Sam shouted, as Emma said, 'We've been over this, Roo.'

'Sorry,' Ruby said, quietly. She was exhausted, Emma could tell.

'Was Yahya's mum nice too?' Sam asked Emma.

'She's lovely,' Emma said.

If Hanan hadn't been there, Emma suspected she'd have shouted at Sam, who'd then have burst into tears. Ruby would have gloated about telling on him and knowing that they weren't allowed to use the hose. Emma would no doubt have lost her temper with Ruby too (sometimes her smugness could be a little wearing) and then they'd have eaten dinner in silence, been subjected to a short angry bath and then once they were in bed, Emma would've cracked open a bottle of wine and wondered where the fuck Paul had got to.

Instead they'd all laughed until their stomachs hurt and Sam had almost peed himself, and Emma felt like she'd made a real friend.

'It's only clothes,' Hanan had said, as they'd undressed the boys in the downstairs loo. 'They'll dry.'

And she was right; it was only clothes. The garden was a swamp now, but Emma couldn't remember the last time she'd had so much fun.

'Can we have two chapters?' Sam asked, his voice muffled by the blankie-wrapped thumb in his mouth.

'Just one,' Emma said. 'You two are exhausted.'

'I'm not even tired!' Sam said.

Emma glanced down at him. His eyes were already closed. She opened the book and started to read.

Before Emma had even finished one chapter, Ruby was asleep too. Emma had left her in her and Paul's bed, but carried Sam to his own bed, his little hand reaching up to pat her cheek as they'd crossed the landing. Paul could take Ruby back to her own bed when he got home. Back downstairs, Emma swiped a crust of toast through a puddle of ketchup on Sam's plastic Paw Patrol plate and folded it into her mouth. She should text Paul and ask for his ETA.

She yanked the dishwasher open and pulled out a glass. And then she opened a bottle of wine.

Emma wasn't sure what time Paul had come home, just that it was late. She'd heard him come in – stubbing his toe on the corner of the bed and muffling a 'fucksake', pulling open the squeaky drawer to get a new pair of pants to wear in bed, groaning as he sank into the mattress. She'd listened to it all with her back to him and her eyes closed, breathing steadily so he didn't suspect she was still awake.

She'd been looking forward to him coming home too. Thought maybe they could have had a glass of wine together and sat at the kitchen table talking about their day, the way they used to in London. Sometimes they'd intended to just have one drink and then move to the lounge to watch TV or up to bed for an early night, but they'd found themselves talking – talking until it was time to head up to bed anyway. She missed it. She missed Paul. He'd been working such long hours since they'd moved north. And she knew he was trying to establish himself, knew it would get better. But she still felt like they were growing apart. Or not even growing apart really. Being stretched apart. Paul was being stretched away from her and she didn't know when he was going to snap back.

She still needed to think about the lube too. About what it meant. Beyond that he used it for wanking. But when? Emma was always around and he certainly wasn't using it with her. She'd have to ask him about it, but the thought of that was almost hilarious. How does a person even bring that up in conversation when they haven't talked about anything other than kids or bills for months?

Emma wondered if he missed her too. If he even thought about her. If he remembered when he'd climb into bed and curl around her like a comma, his thigh slung over her hip, hand flat against her belly, lips pressing into the side of her neck. She'd loved it. Loved how safe it made her feel. And she loved it when she could feel his dick hardening against her bum. She used to wriggle a little, pretending she was just making herself comfortable, waiting for his answering moan before he'd flip her over and they'd both laugh as he'd push her T-shirt up and slide down under the duvet.

When had that last happened? She couldn't remember. A few weeks ago, he'd come in late after some work function at a hotel in Albert Dock – smelling of beer and cigs and garlic – and pressed up against her, but she'd rolled away instead of pressing back, and he'd turned over and been snoring within seconds. He probably didn't even remember it. Or maybe that's when he'd bought the lube – because he thought Emma wasn't interested. She needed to make sure he knew that wasn't true.

She shuffled closer to him, but his breathing was slow and heavy. She could tell he was almost, if not already, asleep. She'd wanted to tell him about Hanan and the kids. Wanted to tell him about school and Sam meowing. Wanted to tell him she'd had a really good day and ask him about his. Maybe at the dining table with a glass of wine. Or in front of the TV with her feet in his lap as he pressed his thumbs into her arches and wiggled his fingers between her toes until she had to yank them away. She couldn't remember the last time they'd done that either.

Chapter Nine

After dropping the kids at school the following morning, Emma went home for Buddy and then down to the beach again. She sat on the rocks as the Border Terrier ran wildly, teeth bared, ears flying back in the breeze.

Emma thought back to her conversation with Hanan: what did she want from life? Maybe she just needed to work. She'd known exactly who she was when she'd had a job. Work Emma had been more together, more organised, more confident than Housewife Emma. She'd known she was good at her job, but it was always challenging, she was never bored. Well, hardly ever. Now she seemed to be bored most of the time. No one told you how tedious much of parenting was. Not just the constant washing and tidying and wiping faces and bums, but also listening to Sam talk about Minecraft. Or Lego. Or to Ruby reading. She was a great reader, but the books the school sent home were dull as fuck. And Emma still hadn't managed to read anything herself. Ruby had asked if they could go and join the library, but they hadn't got round to that either. Just the day to day *stuff* seemed to suck up all of Emma's time.

And what made it worse was that Emma knew she was meant to find the stuff rewarding. Quality time with the children. Walking on the beach or in the park. Playing in the garden. Even bath time. But she always caught herself thinking about all the things she could be doing instead. And not even valuable, useful things like cleaning or the laundry or organising all the paperwork she'd meant to do before the move, but had instead shoved into a big blue Ikea bag and brought with them – no, she fantasised about sitting at the table with a coffee. Or watching an episode of Bake Off without the kids interrupting or Emma herself falling asleep.

It probably made her a terrible person. It almost certainly made her a terrible mother.

Emma called out to Buddy, who stopped dead, stared at her, then took off in the direction of Hilbre Island. The kids had been asking to walk out there since they'd first arrived in West Kirby, but they hadn't got around to that yet either.

'Fuck's sake,' Emma said. She could run after him, but he'd probably think it was a game and have her chasing him all round the beach. Or. She could just leave and hope he came after her.

'OK, bye!' she called, jangling his lead, as she walked towards the slipway. 'See you at home!'

Buddy stopped again and looked back at her, his head on one side. By the time Emma had reached the promenade, he was jumping up at her heels and trying to grab the lead in his mouth.

'Idiot,' Emma said, affectionately.

She turned towards home, before remembering she'd used the last of the milk, and pivoting back in the direction of the town centre.

Forty-five minutes later, she'd been to the butchers, the grocers, the chemist, and the greengrocers. This was one of the things she'd wanted when they'd moved – local shops and local produce, not having to support the big bad supermarkets.

But big bad supermarkets were quicker, she had to admit. And cheaper. She turned down a side street that she suspected was a short cut to the main road. It had looked like a normal terraced residential street as she'd headed into it, but there was actually a parade of shops along the right hand side. How had she never been down there before?

The first shop was Saucer, a small coffee shop with forest green bi-fold doors dotted with flyers and posters, the compact seating area in front bordered with planters full of flowers. She got herself a coffee, sat outside, and watched the world go by. It was the most relaxed she'd been for weeks.

Chapter Ten

Matt had tried to convince Jools to give up her book club while she was ill, but she had flat-out refused. For a start, she wanted to keep everything as normal as possible, for herself, for the girls, and so that her friends didn't actually get wind of the cancer. If she cancelled book club, questions would be asked. And questions lead to gossip and the last thing Jools wanted was gossip about her health.

She had decided, however, that she would try to keep the evenings a little shorter – focus more on the books and less on the chat. They could chat at the school gates, there was no need to do it at home too. Though she didn't know if it would work. Once Eve got going – and got a couple of gins down her – they were in it for the long haul.

Sofia had offered to put the girls to bed when she noticed that Jools's eyelids were drooping over dinner. Jools usually loved to do it herself, but she definitely did fancy a quick nap before book club. She crawled into her bed and immediately fell to sleep.

Maggie sat in Jools's lounge by herself. She'd arrived a little early, hoping to catch Jools alone and see if they could get over the awkwardness between them. But the nanny, Sofia, had answered the door and said Jools was having a nap. She'd shown Maggie into the living room, got her a glass of wine, and then run up the stairs two at a time.

Jools's middle daughter, Eloise, had come in to ask some questions about Amy – was she in bed already? Who was looking after her? Could she maybe have one of Amy's puppies? – but then she'd wandered off and Maggie was alone again.

She envied Jools. She'd always envied Jools. For pretty much everything. But right now she was envying the fact that she'd had a nap. Maggie would have loved a nap, but she'd made Amy's dinner, helped her with her homework, given her a bath and washed her ever-knotty hair, helped her with her school reading book, then read the fun book they were reading together, and then cuddled her until she was almost asleep.

Maggie did sometimes fall asleep too, waking up hours later with a stiff neck and a dead arm, but it was hardly restorative. She didn't imagine that was Jools's current circumstance. Maggie had seen Jools's bedroom – it was a sanctuary, like a boutique hotel room. Maggie and Jim's room was messy and tired and had mildew curling around the tops of the wallpaper. Even though Jim was a builder, he never seemed to have time to fix anything around his own house.

She was topping up her wine when Sofia came in and apologised on Jools's behalf.

'She's very embarrassed,' Sofia said. 'She meant to set an alarm on her phone. But forgot.'

Maggie was about to say 'she must've needed it' but that was exactly what her mum would have said and Maggie was still smarting from Nick's comments about their similarities. Instead she said, 'It's not a problem.'

'Is Amy with your husband?' Sofia asked. She was still standing near the end of the coffee table where she'd placed the wine earlier.

'Sit down,' Maggie suggested, gesturing at one of the other chairs. She half expected Sofia to say she wasn't allowed on the living room furniture, but instead she perched on the edge of the chair opposite Maggie's and smiled.

'My brother's looking after her actually,' Maggie said. 'Husband's working tonight.'

Sofia asked about Jim's job and by the time Jools appeared, they were deep into a conversation about Polish builders, both laughing, and Maggie was on her third glass of wine.

'Sofia, I think Eloise was calling you,' Jools said.

Sofia sprung to her feet. 'Sorry, I'll go up now.' She smiled at Maggie. 'It was nice talking to you.'

'You too,' Maggie said.

She watched Sofia leave the room and then turned to look at Jools. She didn't look like she'd just got up. She was wearing a black jumpsuit and leopard print ankle boots with a heel. Her beautiful hair was pulled back in a low ponytail and she was wearing the sort of make-up that made you look like you weren't wearing any and which Maggie had never been able to master.

'So how are you?' Maggie started. 'I—'

She was interrupted by a knock at the door.

'So you're actually telling me that you'd choose romance over passion?' Eve asked Flic.

Flic's cheeks were pink. 'Yes! And I think you probably would too.'

'I wouldn't,' Eve argued. 'If I had to choose between Darcy and Heathcliff, it'd be Heathcliff every time.'

'Even though he's a sociopath?' Jools asked.

'Psychopath, in my opinion,' Flic said. 'He kills the puppy.'

'Because he's passionate,' Eve says. 'Darcy's repressed and

obnoxious and the only reason anyone finds him remotely attractive is Colin Firth.'

'That's not true,' Maggie said, laughing. 'The book was popular for a long time before the wet shirt thing.'

Eve flapped her hand. 'I just can't believe anyone would choose a wet lettuce like Jane Austen over Emily Brontë. Needlework versus the dark and stormy moors.'

'I'd rather take a turn around a rose garden than try to slit my wrists on a broken window,' Maggie said. 'But that's just me.'

'It's not passion, it's petulance,' Flic said.

Eve rolled her eyes. 'This is all because you're not passionate about anything.'

'I am!' Flic said. Her cheeks were a much deeper pink now.

'What are you passionate about?' Eve challenged her.

Maggie topped up her wine glass and realised she'd drunk a full bottle. How had that happened?

'I'm passionate about baby-wearing,' Flic said.

'Oh my god,' Eve groaned.

Flic laughed. 'I'm passionate about music.'

Flic had surprised them all by recently admitting to being a huge fan of hair metal. Eve said it was her dream to go to a gig with Flic and just watch her in the mosh pit.

'OK,' Eve said. 'You can have that one. What about you two?' She gestured at Jools and Maggie.

'I'm passionate about lots of things,' Jools said. 'Family. Parenting.'

'Jesus Christ,' Eve said.

'Travel,' Jools added. 'And good coffee.'

'This is depressing,' Eve said. 'Cheer me up, Maggie.'

While Flic and Jools were talking, Maggie had been trying to think of something – anything – she was passionate about, but there was nothing.

Well, there was Amy, of course. But that was basic. If Eve had asked her ten years earlier, she probably would have said Jim. But that certainly wasn't true now. And it probably hadn't been true then either.

'Nothing?' Eve prompted.

'Days like today when it's cold but sunny and the air feels crisp,' Maggie said, looking the length of the room into the garden. 'I'm passionate about that.'

'I'm sorry I even asked,' Eve said. 'You're all useless.'

Chapter Eleven

'I hate him!' Ruby screeched from the corner of the dining room.

'That's not very kind,' Emma said, from the stove.

She'd accidentally turned on the grill instead of the oven, which meant the kids' oven chips were still frozen, and the baking tray she'd left under the grill was burned black and billowing eye-melting smoke.

'What's that smell?' Sam called from the hallway where he'd been banished by Ruby.

'You!' Ruby bellowed.

Emma smothered a laugh. 'I just burned a pan, sweetie, don't worry about it.'

'When's Daddy home?' Sam asked, peeping around the door.

'Get out!' Ruby yelled.

'Rubes,' Emma said. 'Get a grip.' They were approaching half-term now and both children were exhausted and crotchety. Emma wasn't feeling much better herself.

She shook the oven chips on the tray and put them back in the oven. 'Sam. I'm not sure when Daddy's back. He said he wasn't going to be late, but I don't know what time it'll be.'

'Before my bedtime?' Sam asked.

'I don't know, hun. I hope so.'

'OK,' Sam said, cheerfully, and went back to his Lego.

'You shouldn't be nice to him, Mum,' Ruby said, sidling up to Emma. 'He ruined my picture.'

'It was an accident,' Emma said, even though she knew it probably hadn't been. 'And he's little.'

'He's not that little,' Ruby said, but her voice had already softened. 'He's five! Can I do something?'

Emma leaned over and kissed the top of her daughter's head. 'Want to do the peas?'

While Ruby was emptying the peas into a microwavable dish, Emma heard the key in the front door and Sam shouting 'Daddy!'

She poured herself a glass of wine.

Dinner was already on the table when Paul came down from his shower. His hair was still wet and curling against the collar of his T-shirt. He hadn't shaved, but Emma could smell the shower gel he'd bought in duty free when they went to Madeira in the summer. Lemons and a hint of tobacco. They'd had some good sex in Madeira. There'd been a problem with the main building of the hotel so they'd been upgraded to a villa. The kids had their own bedrooms and they were a couple of rooms away from Emma and Paul's. The sun and the sea and the wine – and Paul being away from work – meant that they were more relaxed than they had been for a long time. Most nights, they'd crawled into bed not long after Ruby and Sam had.

In fact, was that the last time they'd had sex? That might've been the last time they'd had sex.

'Busy today?' Emma asked.

Paul shrugged. 'It's always busy. Today wasn't bad though. Not like yesterday's sh—'

'No swearing, Daddy,' Ruby said.

Paul grinned and reached over to ruffle her hair. Ruby jerked her head away and smoothed it back down.

'What happened yesterday?' Emma asked.

'We're doing a big deal,' Paul said, rubbing a hand over his damp hair. 'But the guy at the club's being a—'

'No swearing, Daddy,' Emma said, raising one eyebrow at him.

'Difficult,' Paul said, smiling. 'He's being difficult.'

'Anyone I'd have heard of?' Emma asked. It was unlikely. But possible.

'Actually, maybe,' Paul said. 'I'll tell you later.'

'Why can't you tell us now?' Ruby asked, frowning.

'Because it's not official yet,' Paul said. 'And little jugs and all that.'

Ruby rolled her eyes. She hated being left out of anything.

'I don't want to talk about my boring job anyway,' Paul said, reaching out and poking her gently in the side. 'Tell me about school.'

'I hate it,' Sam said.

'You do?' Paul looked over at Emma.

She stared back at him. She'd told him. More than once. She'd met with the head who had referred Sam to a psychologist who was coming to see them at home. The head agreed that it was probably just a settling in issue, but better to nip it in the bud if possible. Emma wondered if Paul had been listening even as she'd been saying it.

'I want to stay home with Mama,' Sam said. 'Can I stay home with Mama?'

'No, you can't,' Emma said.

'So who's the player then?' Emma asked, once the kids were both in bed.

Paul was stretched out on the sofa, his feet up on the coffee table, *Grand Designs* on the TV. Emma was sitting in the armchair, her feet curled up underneath her, but she was considering joining Paul on the sofa. Maybe. Over the past few weeks since she'd found it, she'd tried so many times to think of a way to ask Paul about the lube and eventually decided not to. His wanking habits were his own business. It wasn't like she didn't have her own *me time* every now and then.

Paul looked up. His glasses had slid down to the end of his nose and he peered at her over the top of them. His hair had dried fluffy and he looked a bit like a sexy owl. He was still so gorgeous. Emma had always fancied him, since the first time they'd met – at Emma's work Christmas do. At the time, Paul was best mates with Carl, one of Emma's colleagues. Carl's girlfriend had moved out unannounced while he was at work earlier that week, so Paul had come along with him to both help him drown his sorrows and stop him going completely off the rails. Emma had got talking to him at the bar and had kept talking to him for most of the night. The following day he'd sent her flowers and they were living together within three months. He'd hardly changed at all, which was a bit galling since Emma felt like she was an entirely different person.

Emma moved to the sofa.

'The player you're signing,' Emma repeated.

'Oh. Yeah. Matt Jackson. He lives off Grange Road. You know near that wine place? His kids go to Hillcrest.'

'Oh my god,' Emma said. 'I know his wife. I mean, I don't know her. God, she's a bitch.'

'Yeah?' Paul said, folding the newspaper and leaning forward to put it on the coffee table. 'How?'

Emma turned on the sofa so she was facing Paul. 'She's like the Queen Bee of the school. She runs an exclusive book club. Invitation only.'

Paul laughed and Emma felt something loosen in her chest. It couldn't have been that long since she'd seen him laugh, could it? But it felt like maybe it was.

'Fuck off!'

'No! I know! That's what I said.'

'What does she look like?' Paul said.

'Like . . . a footballer's wife. Long, shiny, blonde hair. Tan. Teeth. You know.'

Paul smiled. 'I do.'

Emma didn't dare think about what she might look like. In her saggy tracksuit bottoms and oversized stripy T-shirt that she'd flopped a bit of ketchup on during dinner. Her hair pulled back into a ponytail. No make-up. She wasn't sure if she'd even cleaned her teeth that morning. She knew she'd intended to, had possibly made it as far as the bathroom, but she had a sneaking suspicion that one of the kids had called her and she hadn't done them. She wasn't even sure she'd put on deodorant, now that she thought about it. She knew she hadn't moisturised. In fact, she thought maybe she was out of moisturiser. Jools Jackson probably used Crème de la Mer. Or that one made from baby foreskins.

But Paul didn't care what Emma looked like. In fact, he used to say he loved her most when she was all relaxed and cosy at home. Although maybe he didn't mean quite this relaxed. She should probably try a bit harder.

Paul leaned forward and topped up Emma's wine, emptying the bottle. Emma smiled to herself. That was one of Paul's tells. He wanted to have sex. It wasn't ideal that he felt like he had to get her tipsy first, but it was fair enough really. She definitely found it hard to relax enough to really go for it. She was tired. She worried that the kids would overhear. And apart from anything else, after a day of being bothered by the kids the last thing she wanted was someone else pawing at her. But she knew that wasn't the healthiest way of looking at it. So she shuffled along the sofa towards Paul and put her head on his shoulder. He made a surprised sound, but relaxed against her, his hand brushing against her thigh. Emma felt a frisson of . . . something, run up between her legs.

'Want to go upstairs,' she murmured.

'Thought you'd never ask,' Paul replied.

Emma slumped slightly as Paul leapt to his feet and grabbed their wine glasses off the table, before heading out of the room.

As Emma hauled herself to her feet, she glanced at the pile of mugs on the coffee table that should be in the dishwasher. On her way out of the room, she spotted Sam's school sweatshirt where he'd pulled it off and left it on the floor. It should've gone in the wash, she wasn't sure if he had a clean one. On the way up the stairs, she remembered that she'd promised to do Ruby's reading with her and had then forgotten all about it – they'd have to do it in the morning. She'd have to wake up a bit earlier. She didn't even want to know what time it was now. It was fine.

Paul was already in bed when Emma reached the bedroom. The lights were off, but the streetlight was glowing through the too-thin curtains. She needed to order new ones, but she wasn't sure how you measured for curtains exactly.

Usually when Emma came up to bed and Paul was already there, he'd have his back to her and, she assumed, his eyes closed. But tonight, now, he was on his side, turned towards her, his head propped up on his hand.

'*Draw me like one of your French girls*' popped into her head, and Emma stifled a laugh. No, not a time for laughing. Sex time. Right. Emma pulled her T-shirt over her head, only stopping to wonder which bra she had on when it was too late. She just had to hope it wasn't her saggiest, most greying. She looked down. It was. She pulled it off fast and saw Paul's eyes widen almost imperceptibly. It was good to know he still liked her boobs. But she had good boobs, even she knew that. She wriggled out of her trackies in what she hoped (but doubted) was a passably sexy way and then clambered under the duvet.

'Hey,' Paul said.

'Hey.' Emma wriggled across the bed towards him.

She never really knew how to do this bit. How to get from 'here we are in bed together, quick kiss, night!' to sex. Being sexy. She'd read an article about it in a magazine once, but one of the suggestions was to get your partner to play with your nipples while you watched TV, which was one hundred per cent one of the worst ideas she'd ever heard in her life.

Now she pressed herself up against Paul and sighed into his neck. She felt almost shy. Which was ridiculous. They'd been together for ten years. He'd seen her shit herself during labour with Ruby. There was absolutely zero mystery any more. She sucked his earlobe into her mouth and appreciated his resulting groan.

'Hi,' Paul said again, shuffling down the bed slightly and kissing her neck. She tipped her head back a bit. Paul always went to town on her neck and it wasn't that she didn't like it – it was fine – it just didn't seem to do as much for her as Paul seemed to think it would. She tipped her head back and moved her mouth to his. Kissing. Kissing she could do. They were good at kissing, always had been. Sometimes during sex, Paul got a bit slobbery and over-eager, but that was OK. She could work with that. She pushed her hand into his hair to make it easier to hold him back a little, but it wasn't necessary. It was a good kiss. Soft, but deep and slow and, yes, sexy. Emma sighed against his mouth. Kissing was good. They should kiss more. Why didn't they kiss more?

'Mummy?'

Shit.

Paul was still kissing her. She turned her head and wriggled out from under him.

'What's the matter, sweetie?'

Ruby was standing in the doorway, the head torch Paul's dad had given her for Christmas in her hand, the light turned to red.

'What are you doing?' Ruby asked.

Emma couldn't quite see her face, but she could picture it: eyebrows drawn together and bottom lip pouched out, her hair tangled at the crown of her head, fingers tugging at the bottom of her pyjama top.

'We were just having a cuddle,' Emma said, reaching over the side of the bed and groping on the carpet for her T-shirt and knickers.

'Have you got pants on?' Ruby asked Paul.

Paul laughed. 'Not right now, no. I was a bit hot.'

Emma smiled as she slid her knickers up her legs under the duvet. She couldn't even look at Paul.

'Were you hot too, Mummy?' Ruby asked.

'Very hot,' Paul said and Emma snorted, swinging her legs out of bed.

'Let's get you back to bed, pickle.' She chivvied Ruby out of the room and across the landing, back to her own room. She turned on the lamp on top of the bookcase at the foot of Ruby's bed.

'What's up?' she asked her daughter, as she climbed back into bed.

'I had a bad dream,' Ruby said, her bottom lip quivering. 'A monster came and then I woke up but the monster came again cos I was still asleep and then when I woke up, I saw a shadow and I thought the monster was in my room so I got my head torch and I came to find you.'

'Wow,' Emma said, stroking Ruby's hair back from her forehead as she eased her back onto her pillows. 'That sounds super scary.'

'It was,' Ruby said, in a tiny voice.

'I'm not surprised you came to find me.'

'Good job I had my head torch.' Ruby yawned.

'Yep. Very sensible.' Emma leaned over and kissed her daughter's forehead. 'Do you think you can go back to sleep now.'

'Yes.' Her eyes were already closed. 'But what if the monster comes again?'

'Just think happy thoughts and I don't think it will. Monsters hate happy thoughts.'

Ruby smiled. 'Cos they're so mean?'

'Exactly that. For monsters, happy thoughts are disgusting. Like broccoli.'

'Or olives.'

'Or olives, yes.' Emma loved olives. She kissed Ruby again and tucked her duvet into her sides. 'Love you.'

'Love you,' Ruby echoed, almost asleep already.

Emma turned off the lamp and tiptoed to the door and back across the landing, pulling her T-shirt off on the way. Back in the bedroom, she climbed straight into bed and pressed right up against Paul, hooking one leg over his hip.

He was fast asleep.

Chapter Twelve

Maggie and Amy were dancing to Ariana Grande in the kitchen when Jim came home. Nick had gone with Maggie to pick Amy up from school then headed over to Liverpool to meet an old friend for dinner. Maggie envied him; it was ages since she'd been out for dinner with a friend. Jim seemed to think book club met all of Maggie's social life needs.

Jim dropped his jacked over the back of a chair and then flicked the radio off without even speaking. Maggie and Amy stopped dead in the middle of the room.

'Bad day?' Maggie asked.

'I'm knackered,' he said, rubbing his hands over his face. 'Shouldn't she be in bed?'

'We've been dancing!' Amy said.

'I'm going to get a shower,' he said, ignoring his daughter and heading upstairs.

'Do I have to go to bed?' Amy asked, sitting down at the table. 'I've got my reading book . . .'

Maggie laughed. Literally the only time Amy was ever keen to do her homework was when it would work to stall bedtime.

'Fifteen minutes,' Maggie said.

When she heard the shower start to run, she turned the

radio back on. Amy slid off the chair and danced towards Maggie, a cheeky smile on her face.

'Does Daddy hate his job?' Amy asked, as Maggie twirled her under her arm.

'He doesn't hate it. It's just hard work. And sometimes the people he works for are annoying.'

'Louis is annoying,' Amy said. 'He threw Puppy in a tree.'

'Oh no!' Maggie said, reaching for Amy's other hand so she could twirl her the other way. 'What did you do?'

'Sam got him down.'

'Sam the new boy? How did he do that?'

'He threw a stick and it hit Puppy and he fell out and I caught him.'

'Wow, smart thinking from Sam!'

'He's nice,' Amy said, still twirling.

The song ended and Maggie said, 'Go upstairs now. I'll get milk and a biscuit and be up in a min. And take all the puppies! All of them, I mean it.'

Amy laughed and ran through to the conservatory to start collecting. Maggie was making a note in Amy's school reading diary ("Amy read well tonight", even though Amy hadn't read at all) when Jim's phone started ringing in his jacket pocket. He'd set it with the most obnoxious ringtone and it went on and on, way past the point Maggie expected it to stop. It stopped briefly and then started up again. Maggie fished it out of Jim's pocket, intending to turn the ringer off, but instead she saw his latest text message.

It was from someone named Eve and it said, simply: 'Tonight?'

Maggie stared at it, gripping the edge of the dining table until her knuckles ached. Eve. Maybe it wasn't Eve from school, from book club. Maybe it was an Eve from work. An Eve he'd never mentioned. Maybe it was Steve and he'd fucked up the name when he typed it into his phone. Or – Maggie frowned down at the phone – maybe it actually did say Steve and she just wanted . . . No. It definitely just said Eve. With a capital E.

'Mum?' Amy said. She had two puppies under each arm.

'On my way,' Maggie told her.

'Have you seen my phone?' Jim asked, putting his head – his hair wet – round the door of Amy's bedroom, where Maggie and Amy were sitting on Amy's bed, leaning up against the headboard, reading a Clarice Bean book that Amy liked a lot more than the book she'd brought home from school.

'It's on the dining table,' Maggie told him. 'And I'm done.' *In more ways than one*, she thought to herself. 'Do you want to say goodnight?'

Maggie kissed her daughter's forehead and then stood up, switching places with Jim. She couldn't get out of the room fast enough.

Downstairs, she packed Amy's school bag and set out a clean uniform, before putting the dinner dishes in the dishwasher and the day's dirty uniform – along with the clothes Jim had discarded on the bathroom floor – in the washing machine ready for the morning. She wanted to look at his phone again. She wanted to see if she could guess his pin – it was probably their anniversary or Amy's birthday. But she also didn't want to snoop.

But Eve. Could it really be Jools's Eve? She'd pretty much stolen Jools from Maggie and now she wanted her husband too?

Maggie was in the conservatory with her wine and her craft box when Jim came downstairs. She heard his footsteps on the quarry tile in the kitchen as she squirted glue onto the pebble she'd found earlier, the pebble for the father's head in the picture.

Jim's footsteps stopped. And then nothing. Maggie drank some wine and pressed the pebble onto the board. The picture was a family of three. Their family. Amy had asked for it, even though Maggie had made her a few pictures already: one of a little girl, one with a little girl and a puppy, one with their whole family including Grandma and Nana.

'Mags,' Jim said from behind her.

She half-turned in her chair, looking back at him. He was still really good-looking. His work, along with five-a-side on a Sunday morning kept him fit and muscled and he knew what clothes suited him, which still somehow surprised Maggie – he was better at dressing himself than she was. Right now he was wearing black jeans and a long-sleeved grey shirt that showed off the definition in his chest.

'I've got to go out,' he said. 'Probably be a late one.'

She nodded. 'OK.' Nick would be back soon anyway, and if Maggie was honest with herself (which she rarely was), she preferred Nick's company anyway.

Jim didn't say he had a work thing or that he was going to meet the lads. He just . . . left. Maggie heard the front door close and wondered what she'd do if he really was having an affair; if he was sleeping with Eve. She'd like to think Eve wouldn't do it to her, but she wasn't sure. She knew Eve had a different standard of morality to the rest of them, particularly Flic – Eve had reduced Flic to tears of frustration during a discussion of sex as a commodity when they read *Moll Flanders*. If Eve thought it was just sex, or if Jim had told her they were separated, Eve wouldn't hesitate. And while it made Maggie want to smash her head in with one of the pebble pictures, it wasn't Eve's responsibility to be faithful to Maggie. It was Jim's.

Maggie pulled the pebble off the board and threw it hard at the wall. It landed with a pitiful *dink* and dropped to the ground. Maggie shook her head. She couldn't even do anger right. But anger wasn't actually the main emotion she was feeling. No, that was relief.

Chapter Thirteen

'What time's the appointment?' Matt asked Jools.

He was lying behind her in bed, drawing on her back with his index finger. They'd done this for as long as they'd been together. The first time he'd told her he loved her he hadn't actually said it, he'd written it on her back with his finger. She hadn't guessed it – he told her later.

'You don't need to come,' Jools said, her eyes still closed. 'Eve's coming with me.'

Matt dipped his head and kissed her shoulder.

'You're crazy if you think I'm not coming.'

'Babe, you can't come.' Jools rolled onto her back and looked up at him. The room was still dark, but she could see the shape of his face and she knew it so well anyway, she didn't need to see him to be able to picture his expression perfectly. Currently a combination of hurt and stubborn, she imagined.

'No, listen,' she said. 'We want to keep this quiet, right? And you're distinctly recognisable, particularly now with all the transfer rumour stuff in the papers.' She brushed her thumb over his cheekbones, her fingers over his jaw. 'I'll be fine with Eve. And I'll call you straight after.'

'I should be there,' he said.

'It's fine. It's the first one. It won't be so bad. You can come next time, after the deal's done.'

He kissed her, his hand curling over her side, fingers pressing into the spaces between her ribs.

'Are you scared?'

She closed her eyes. 'I don't think so. Maybe a bit? Really I just want to get it over with. I hate this limbo. And I hate thinking of all these little cancer bastards crawling around inside me. I want the fuckers dead.'

Matt rested his forehead against the front of her shoulder, letting his lips drift over her skin.

'And I'm a bit scared I might get really sick. And be a rubbish wife. And mother. And look like shit. And smell like puke. And—'

Matt kissed her. 'I don't give a shit. I love you. All of you. The kids will be fine. I'll be fine. You just need to focus on getting better.'

'You're the worst,' Jools said.

Matt reached up and brushed away the tears that had started to pool in the outer corners of her eyes.

'I love you. More than anything.'

'More than football?'

Matt laughed. 'Little bit more than football, yeah.'

'We need to get up,' Jools said, wiggling a little underneath him.

'Not yet.' He dipped his head to kiss the top of her breasts. 'These fellas are going through some shit today. I need to give them a bit of moral support.'

'Fellas?' Jools said, laughing. But she was already curling her body up to meet Matt's mouth.

'I've got Coke. And cheese,' Eve said, holding her bag out awkwardly in front of her. 'Biscuits – those nice ones from Aubergine. And chocolate. Oh and ginger biscuits and some ginger sweets I read about online, but they look disgusting.'

'Thank you,' Jools said. Her stomach was churning with nerves. She hadn't been able to eat anything that morning or much of anything the night before either. This was it. This was the start of her treatment and either the first day on her way to recovery or . . . not. Her doctor was optimistic – apparently the type of cancer she had wasn't aggressive and it responded well to chemo, but of course cancer was unpredictable.

'I've brought a scarf in case you get cold,' Eve said. 'And socks. And some magazines – the new *Vogue*! And some chav mags – and a book a woman was going on about at work. Like *Fifty Shades* only better, she said.'

'I'm not reading smut while I have chemo,' Jools said.

'You can take it home.' She lowered her voice. 'I read that chemo can fuck with your sex drive, so.'

Jools nodded. She'd been worried about that. And then felt guilty for worrying. Her sex drive was really the least of her problems at the moment.

'Are you nervous?' Eve asked her.

Jools shifted on the chair. 'A bit. I just want to get on with it really. I hate not knowing how it's going to affect me. And the sooner I start the sooner it'll be over.'

'I'm shitting myself,' Eve said. 'But I know it's not about me.'

Jools laughed. This was why she'd wanted Eve to be the one with her. Eve wouldn't be big, wet eyes and worry and sympathy. Eve was cheese and chocolate and socks and smut and piss-taking.

'How long are we going to be here?' she asked. 'I keep forgetting.'

'Hours,' Jools said.

'Mrs Jackson?' a nurse said from the doorway.

Jools's stomach flipped over as she stood. This was fine. This was good. This was dealing with the problem. Kicking cancer's arse. She could do this.

Eve squeezed her arm as they stopped for another dollop of antibacterial hand wash and then followed the nurse into a private room. It was wide and bright and could almost be a hotel room, if it wasn't for all the medical equipment.

'Can I get you a cup of tea, lovey?' the nurse asked. 'And there's a menu on the table if you'd like something to eat.'

'Tea would be lovely,' Jools said. She wanted to laugh. *Tea would be lovely*. She was about to have chemo, she wasn't at a social function.

'I'll bring a pot,' the nurse said.

'Thank you for coming with me,' Jools said, not for the first time, once the nurse had left.

'Oh shut the fuck up,' Eve said, reaching for the menu on the table. 'Of course I was going to come with you. What did Matt say?'

'He wanted to come. Of course. But I told him he's too conspicuous.'

Eve laughed. 'Bet he loved that. Holy shit. You can order grilled sea bass! Chocolate torte!'

'I'm not hungry,' Jools said. 'And Matt was great. I just hope I don't turn into a gross, vomiting mess.'

'Eh, you know he'd love you anyway,' Eve said. 'The two of you are a horrible disgrace.'

She passed the menu to Jools and then reached into her bag on the floor between her feet and pulled out a Twirl. 'Want half?'

Jools shook her head. 'Seriously. Not hungry.'

'So,' Eve said, through a mouthful of chocolate. 'I'm sort of seeing someone.'

'Oh my god. And you've waited 'til now to tell me?'

'I was actually going to wait 'til they started pumping you with the stuff, but apparently that's not happening anytime soon, so. Don't judge me . . .'

'Oh god,' Jools said.

The nurse chose that exact moment to return with the tea, which came on a tray with a jug of milk, a bowl of sugar lumps, and a plate of biscuits.

'We're not in Kansas any more,' Eve said, screwing up her Twirl wrapper and throwing it in the bin.

'I'll be back in a minute,' the nurse told Jools. 'Just need to sort out your medications. It's only just arrived.'

'So . . .' Jools said, once the nurse had gone.

'He's married,' Eve said. 'But not happily. I know. It's bullshit. But it's not a relationship, it's just sex. Really good sex.'

Eve hadn't lowered her voice at all and it was loud at the best of times. Jools shushed her.

'Oh god, don't shush me!' she said. 'I'm not going to go into detail. Unless you want me to? Also who's going to hear me?'

'I really don't,' Jools said. 'And I don't know! You don't know how thin the walls are.'

Eve rolled her eyes. 'I know you won't approve. And that's fine. But I wanted to tell you anyway because I love you. And also I need someone to talk to about him. Show off when he's amazing, complain to when he's a dick. You know.'

'Where did you meet him?' Jools reached for the tea, which was still too hot but just about manageable if she held the cup by the rim.

'School,' Eve said.

'You've known him since school?'

'Christ, no. Hillcrest.'

Jools tried to shuffle up in her seat, but she couldn't because of the tea. 'Do I know him?'

'You've probably seen him, yeah. He doesn't do the school run often, but he was at the summer barbecue. He's called Jim.'

'Jim,' Jools said. 'Maggie's Jim?'

'Your Maggie? From book club? No. Her husband's not Jim, he's . . .' She screwed up her face in concentration.

'Jim. Her husband's Jim.'

'Really? It can't be the same one then.'

'Why not?'

'I've seen Maggie's husband, haven't I? I would've noticed if . . . What's Maggie's daughter called?'

'Amy.'

Eve made a humming sound.

'You know it's him. Stop pretending you don't.'

'I didn't before just now, I promise.' She bit the skin around her thumbnail.

'You have to stop seeing him,' Jools said.

'Oh come on! Why?'

'Why?' Jools leaned forward, bumping the table, tea sloshing over the side of the cup. 'Because Maggie's our friend! How are you going to face her at book club when you've been fucking her husband?'

'Like this?' Eve smiled beatifically.

'Oh my god,' Jools said. 'You're the worst.'

'OK, I'll tell him we're done. For you. Cos you played the cancer card.'

'I did not!'

'No, but you were thinking about it. I could tell.'

'I've got a different card, actually.'

'Yeah?' Eve poured herself a cup of tea.

'He made a move on me once.'

'No!'

Jools nodded. You remember when I did that stall on the summer fair? He cornered me in the stock cupboard.

'*He Cornered Me in the Stock Cupboard*,' Eve recited dramatically. 'I think I've read that book.'

'Shut up!' Jools swatted her friend's arm. 'He told me I was beautiful and sexy and he could, you know, show me a good time.'

'Did he actually say that? Cos that's killing my lady boner.'

'I don't remember what he said exactly, but that was the gist. I told him I was married and not interested and said I had to get back to the stall and that was it.'

Eve was still stirring her tea, even though the tiny amount of sugar she'd added had to have dissolved already. 'Oh! Is that when you started being weird with Maggie?'

Jools winced. 'Yeah. I was going to tell her. I thought I should tell her, you know?'

'You're too nice.'

'And then I just couldn't. I didn't think she'd believe me, for one. So then I just felt really guilty about it. And whenever she mentioned him it made me feel weird, so I just stopped seeing her so much. Shitty, I know.'

'I mean, it's fair enough. Her husband did try to scuttle you in a cupboard.'

'He did not. God, Eve.'

They sat in silence for a few seconds before Jools said, 'That's made you want him more, hasn't it?'

'It really has,' Eve said. 'I don't know what's wrong with me. It's a sickness.'

And right on cue, the nurse arrived with Jools's chemo.

'Who is that?' Emma asked Beth as a man appeared in the playground. He didn't seem to have a child with him, but he did have swept back dark hair, square black-rimmed glasses and long legs in tight black jeans.

'Oh my god,' Beth said. 'I've never seen him before. Maybe he's a new teacher?'

The man had stopped just inside the gate and turned back to look down the road. A small girl ran under the arm he was holding the gate open with and grinned up at him.

'Can I go and play?' she asked, holding a large floppy dog.

The man's face cracked into an enormous smile and he said, 'Course.'

'Is that Amy?' Beth said, squinting over and making no attempt to hide her interest.

'I think so,' Emma said. 'The dog's a bit of a giveaway.' She watched as Amy ran across the yard towards Ruby, who had been standing alone under a tree. Amy threw her toy dog up towards the branches and Emma could hear Ruby's laugh as clearly as if she was standing next to her. She saw one of Jools's daughters – Violet she thought her name was – standing watching and made a mental note to mention it to Ruby later so that Ruby could perhaps include her in future.

Beth made a growling sound and Emma tore her eyes away from her daughter and looked back over at the new guy.

'You think he's hot?' she asked Beth.

'You don't?' Beth tipped her head to one side, considering.

Emma tried to look at him without making it obvious she was looking at him. There was definitely something about him, but he wasn't exactly good-looking. All his features seemed a little too big for his face. In fact, not just his features: his arms were too long, his hands too big. He looked a bit like a puppet. But it sort of looked good on him.

Emma could tell the other mums were all checking him out too. The atmosphere had changed as soon as he'd appeared. He was still standing just inside the gate. But there were so few dads – or men at all – on the school run, maybe they were just startled.

'Maybe Maggie's hired a manny,' Beth said. 'Maybe he's a lonely widower looking for a soulmate.'

'Or, you know, just a man doing a job.'

'You should go and introduce yourself,' Beth said, bumping Emma with her shoulder. 'Since you're new too.'

'Oh my god,' Emma said. 'Imagine.'

'I wasn't joking. Go on.' She gave Emma a little push in the small of her back.

'No way. I'm not humiliating myself in front of all these people. Women.'

'Women are people too,' Hanan said. Emma hadn't even noticed her approaching. 'What are we doing?'

'We're looking at the new hot new guy,' Beth said.

'Is he hot though?' Hanan asked.

'That's what I said!' Emma turned and smiled at her.

'I think Emma should go and introduce herself, but she's . Emma's too chicken.'

'I'm not chick—'

Hanan interrupted her with a chicken noise.

'You've got to be joking,' Emma said.

Hanan grinned at her and made the noise again.

'You're a grown woman! A mother!'

'Bwak,' Hanan said.

'Oh my god.'

Emma set off across the playground without looking back. Or, in fact, in any direction. She could tell everyone was watching, could almost hear them talking about her; where she was going, what she was planning to do. Although that might have been her overactive imagination.

'Hi!' she said when she reached the guy, who was, it turned out, objectively hot. Beautiful brown eyes. Wide, soft-looking lips. And a jawline she wanted to run her fingers over. It had clearly been too long since she'd had sex.

On the way over, Emma had planned to say 'Are you new here?' and then, at some point, 'Me too.' What actually came out of her mouth was 'Are you me here?'

'Sorry?' He looked a little confused and a little amused.

Emma blinked and shook her head. 'Sorry. I meant new. Are you new here? Because I am too. And we were wondering . . .' She turned and looked back at Hanan and Beth. Beth gave her a thumbs up and she felt her face heat up.

'Oh!' he smiled. He had really nice teeth. 'Yeah. Sorry. No. Not really. Or maybe a bit.' He shook his head as if to clarify his thoughts. 'The little girl with the dog—'

'Amy,' Emma said.

'Oh you know her? Cool. She's my niece. I'm Maggie's brother.'

'Ah!' Emma said. 'That makes sense. I'm Emma. Do you want to come and . . .? I know it can be weird standing on your own when you don't, um, know anyone.'

'Cool,' he said, following Emma across the playground to where Hanan and Beth were waiting. Beth looked flustered already. Hanan was smiling in a way that suggested to Emma she might be planning to break out another chicken impersonation.

Emma introduced him to the other two women and then all three of them stared at him.

'Oh!' he said. 'Yeah. God. Sorry. I didn't say, did I? Nick.'

'Maggie's brother,' Emma said and watched both sets of her friends' eyebrows shoot up.

'Have you moved here?' Beth asked. 'Or are you visiting?'

Before Nick had a chance to answer, Miss McCarry opened the door behind them and walked out into the yard, blowing her whistle on the way. All the kids stopped absolutely dead and silent.

'Woah,' Nick murmured.

'I know, right?' Emma whispered back. 'It's impressive, but also sort of chilling.'

Miss McCarry blew her whistle again and the children immediately sorted themselves into lines for each class.

'This is freaking me out,' Nick said.

'I always think I should get a whistle for home,' Beth said. 'Since they take no bloody notice of me.'

'I've said "one two three, eyes on me" before now,' Hanan said. 'That works. Although I said it to my husband once, he wasn't keen.'

The children all started filtering to their various classrooms, Sam stopping to hug Emma's legs. She bent to drop a kiss on the crown of his head before gently pushing him in the direction of the door.

'He's doing a lot better, isn't he?' Beth said.

'Yeah. We still have tears at night sometimes. And sometimes in the mornings. But I'm not prising him off the door frames any more.'

'Sounds like my ex,' Nick said, before shaking his head. 'Sorry. No brain to mouth filter.'

'We're going to go and get a coffee,' Beth said. 'Would you like to come?'

'Thanks,' Nick said. 'But I said I'd wait for Maggie. She was running late so she told me to go on without her. You know, like in a war.'

'Ah,' Emma said. 'Well. Hope she doesn't leave you too long.'

The three women started to drift away, Beth and Hanan pushing their buggies.

'Good to meet you all,' Nick said. 'Have a good day.'

'See you later,' Emma said. 'Soldier.' When she'd said that in her head, she'd planned to salute. But she couldn't bring herself to do it. And the 'soldier' had been mortifying too.

'Jesus Christ,' she muttered under her breath, as the three of them shuffled into single file to get through the gate.

'Was that you flirting?' Hanan asked, once they were walking side by side again. 'Because if it was . . .'

'God, no, not flirting,' Emma said. 'And shut up.'

Chapter Fourteen

Maggie tried not to notice how Jim was coming home later and later. He kept missing bedtime with Amy and she'd even allowed Maggie to take over a little bit of their routine – singing a song she'd learned in nursery. It made Maggie's heart hurt. Maggie was also aware that she hadn't seen Jim's phone since the day the text message from Eve had popped up. He never left it lying around any more. He took it with him even if he went to the loo. She knew he was having an affair, she was almost sure of it. But a little voice in the back of her mind (her mother's voice) told her there could be a perfectly innocent explanation. Maybe it was right?

Nick had been spending a lot of time in Liverpool looking for a flat – he'd decided to stay up north, but said West Kirby was too small for him – and hanging out with his friends. Maggie hadn't told him about Eve, but whenever he came over he asked Maggie questions about her marriage. Questions she'd asked herself over the years, but now she found herself thinking about them all the time. Why had she married Jim in the first place? Why had she stayed married to him? Did she really think this was it for her for the rest of her life?

Maggie had fancied Jim the first time she saw him. She was out with a group of friends from work, and he was with a group of his mates. They'd started off at opposite sides of the pub, but over the course of the evening had gravitated together to form one raucous, stumbling, laughing group. Maggie couldn't remember much about it apart from Jim handing her a bottle of Smirnoff Ice and then, later, falling backwards off a chair and lying on the floor laughing. That's how she'd pictured him when he'd texted her a couple of days later: on his back on the sticky pub carpet, looking up at everyone, his eyes bright, mouth wide open with laughter.

For their first date he took her to a pub in Parkgate. They sat outside, looking out over the marsh, watching seagulls swooping down to steal people's chips, before ordering fish and chips themselves, curling over to protect them from the birds. They'd bought ice creams and walked along the front. If Maggie closed her eyes, she could still smell the salty air, taste the mint choc chip ice cream, feel Jim taking her hand and squeezing. She'd felt safe. And happy.

The first time he'd yelled at her, he'd been drunk. Had come staggering round to her tiny flat after post-work beers and picked an argument about something stupid. Something so stupid she couldn't even remember. An advert maybe? Or something she was watching on TV that he didn't rate. He'd called her a fucking moron, said he didn't know what he was even doing with her, and then he'd fallen asleep on the sofa. In the morning he'd brought her a cup of tea in bed and didn't remember anything about it. He'd been back to his usual self, funny and kind and loving. She thought it was just the drinking.

They'd been together just over a year when he proposed. He'd planned to propose in Paris – at the top of the Eiffel Tower he said, even though he admitted it was a cliché – but he'd ended up proposing in bed one night, just after they'd had sex. She was resting her head on his chest, already seventy-five per cent of the way to sleep, when he'd said, 'I want to marry you. What do you think?'

The wedding was small and cheap, but the reception had been fun. All their friends in their local, laughing and dancing and toasting them. Maggie remembered it as a blur of happy and proud faces. Of too many drinks. Of Jim's hands on her waist. Her dad hugging her and giving her an envelope that, it turned out, contained a cheque for £1000, of being the last to leave, sitting on a velvet covered sofa, her head on Jim's shoulder, eyes drooping as he laughed with the bar staff and then literally carried her up to bed.

The first time she'd suspected he was seeing someone else was deeply unoriginal: there'd been a smudge of lipstick on his collar. But she told herself it could have happened easily – a colleague could have leaned in for an air kiss and misfired. Maggie had certainly fended off kisses and more from men she'd worked with over the years, it didn't have to mean anything. She didn't mention it to him because she knew even the question would infuriate him.

The next time had been a comment from a friend – or someone she'd previously considered a friend. A group of them had spent the entire day in a beer garden. Lots of them had kids at the same time and they'd all been playing together – running around, hiding under tables, screeching with laughter and occasionally reappearing red-faced and sweaty for an ice lolly or a fruit shoot. Maggie had a few vodkas and then stopped. The sun made her sleepy and spaced out anyway and she knew she'd be the one getting Amy to bed when they got home. Jim was hammered, lying on the grass with his eyes closed. Their friend Claire had come to sit with Maggie, staggering in her heeled sandals, her eyes unfocused. She'd clambered up to sit on the table, her feet on the bench next to Maggie.

'You know he's fucking Selina, right?' she'd said, holding up her bottle of beer like she was making a toast.

Maggie had immediately looked over at Jim, expecting him to have heard and be heading over to them in a fury, but he was still on the grass, most likely asleep.

'No,' Maggie had said. She knew she should have said she knew he wasn't. But no had been all she'd been able to manage. She felt the vodka from earlier burning the back of her throat. Ignoring Claire, she'd got up, found Amy and got a cab home, leaving Jim with his mates.

The next day she told him what Claire had said and he laughed and said, 'She was arseholed, why would you listen to her?'

But he hadn't denied it.

Chapter Fifteen

'Mummy?'

'Hmmmph?'

Emma had been deeply engrossed in a dream about Chris Hemsworth and a bottle of cocoa butter and she couldn't believe she had to wake up.

'Mummy?' Ruby said again, adding a small hand to shake Emma's shoulder.

'Jus'a'min,' Emma mumbled, her face pressed into the pillow. Chris Hemsworth's back muscles under her slippery hands. Chris Hemsworth's lips on her neck.

'We're going to be late!' Ruby said, her voice becoming shrill.

'Ruby!' Emma said, rolling onto her back and scrubbing her hands over her face. 'Could you just let me wake up?'

'But it's eight o'clock,' Ruby said, indignant.

'What?' Emma said, opening her eyes. Watery golden sun was bleeding around the edges of the curtains. It didn't look like eight o'clock. Emma groped around her bedside table for her phone and squinted at the too-bright screen.

'Oh fuck.'

She turned her head and saw that Paul was still in bed, flat out.

'Paul.' She stretched her leg across the bed and pressed his calf with her toes.

He groaned and pulled his leg away.

'You go and get dressed, Rubes,' Emma told her daughter. 'And maybe wake your brother up?'

'I am dressed,' Ruby said. 'And I did already. He's wet the bed.'

'What?' Emma started to sit up. This was all too much to take in when her head was this fuzzy.

'He wet the bed. And his pyjamas. I told him to take them off, but he cried.'

'God,' Emma said. 'OK. Just . . . I don't know. Go and read your reading book or something. OK? I'll sort Sam out.'

'We're going to be late,' Ruby said, walking out of the door. 'Mrs Walker said that she's going to start putting people in the late book and—'

'Ruby!' Emma snapped. 'Please just go downstairs and let me get ready.'

Emma saw her daughter's lip quiver, but then she was out of the room and heading down the stairs.

'Shit,' Emma said.

'I can't believe you didn't wake me!' Paul shrieked fifteen minutes later in the kitchen, yanking a teabag out of his travel mug, his hair wet from the shower, shirt still unbuttoned, tie loose around his neck.

'I mean, I did,' Emma said. 'I can't believe you didn't set an alarm.'

'My phone ran out of charge,' he said. 'But I thought you had an alarm set too.'

'Nope,' Emma said, popping the p. 'I wake up when yours goes off. Can you stop yelling. These things happen.'

'I've got a fucking meeting this morning,' he said.

'Daddy!' Ruby shouted from the front room where she was reading her book in front of the TV.

'Sorry!' Paul called back, before turning back to Emma. 'My wallet?'

'I am not your fucking valet,' Emma said, through her teeth. 'It's probably on your bedside table where it always is.' *Try behind your lube,* she mumbled under her breath, as she ran up the stairs, dodging a Lego helicopter Sam had left there, presumably as some sort of passive aggressive murder attempt. When she got back downstairs with the wallet, Paul was already at the door, satchel over his shoulder, briefcase in one hand, travel mug of tea in the other.

'Have a good day, darling,' Emma said, sarcastically, tucking his wallet into his jacket pocket.

He stepped out onto the path and then turned back.

'I need to take Matt Jackson and his wife out for dinner. With you too. Can you get a babysitter for Friday night?'

Emma's stomach dropped. She opened her mouth to ask for more details, but the door was already closed, with her husband on the other side.

After the school drop off – they'd been half an hour late and Emma had been warned to expect a letter in both Ruby and Sam's school bags at pick-up, which Ruby was not at all happy about – Emma had got home and filled the dishwasher, stripped Sam's bed and put the sheets and duvet cover in the wash, propping his mattress up against the radiator. She'd trawled the house with a big plastic storage bucket, collecting every bit of loose death-trap Lego. And then she'd roused Buddy from his basket, clipped on his lead, and headed for the beach.

It was another perfect autumn day: brisk and bright. Too warm for a winter coat but a bit too nippy for no coat at all. Emma was wearing her yellow mac that she suspected made her look like the kid from *It*. At the beach, she watched while Buddy ran wildly through puddles and barked at seagulls and wondered just how awkward the Jackson dinner was going to be. She'd hated those dinners when they were in London. Paul was always self-consciously blokey – talking and laughing too loudly – and Emma and the wives never had anything in common.

Once, a footballer had slid his socked foot up the inside of Emma's bare leg and she hadn't known whether he was making a pass at her or had mistaken her leg for his wife's. Another time, the wife had asked Emma to go to the bathroom with her and then made her hold the door closed while she did cocaine off the vanity unit. Paul had promised Emma that she wouldn't have to do them any more once they'd moved. She hadn't entirely believed him – it was part of his job – but still. And not only did she have to do dinner, she had to do it with Jools fucking Jackson.

And she was meant to have made the appointment with the psychologist for Sam – even though she was sure he didn't need one – and find a new dentist for all of them and there was something else she'd forgotten, nagging at the back of her mind. She hoped it wasn't anything too important.

She turned to look for Buddy and spotted him wriggling on his back on top of a dead seagull. Marvellous.

Chapter Sixteen

Maggie was late. Again. She'd woken up suddenly at six and realised Jim was still in bed next to her. He usually left for work at 5.45, his alarm going off at five. For a second, she thought about ignoring it and going back to sleep – or trying to go back to sleep – but she couldn't do it.

'Jim,' she whispered, shuffling across the space between them until she could feel the heat emanating from his body. 'Jim.'

He huffed in his sleep, but she knew he wasn't anywhere close to awake. She reached for his shoulder and pushed lightly. 'Jim.'

The thing Nick had said about Simon floated through her head: *I looked at him one day and I couldn't remember why I was with him.*

Jim jerked, huffing again, and said, 'Wha'?'

'It's six.'

'What?'

It was still dark, she couldn't see him at all.

'Six o'clock.'

'Oh for fuck's sake.' He rolled onto his back and Maggie knew he'd be rubbing his face with both hands, stretching his legs down the bed.

She shuffled back to her side.

'Sorry.'

'Fucking phone,' he said and then the room was briefly illuminated by the light from the screen. 'Switched itself off,' Jim said.

Maggie snuggled further under the duvet. She didn't need to get up until seven. She could get another hour's sleep if Jim left soon. The mattress shifted as he clambered out of bed, groaning and muttering. He'd slammed the wardrobe door, swore violently when he'd banged his leg on the bottom of the bed, and then finally he was gone and Maggie could relax. But she'd relaxed too much and didn't wake again until eight. They had to be out of the house by half past.

On the way to the bathroom, she crept into Amy's room and up to the bed. Amy wasn't even visible among the dozens of soft toys she'd filled her bed with. Maggie pulled the duvet back and moved a Cookie Monster, Toothless from *How to Train Your Dragon*, and at least three different puppies before her daughter's sleeping face was visible.

'Baby,' Maggie said. 'You have to wake up.'

Amy's eyebrows pulled together in a frown, her lower lip pouting out. Maggie could smell her breath and it still smelled the way it had when she was tiny: like milk and something biscuity.

'Baby,' Maggie said again, pushing Amy's tangled hair back from her face. 'You've got to wake up. We'll be late.'

Amy groaned and it sounded like Jim.

Maggie knew the road to the school would be crammed with cars – people started arriving not long after eight, which was ridiculous, but it was eight forty now. She pulled in and parked on the side road on the far side of the green.

'I think I need my PE kit,' Amy said, as Maggie opened her door from the outside.

'What? Haven't you got it?'

Amy shook her head. 'Sorry. I forgot.'

'OK. Don't worry. After you go in I'll go home and get it and drop it back at the office.'

'Will they tell me they've got it?' Amy asked.

Maggie reached for her daughter's hand as they crossed the road towards the green. 'I'll ask them to do that. Or you might have to go and ask them at break.'

'OK.'

Maggie skidded a little on the gravel path in her heeled boots and steadied herself with a hand on Amy's shoulder. Other parents and children were still walking up the road, so the whistle obviously hadn't gone yet.

'We're not late,' she told Amy. 'It's fine.'

'Can I go and walk up with Flora?' Amy asked, spotting her friend heading up the other side of the road with her mum pushing the double buggy that Maggie knew contained her twin boys.

'Not yet. Wait 'til we're a bit closer. You can't cross the road on your own anyway.'

They were about to cross the road when Maggie heard the first whistle, which meant they only had two minutes to get to school. Still holding Amy's hand, she stepped out between two parked cars, looking left to make sure no one was attempting to drive up to the school. The parked car to her left started to move: slowly at first and then suddenly jerking back so quickly that Maggie had to jump out of the way, pulling Amy along with her. Amy yelped with fear and Maggie's stomach flipped over as she pushed her daughter back onto the pavement, stormed to the front of the car, opened the passenger door and punched the person in the seat.

★

'What on earth were you thinking?' Mrs Walker, the head, asked her. They were sitting in Mrs Walker's bright, plain, organised office. Maggie had both hands wrapped around a cup of hot, sweet tea, but she was still shaking. Not just her hands, but everywhere. Her teeth were chattering with it.

'I don't know,' she said. 'It was like an out of body experience.'

'Ms Catchpole is very upset,' Mrs Walker said, sipping from her own mug of tea.

Maggie knew exactly how upset Ms Catchpole – Mandy – was, because she'd leapt out of the driver's side and screamed that Maggie was a 'stupid bitch' who shouldn't have been crossing behind the car at all and certainly shouldn't have smacked Mandy's boyfriend. Maggie still couldn't believe she'd done it.

'Is everything OK at home?' Mrs Walker asked and Maggie had that feeling again. The out of body feeling. She was no longer a thirty-year-old woman, sitting in the office of the head of her daughter's school, but a fifteen-year-old girl who'd just spat in her best friend's face in the playground. Even now, remembering it made her shudder.

'Fine,' she said and drank some tea.

She glanced at Mrs Walker over the top of the mug. She looked concerned. Maggie had always hated people looking at her like that.

'Honestly,' she said. 'Everything's fine. I just overslept. I'm tired and we didn't want to be late and, honestly, she could've hit us with the car. She didn't even look.'

'I appreciate that,' Mrs Walker said. 'And I will be speaking to Ms Catchpole as well. But this isn't actually the first time I've had . . . concerns.'

'About me?' Maggie asked before she could stop herself.

'About Amy,' Mrs Walker clarified. 'She often seems subdued. She doesn't really have any friends apart from Flora Wilson. She's . . . timid, I think would be the word.'

'Timid,' Maggie repeated. She'd never thought of Amy as timid. Amy was gentle and kind and funny and sometimes horrendously stubborn. But never timid.

'Perhaps you might suggest she spend more time with some of the other girls?' Mrs Walker said. 'Arrange some playdates? Get her out of her shell a little. Do you know Emma Chance at all? She's new to the area. Her daughter Ruby's in Amy's class? And apparently they've played together a little.'

'I don't think so,' Maggie said. She could vaguely picture a new mum – shoulder-length dark blonde hair, one of those bright yellow coats everyone seemed to have – but she'd never spoken to her.

'I was thinking it might be an idea for you to get Amy and Ruby together? Ruby's friendly with Flora too, but it would be nice if the three of them could spend some time together. Obviously it's up to you and Mrs Chance . . .'

'Right,' Maggie said, nodding. She'd almost finished her tea now without even realising she'd been drinking it. 'Yes, OK, I'll talk to her.' She glanced out of the window. It had started to rain.

'Amy is a lovely girl,' Mrs Walker was still talking. 'I just think she'll blossom more with more friends.'

Maggie wondered if she could ask Jools to bring Violet round to the house. Or maybe it would be better if they went to Jools's house, although she could hardly invite herself. And Jools wouldn't want to have Flora Wilson round for a playdate. Amy and Violet had played together as toddlers, but once they'd both started at school, they'd seemed to drift apart. Maggie had wondered what had happened, but since the same thing had happened between her and Jools, she hadn't been too surprised.

'Are you sure you're all right?' Mrs Walker asked.

Maggie leaned forward and put her mug down carefully on the coffee table. It still made a sharp ringing sound against the glass and Maggie winced.

'I'm fine. Thank you.'

'Perhaps you might like to call Ms Catchpole too,' Mrs Walker suggested.

What Maggie actually wanted to do was lie down on the floor and have a little nap. Maybe stay there until it was time to collect Amy. But she had to get the PE kit. The thought of going all the way home and then coming all the way back again was too much. Even though it was only five minutes each way.

'Yes,' she said, standing. 'Thank you.'

At the office door, Mrs Walker steered Maggie with a hand on the small of her back and then, as she said goodbye, gave her upper arm a quick squeeze.

Maggie had no idea why, but it made her want to cry.

Jools couldn't get out of bed. Her limbs felt stiff and heavy, her head fuzzy. She'd been warned that the chemo might knock her out and that it might get a little worse each time, but she'd felt so well after the first round that it had obviously lulled her into a false sense of security.

Matt had an early call and had left her sleeping and when Eloise had clambered into bed with her, chattering about a game Violet had shown her on her iPad, Jools had listened for a while and then asked her to go and get Sofia.

Sofia had stood at the side of Jools's bed, listening, then she'd taken the girls downstairs and come back up with a cup of tea, a plate of toast and a bowl of fruit salad for Jools, along with Jude the Obscure, the book Jools was reading for book club. It had been Eve's choice and Jools really wasn't enjoying it at all. It was much too depressing. It had been her idea to read classics for book club, but that was before her diagnosis and she was almost regretting it now. She'd love to be able to read something light and fun. Maybe something romantic or sexy. But no, she was stuck with poor Jude and his dead kids. She picked up her phone instead.

Maggie recognised Eden, Jools's youngest daughter, before she saw Sofia. They were sitting in the corner of Saucer with a colouring book open on the table between them, Sofia's head bent in concentration. Eden looked confused when she saw Maggie looking at her, a tiny frown line appearing between her eyebrows, her mouth dropping open. Maggie waved at her, then watched as she muttered something. Sofia looked over at Maggie, smiling.

'Can I get you a drink?' she asked Sofia from across the room.

Sofia shook her head. 'I'm good, thanks.'

Maggie bought herself a coffee and a slice of chocolate cake before heading for a table on the other side of the room.

'Maggie!' Sofia called and then gestured with her eyebrows.

Maggie crossed the room again, smiling.

'Sorry,' she said, sitting at the third side of the square table. 'I didn't want to interrupt.'

'Jools asked me to talk to you,' Sofia said. 'About bringing Violet round for a play with Amy?'

'That's funny,' Maggie said. 'I was planning to ask Jools about getting them together.'

'You'll let me know when's a good time?'

'You'd be bringing her?' Maggie clarified. 'Not Jools?'

Sofia bit her lip as she glanced at Eden. 'Jools is not available so much. She has appointments. So she asked me.'

'Oh OK,' Maggie said. She'd love to ask what appointments, but no doubt it was eyelash extension or botox or something. 'That sounds good anyway.'

Maggie looked down at her cake. For a second there she'd thought it had come from Jools. That Jools would want to bring Violet over, and the girls would play and Maggie and Jools would talk and maybe get back a bit of the friendship they'd lost over the past few months. She should have known better.

Emma had spent the day sitting at her dining table, staring at her laptop. She'd intended to see if she could find any freelance opportunities, maybe email some of her old contacts, instead she'd started reading lifestyle blogs and hadn't stopped until the alarm on her phone alerted her that it was time to go and get the children. Her neck had been stiff, her eyes dry and itchy. And she'd wasted an entire day. So she was relieved to be outside. The earlier rain had stopped and while it was still a bit chilly and damp, the sun was struggling to emerge and the air smelled of ozone. Emma breathed in deeply.. She should start running, she told herself not for the first time. Or maybe swimming. Something anyway. She needed something.

'Excuse me,' a woman called from the opposite side of the road. 'Are you Emma Chance?'

Emma stopped and blinked at her. 'Yeah. Hi. Sorry, I don't . . .'

The woman crossed the road to join Emma. 'You're Sam and Ruby's mum, right?'

Emma nodded. She recognised her now: Maggie. She'd seen her at the school gates. And Beth had told her about her. She was one of Jools's friends.

'Sorry,' Maggie said, as they headed along the prom towards the school. 'I had a meeting with Mrs Walker this morning and she suggested I have a word with you about our daughters? Getting them together? I'm Amy's mum. God, sorry, I'm not making much sense.'

'Oh!' Emma said. 'No, that sounds good. I know Ruby likes Amy. She's talked about her at home.'

'Oh I'm glad,' Maggie said. 'Mrs Walker's worried that Amy doesn't have enough friends and that maybe your daughter might . . . They're both friends with Flora Wilson?'

'Oh yes!' Emma said. 'Ruby loves Flora.'

'Amy does too. You could come round to mine – I can ask Beth about Flora. I was talking to Sofia – Jools's nanny? – and she mentioned bringing Violet round too.'

'Sounds great. Thanks.'

When they got to school, Maggie followed Emma over to Beth. Emma noticed Beth's eyes widen at the sight of the other woman, but she was perfectly nice when Maggie suggested getting the girls together.

'Wow,' Beth said, once Maggie had confirmed that Beth was up for it and headed back across the playground to Flic, who was sitting on one of the picnic tables, breastfeeding her baby. 'She must've fallen out with Jools badly if she wants to slum it with us.'

'Beth!' Emma laughed, covering her mouth with her hand. 'She said one of Jools's daughters will be there too.'

'Yeah, with the nanny. Not with Jools.'

Emma shushed her. Sofia was over near the gate, but Beth's voice wasn't quiet.

'Still,' Emma said. 'It's a good thing. It'll be nice for the girls to get together.'

Beth smiled at her. 'Yeah, you're right. Sorry, I'm being a cow. I've just been around these women much longer than you. I don't trust any of them.'

'That's probably wise,' Emma said. But she hoped Beth was wrong.

Chapter Seventeen

'Ooh!' Eve said, reaching for a long, dark wig. 'Can I try this one?'

'Sure,' Angie, the stylist, said. 'Try on anything you like.'

'But don't forget we're actually here for me,' Jools said, running her fingers over a short cropped wig.

'As if I would,' Eve said. She pulled the wig off the stand and arranged it over her own short hair, turning to pout at Jools. 'What do you think?'

Jools laughed. 'It's not really you.'

'Have you got anything in pink?' Eve asked Angie.

'My customers tend to favour more natural colours,' Angie said, passing Jools a look book. Jools sat down on the sofa in the window and flicked through, trying to find a wig that looked as close to her own hair as possible. She'd thought about trying something different – Eve had suggested a shoulder length bob – but apart from deciding to try a sweeping fringe, she wanted to stick with her own look. She didn't want anyone asking about it, or noticing anything at all. And these wigs were so good, she hoped she might get away with it. That was also why they were so expensive, but, as Eve had said on the way in the car, it's not every day you get to replace your hair.

'Has your hair actually started falling?' Angie asked Jools.

Jools reached up instinctively. There'd been hair on the pillow when she woke up that morning. Hair sliding down her back and tangling in the plug when she'd showered. You couldn't tell looking at her, but it was definitely starting to fall out. The thought of it made her feel sick. Which was why she'd made this appointment.

'A little,' Jools said. 'Not much.'

Eve was trying on a short black bobbed wig. 'Do I look like Louise Brooks?' She reached for her phone and snapped a selfie.

'Don't post that,' Jools said.

'I'm not going to tag it,' Eve said, tapping her phone.

'I know,' Jools said. 'But don't post it.'

Eve stared at her. 'OK.'

'I just—'

'I know. I'm sorry.' Eve crossed the room and sat on the sofa next to Jools. 'I wasn't going to tag it. You know that.'

'I know. And I know I'm being paranoid.'

'You could just tell people, you know,' Eve said, taking the look book from Jools and putting it down on the seat next to her. 'People would want to help.'

Jools shook her head. 'I know they would. But they'd also want to know my prognosis. They'd look at the girls with their heads on one side and wonder if Matt would marry again after I'm gone. I don't want any of it. The oncologist said it could all be over in less than a year if we're lucky. No one needs to know.'

'OK,' Eve said, standing again. 'Let's find you a wig then.'

Despite finding the one she wanted almost immediately, Eve had made Jools try on almost every wig in the shop. She'd insisted on taking photos of a few of them and sending them to

Matt because Jools looked so beautiful. There wasn't a single colour or style that didn't suit her. And Jools had laughed so much she'd cried and it had made Eve's heart hurt.

'You make me sick,' she said on the way back to the car. 'I don't know how you still looked gorgeous in that short blonde one. It made me look like Boris Johnson.'

Jools snorted, just like she'd snorted when Eve had tried it on. 'It did not. And anyway, you're not allowed to be sick. I've got cancer.'

'Way to keep it on the DL,' Eve said. But they were in Eve's car, so it wasn't as if anyone was going to overhear. 'And you're going to have to stop playing the cancer card eventually, you know? It's getting old.'

'The only way I stop playing it is if I die,' Jools said. She'd been testing the idea out mentally, emotionally, over the last couple of days and she'd managed to downgrade her response from total panic to a feeling of mild terror with a side of vomit.

'You should at least tell book club,' Eve suggested. 'They could help with the girls. Make you food. Do other things that women do for each other on TV and in films. Pillow fights, face masks, I don't know.'

Jools shook her head. 'I don't want any of that. Particularly not pillow fights. I just want everyone to act like everything's OK. To treat me like everything's OK.'

'But,' Eve said.

'I know. But that's the way I need it to be. OK?'

'OK.' Eve picked up her phone and poked at it for a bit before looking at Jools again. 'But why?'

'Why are you so annoying?' Jools said.

'I don't know. Always have been. Just . . . can you tell me? Because I don't get it. If it was me, I'd want everyone to know. I'd want every man I've ever slept with to send me flowers.'

'You'd have to hire somewhere to put them all,' Jools said.

'You're funny. And I'd want people to cook me food and take me out and basically coddle me until I felt better or got better. I don't get why you want to do all of this alone.'

'I'm not alone,' Jools said. 'I have you. And Matt. Sofia's great. She shields the kids and distracts them. It's fine. I'm fine. I definitely don't need flowers from ex-boyfriends or meals from the neighbours.'

'Well, you've only got one ex-boyfriend and you don't know your neighbours, right? But you know what I mean? Wouldn't it be easier to tell people than to try to hide it?'

Jools shook her head. 'Matt . . . we have an image.'

'Oh my god,' Eve said. 'Fuck off. You're not Posh and Becks.'

'Shut up. Not like that. Like . . . it's not Matt. It's me. It's just easier for me if I control everything.'

'But you can't control everything,' Eve said. 'That's not possible.'

Jools stared down at her fingers. The skin around her cuticles was dry, but her manicure still looked perfect.

'I can't control cancer,' Jools said. 'But I can control how I deal with it. And this is how I want to deal with it.'

'Mummy got in trouble for hitting,' Amy said without even looking up from her bowl of spaghetti Bolognese.

Without thinking, Maggie shushed her before turning it into a laugh. 'I didn't really.'

'Who'd you hit?' Jim asked Maggie, also without looking up from his plate.

'Did you really?' Nick asked, reaching across the table for the parmesan.

'Someone nearly hit us with their car,' Amy said. 'And Mummy jumped over! And pulled the door open! And—' She clapped her hands.

'Amy!' Jim yelled, dropping his fork on his plate.

Amy and Maggie both jumped, but only Amy burst into tears and fled from the table, running up the stairs to her room. They sat in silence until they heard her door slam.

'She's got a hell of a temper,' Jim said. 'Gets it from you, eh?'

Maggie bit the inside of her cheek, digging her fingernails into her thighs under the table. She didn't even dare look at Nick.

'Did you really smack someone?' Nick asked her.

Maggie forced herself to take a breath in and then out. 'Yeah. I mean, I barely touched them really. Mandy totally overreacted.'

'You smacked Mandy Catchpole?' Jim said.

'No,' Maggie said, stabbing some pasta and twirling it round her fork. 'Her boyfriend.'

'Oh that wanker,' Jim said. 'He was in the Railway last weekend. I thought he could do with a smack actually.'

'I've got to ring her. Apologise.'

Jim shrugged. 'I wouldn't. Fuck 'em.'

'I have to see her every day at school—'

'I take Amy to school too. And pick her up.'

'I know you do. I just mean, I do it almost every day. So I see her a lot more than you do. And I don't want Amy to not get invited if Georgie has a party, that kind of thing.'

Jim finished his pasta and dropped his cutlery on his plate. He leaned back in his chair, arms folded, and looked over at Maggie.

'You don't need to grovel though. Just say you're sorry you smacked the dickhead and leave it at that.'

'I wasn't planning on grovelling.' Maggie pushed her chair back and reached for Jim's plate, sliding it under her own, before carrying both of them through to the kitchen. Nick was still eating, so Maggie would usually stay at the table, but she didn't want to argue with Jim in front of her brother.

Jim followed her into the kitchen and came up behind her, pressing her against the counter, his hands on her waist.

'Fancy a bit while the brat's having a tantrum?'

'Nick's in there,' Maggie said, embarrassment pricking between her shoulder blades.

'He'll make himself scarce,' Jim said. 'He's not daft.'

He kissed the back of her neck and ground his hips against her bum.

'Amy'll probably be down in a minute,' Maggie said. 'She didn't finish her tea. You know what she's like with her food.' She wanted to ask about Eve, suggest he go and try this with her instead, but she couldn't do it. Not with a chance of Amy walking in.

'I can be quick,' Jim said. 'Come upstairs.'

Maggie stared at her reflection in the stainless steel of the kettle. She looked pale and odd, although she supposed a kettle wasn't the most flattering surface in which to consider her appearance.

'What's got into you?' she asked him, twisting away a little.

'I like the idea of you smacking that dickhead. S'hot.'

'God,' Maggie said, wondering if Nick had finished eating yet, if he'd bring his plate through or stay at the table for a bit longer. 'It's really not.'

'What are you doing?' Amy said from the doorway. 'Are you cuddling? Gross.'

Jim stepped away and Maggie felt herself sag against the unit in relief. 'I'm just putting the kettle on,' she said.

Jim opened the back door and disappeared into the garden, where Maggie – and Amy – knew he was going for a cigarette.

'What's for pudding?' Amy said.

*

'I can't believe you hit someone,' Nick said, once Amy was in bed and Jim had gone out . . . somewhere.

Maggie shook her head. 'I can't either. I don't know what came over me.'

Nick stared at her.

'Don't,' she said.

'Don't what?'

'He's not like that all the time. Just when he's tired.'

'Is he tired all the time though?' Nick asked. 'He scared the shit out of Amy.'

'She loves him,' Maggie said. 'He's a really good dad.'

'When he's not scaring the shit out of her, I'm sure.'

'Come on,' Maggie said. 'I don't want to talk about this.' She poured herself another glass of wine and leaned over to top Nick's up.

'No more for me,' he said. 'I'm sorry. I'm just worried about you.'

'I know. But we're fine.'

'You really don't seem fine.'

Maggie's hand was shaking as she poured the wine. She put the bottle down and picked up the glass.

'Have you seen Mum lately?' Nick asked. 'I think she wants to come over and see us both together. Kill two birds with one stone.'

Maggie smiled. 'No. She hasn't been over. That would work for me though. It's easier when you're there too.'

'We could take her to lunch,' Nick suggested.

Maggie nodded. 'She'd like that.

Have you told her about Simon? Or that you're staying here?'

'Have you told her about Jim?' Nick said.

Maggie winced. 'Please don't.'

'Let me ask you one thing though,' Nick said, shuffling forward on his chair and resting his elbows on his knees.

'Does he hit you?'

Maggie shook her head. He didn't. He never had. He threatened to sometimes, but then he'd punch the wall or throw a chair or something instead.

'Well that's something,' Nick said.

'He's just got a temper,' Maggie told him. 'But he'd never go that far. And apparently I have too.'

'You were protecting Amy,' Nick said. 'It's not the same.'

'But it's not that different either,' Maggie said.

'It is,' Nick said. 'You're kind. And gentle. You always have been. He doesn't appreciate you and he doesn't treat you well and I know there's nothing I can do to convince you of that. But I also want you to know that you just have to tell me you're ready to go and I'll help you pack.'

Maggie nodded. 'I do know that.'

She did. She'd always known that. When they were younger, she and Nick hadn't really got on. She'd thought they were opposites – he was so confident and comfortable in his own skin, and Maggie had no idea who she was or what she wanted. But as they'd got older they'd become closer and now Maggie had no idea what she'd do without him. And she prayed she'd never have to find out.

Chapter Eighteen

The West Kirby playground was so much nicer than their nearest one had been in London. That one had been behind Sainsbury's and while it had that bouncy tar stuff on the ground, everything else had been basic – a metal slide, swings and a roundabout. Some toadstools for hopping on. A graffiti-covered climbing frame. And a bench next to the (ever-overflowing) bin. Emma had always hated going there, often had to bribe the children to leave with a packet of biscuits. Sometimes she talked them out of going altogether saying that there were teenagers hanging around – both children were nervous of teenagers.

The playground near the school was different. The wooden equipment was clean, well-spaced, and set on wood chippings on top of the bouncy tar stuff. The top of the slide was basically a fort accessed by a small climbing wall. Beyond it stretched a zipwire. And the roundabout was accessible for wheelchair users.

It was the first bright, dry day after a seemingly endless spell of rain and so pretty much everyone had headed for the park after school.

'This is so much nicer than they're used to,' Emma told Beth. 'They're going to think we used to live in Communist Russia or something.'

'It hasn't been like this for long,' Beth told her. 'It was a shithole for years. And then the council got a European grant or something and did it all up.'

Emma hadn't noticed at first, but now she saw that there was an actual sandpit in the corner, and it probably wasn't even dotted with dog shit. Flic was crouched down next to it, holding her baby under the armpits and letting him flap his feet in the sand. Eve stood just behind her, talking on her phone.

'In the summer there's a water feature,' Beth said, pointing even further beyond the sandpit. 'The kids got soaking wet and crusty but they loved it. We came almost every day.'

'That's brilliant,' Emma said, watching Sam scrabbling in the sand like a dog.

'Sam!' she called, warningly. He glanced up, grinned at her, and then returned to spraying sand everywhere, the children behind him shrieking and hiding their eyes.

'Sorry,' Emma mumbled, glancing at the nearby parents, all seated on the wooden benches around the edge of the park, but with their eyes trained on Sam. And now Emma.

'Don't say anything,' Emma told Beth and Hanan, 'but I've got to go to dinner with Jools Jackson and her husband.'

'Oh my god!' Beth shrieked. 'Why?!'

Emma shook her head. 'Can't really say. But I'm dreading it. And do either of you have a babysitter you can recommend.'

They all headed over to the sandpit while Beth told Emma about a babysitter she and her kids loved and Emma took her details down.

'I'm bored,' Sam said from the sandpit. He was lying on his back making sand angels. Every visible bit of him was encrusted with sand.

'Come on,' Emma told him. 'I'll help you up the slide.'

'Not allowed,' Sam said. 'Ruby's up there.'

'So?' Emma gripped her son under his armpits and hefted him out of the sandpit.

'She said I'm not allowed.'

Emma huffed and escorted Sam over to the slide. She could see Ruby's shiny black school shoes sticking out of the house at the top, like some sort of tiny Wicked Witch of the West. Another pair of feet appeared, shod in white trainers and turned slightly towards Ruby's.

'She's playing with Flora,' Sam said.

'Good for her,' Emma told him. 'But you can still go up there if you want to go up there. Do you?'

'No,' Sam said.

Emma rolled her eyes. 'Well do it anyway.'

Emma knew the other parents would be watching her and there was no way she was going to give up and let Sam go back to the sandpit. Instead she boosted him up the climbing wall, his bum on her chest as he clung to the rope and said 'Mama, I can't.'

'Course you can,' Emma said. 'Just move your feet to the next . . . thingy. I've got you, you can't fall.'

Sam stepped up with one foot before turning to look down at Emma, his eyes wide with panic.

'Don't look down, sweetheart,' Emma said. 'You're almost there. Just one more step and you'll be able to reach the top.'

As Sam moved his left foot, Ruby's face appeared just above him.

'Ugh! Why is he coming up here! I told him not to!'

'And I told him to ignore you,' Emma said in her calmest tone. 'Sam should get the chance to play too and he wanted to use the climbing wall.'

'I didn't,' Sam said.

'But I'm with Flora!' Ruby hissed.

Out of the corner of her eye, Emma saw a small figure whoosh down the slide and run off across the playground.

'And now she's gone!' Ruby wailed.

Emma didn't even have to look to know her daughter's eyes would be brimming with tears.

'Go after her!' Emma said. 'Maybe she's playing tick.'

'My hands hurt,' Sam said. 'Can I get down?'

'I'll push you up,' Emma said. 'Reach for the wooden bit. Rubes, go find Flora and tell her you want to play with her.'

Ruby groaned and slid down the slide, immediately disappearing out of Emma's peripheral vision. Emma held onto Sam until his small fingers managed to cling to the top edge of the wall, at which point she bent her knees and pushed him. He straightened up at the same time and there was a huge clang as he hit his head on the top of the little house and then burst into tears.

'Shit,' Emma said. She turned to look for Beth for support, but Beth was pushing both twins on the swings at the same time. She gave her a grimace of sympathy. Hanan was still in the sandpit with a weeping Mohammed. There was no sign of Ruby, Flora or Yahya.

'I want to get down!' Sam wailed.

Emma wasn't sure if it was her imagination, but it felt like the entire park was watching in silent judgement. She could totally imagine that Eve and Flic were mentally crafting the story they were going to report back to Jools.

'I want to get down!' Sam said again, tears running down his cheeks and dripping off his chin.

'You're going to have to come down the slide, angel,' Emma told the still-sobbing Sam. 'I can't get up there.'

'I can't get down!' He'd swung his legs round now so he was sitting on the edge of the wall. 'Can you catch me?'

Emma stared. She probably could. He didn't weigh much. And it wasn't high. But she had visions of him jumping and either knocking her to the ground or missing her altogether and splatting on the ground himself.

'No, darling,' Emma said. 'I'll come up. Just . . . try to calm down, OK? I'm just going to walk around and see if I can find a way to get up to you. Don't panic if you can't see me, OK?'

Emma could hear Sam whimpering as she walked around the slide. Apart from the climbing wall there was a fireman's pole, but no other way to get up there. When had whoever made kids' playground equipment given up on ladders? What had been wrong with ladders?

'Mama?' she heard Sam call as she reached the bottom of the slide.

'Hang on!'

A glance over towards the benches confirmed what she'd previously suspected, all the other parents were watching her. And she was going to have to go up the slide.

'I'm coming up!' she called to Sam and started to clamber up the metal surface, her shoes squeaking as she slipped. She tensed her arms on the sides and willed herself to get the rest of the way up in one go. *I'll go to the gym,* she promised herself. *If I make it to the top in one go I'll find a gym and build my upper body strength and never—* Her feet slipped again, her knees hit the slide with a loud CLANG and before she could fully process what was happening, she was sliding back down again. She dropped off the bottom of the slide, onto her knees in the wood chippings.

'Fuck,' she breathed, dropping her head.

'You OK, Mama?' Sam called from the top of the slide.

'I'm fine, thanks,' she called back brightly. 'Trying again now.'

She had to do it this time, she knew. There was no way she was spending the rest of the day humiliating herself on a kids' slide. She'd read about women finding the strength to lift cars off their kids, there was no way she was going to be beaten by a slide. The second time she almost reached the top, her feet slipped again, but she managed to grab the wood at the top and then pull her knees up and drag herself over and into the little house.

'Hi!' Sam said. He'd stopped crying. He looked fine. Better than fine, in fact, he looked delighted. 'You're not supposed to go up the slide,' he said.

'I know,' Emma said. 'But it was an emergency. Or I thought it was. Are you OK?'

'Yes thank you. Can I go down the slide on your knee?'

Emma stared at him. She wanted to tell him what she'd just put herself through *because she thought he needed her.* But it was pointless. He was five. He totally expected her to be at his beck and call. And that was fine. It was. She straightened her legs out in front of her and let her son climb onto her knee.

Jools didn't want to go out for dinner with Emma and her husband. She wanted to curl up on the sofa under a blanket and watch old episodes of *Murder She Wrote* that she always kept saved on the DVR for when she just wanted to zone out. But she also wanted – needed – to support Matt. He'd worked so hard and given them this amazing life. And even though he would happily go without her, would, she knew, charm Paul and Emma and anyone else who came within twenty feet of him, she wasn't willing to let him do it alone. Yes, she had cancer, but that didn't mean she had to put her life on hold until she didn't have cancer any more. She just needed to pace herself. She pressed play on the meditation app on her phone and closed her eyes, resting her hands on her breasts. She liked to picture the cancer cells – like frog spawn, bubbling, dividing – and melt them with her mind.

She had to beat it. There was just no other option.

Chapter Nineteen

'You look nice,' Paul said, barely glancing up from his phone.

Nice, Emma thought. She'd been hoping for something a bit better than 'nice', but she knew Paul would be nervous – he always got more nervous about social occasions than business meetings, and Matt was a star player so they both needed to make a good impression.

'You look beautiful!' Ruby said.

'You look like a girl!' Sam added.

Emma was only wearing black jeans with a long-sleeved black V-neck top, but she'd managed to dig out a pair of wine-red suede ankle boots that she hadn't worn for ages and she'd straightened her hair and added a deep red lipstick. The children probably hadn't seen her wear lipstick for months.

'Ready?' Paul asked, standing up, still staring down at the screen in his hand.

'Only if we're planning on leaving the children home alone,' Emma said.

Paul had actually done that once when Ruby was little. Emma had popped out for milk, leaving them both asleep in their respective beds. She'd written a note for Paul just in case, but when he'd woken in a panic, thinking he was late for work, forgetting he had the day off, he'd missed it. And left.

Ruby was still snoring when Emma had got back, but she'd been baffled as to where Paul might be and why he would have left their child. He'd been mortified when he'd realised. Once Emma had stopped clutching her heart with fear over every possible thing that could have gone wrong while neither of them had been home, she'd realised how overworked and stressed Paul had been. That had actually been the first time he'd suggested moving back north, she remembered now. It had taken them years to actually do it.

The doorbell rang and Emma rushed to open it – kicking Sam's school bag out of the way, even though she was sure she'd hung it up once already – and opening the door to reveal Sage, the teenage babysitter Beth had recommended.

'Is that Sage?' Ruby yelled.

'She's been looking forward to seeing you again,' Emma told Sage, as they both headed down the hall to the kitchen.

When Emma had called Sage to ask her about babysitting, she'd invited her round to meet the kids and both of them had fallen instantly in love with her. Emma hadn't been at all surprised. Sage was sweet and funny and wore a bubble gum pink faux fur coat. Even so, Emma had experienced frequent bursts of panic and fear about leaving the children alone with a virtual stranger, but she came with references – she'd looked after Beth's three and she did her school work experience at a local nursery – and Emma really wanted to find someone she could rely on since she hoped to start building a social life for herself at some point.

But not tonight. Tonight wasn't for her. Tonight was for Paul.

Although the kids loved Sage, they still were not at all happy when they realised their parents were actually going out and leaving them alone. Sam had clung to Emma, sobbing, and even

Ruby's lip had quivered a little. But then Sage had revealed she'd brought a jigsaw with her and, along with promises of hot chocolate with marshmallows, managed to coax them back to the kitchen table.

Emma closed the front door behind them and paused for a second.

'They'll be fine,' Paul said.

'I know,' Emma said. 'It's just weird. I haven't left them for a while.'

'I was thinking that we haven't been out on our own for a while,' Paul said, stepping closer. He was wearing a navy suit and a white shirt and he actually looked really hot. Emma leaned back against the door.

'You look beautiful,' Paul said.

'Oh? I thought I just looked "nice"?'

Paul grinned and dipped his head, brushing his lips over her jaw. 'No. Definitely beautiful.'

Emma turned her head and caught his lips with hers. He tasted of coffee. He made a sound against her mouth and pressed her into the door.

'We'd better go,' Emma said against his mouth. 'If the kids spot us . . .'

Paul laughed. 'You're right. We can do a bit more snogging in the cab.'

The restaurant was in Albert Dock with views out across the water to the Liver Buildings. The waiter advised them that Jools and Matt hadn't arrived yet. Emma secretly hoped they'd cancel so she and Paul could have an evening alone.

At the table, Emma fiddled with her napkin and poured herself a glass of water, wondering just how late Jools and Matt would be. Once, in London, a footballer had kept them waiting for three hours. He'd messaged Paul repeatedly with apologies and updates and then, eventually, had said he 'just couldn't swing it'.

Emma spotted Jools as soon as she walked in ahead of her husband. Her blonde hair was piled high on her head and she was wearing a silver shift dress and a necklace that looked like piles of silver balls. Emma shuffled her seat back in readiness for standing and then she saw Jools's husband Matt.

He was beautiful – she'd googled him after Paul had told her about him and she'd been stunned by the photos she'd found. The first page had all been photos of him playing over the last couple of years, in various kits, sometimes with his shirt off. The second page had led her to the scan of the local magazine she'd seen but hadn't fully taken in: pages of photos of him and Jools and their daughters. In their lovely home. The five of them looked utterly relaxed and at ease with one another. In one of the photos one of the girls was sitting on Matt's shoulders, his face scrunched up with laughter. Jools looking up at the two of them adoringly. Emma had stared at it for ages. But he was possibly even better looking in real life.

As Jools and Matt crossed the room, Emma felt the atmosphere change. She glanced around to see that everyone was watching them, but Matt and Jools seemed unaware of it, gliding towards them looking golden and rich.

'Hey!' Matt said, as he reached for Paul's hand. They shook while Jools moved around the table towards Emma. She nodded at Emma and Emma smiled back.

Once they were all seated, the waiter reappeared and, after a bit of discussion, they ordered an expensive bottle of red wine and chatted a little while they waited – small talk about Liverpool, the school, their children.

Matt and Paul were deep in conversation – Paul could talk about football all night. And often did at these things. Emma couldn't think of anything to say to Jools. She wanted to ask her about her hair, her nails, her perfect eyebrows, but the thought of it made her feel like she was back at school, admiring Sara Doyle's hair and shoes and perfume.

'How did you two meet?' she asked Jools eventually, while they were tucking into the main course.

'Tinder,' Matt said.

'We did not!' Jools said instantly, and then grinned at him. 'I got set up on a blind date with Matt's brother, Joe. He had to cancel, but he couldn't get in touch with me – there was a problem with my phone which I hadn't realised. So Matt came to the restaurant to tell me. And then he stayed for dinner . . .'

'And then we got married,' Matt finished.

'How soon?' Emma asked.

'Three months,' Matt said. 'On holiday in Vegas.'

'Wow,' Paul said. 'That's fast.'

'When you know you know,' Matt said. 'How about you two?'

While Paul told Matt how he and Emma had met, Emma finished her food, occasionally glancing over at Jools to see how she was getting on. She was picking at her meal, sipping at water in between.

'Is it not good?' Emma asked.

Jools looked over at her. 'It's fine. I'm just not that bothered about food really.'

Great that Paul brought you to such an expensive restaurant then, Emma thought.

'Emma was telling me you've got a book club,' Paul said, gesturing with his fork, a piece of steak speared on the end.

Emma sucked in a breath and pressed her foot onto Paul's under the table. She really didn't want him to mention the fact that it was exclusive or Jools's inner circle only. She didn't even really want Jools to know that she'd been talking about her at all.

'I have, yes,' Jools said, reaching for her wine. 'It's very small. Just four of us. We've been meeting for a while now.'

'What are you reading?' Paul asked. 'Em's a big reader. Or she used to be anyway. She's had the same book on her bedside table since we moved.'

At that, Emma did actually kick him under the table. He jerked back in his seat, frowning at her.

'I don't have time to read much these days,' Emma said.

'I feel like you have to make time,' Jools argued. She was still looking at Paul, not at Emma. 'It's important to have a bit of . . . intellectual stimulation, I think? Otherwise you can get too wrapped up in the kids and before long, you can name all the CBeebies presenters, but you don't know who the Home Secretary is.'

Paul laughed and Emma seriously thought about kicking him in his other shin. For fuck's sake, all she'd said was that she didn't have time to read, not that she'd given up on the real world in favour of her kids. Although she wasn't sure she did know who the Home Secretary was.

'What *are* you reading now?' Emma asked, realising Jools hadn't answered in her eagerness to get one over on Emma.

'*Jude the Obscure*,' Jools said. 'Thomas Hardy.'

Emma wanted to say 'I know who it's by' but instead she just smiled. 'I haven't read that one. I've seen the film though.'

'You should come along,' Matt said, reaching for the wine and topping up Emma's glass. 'It'd be a great way for you to get to know some of the other mums. Wouldn't it, Jools?'

Emma could imagine how hard Jools was likely stepping on Matt's foot under the table, but her smile never wavered.

'Sure,' she said. 'Give me your number and I'll text over the details.'

Chapter Twenty

Jools knew as soon as she woke up the following morning that her hair was gone. She lay for a few minutes, crying silently, before she sat up and gathered the strands off her pillow with her hands. She didn't feel right about throwing it away, so she fastened it with one of the elastics she always had around the house and tucked it into her underwear drawer.

In the bathroom, she stared at herself in the mirror. Her hair wasn't gone entirely, but enough of it had fallen out that she'd have to shave it and wear a wig or one of the turban things Eve had insisted on buying for her, even though Jools had been equally insistent she'd never wear one. She pulled her remaining hair into a ponytail and snipped through, dropping the straggly ends into the bin, before heading back into the bedroom to wake Matt.

Ten minutes later, Jools was sitting in the middle of the bed, propped up with pillows, while Matt shaved the rest of her hair. She kept her eyes closed, not wanting to see any more of the hair she'd always been so proud of falling down in front of her eyes. It was stupid to be proud of her hair anyway, she knew – it wasn't like she had anything to do with it. But still. She'd always been 'Jools with the long blonde hair'. Who was she now?

Matt's hands were gentle on her head, his fingers brushing over her scalp. She hoped it was a good shape, hoped her scalp wasn't scarred or patchy or odd. No one outside the house would see her without her wig, but Matt would. And she didn't want to look like an alien.

'You look beautiful,' Matt said a few minutes later, dropping a kiss on the top of her head. 'Want to see?'

'No,' Jools said. But she did. Matt led her into the bathroom. She kept her head lowered until she was right in front of the mirror and only then did she look. And she looked fine. She looked like herself only bald.

'This is surreal. I feel like it's for a joke or a play or fancy dress or something. I don't feel like this is really me.'

Matt stood behind her, his arms around her waist, chin on her shoulder. He turned his head to brush his lips over her neck.

'You look like a hot alien. Or a sexy squaddie.'

'Oh my god,' Jools laughed. 'You're ridiculous.'

'I'm serious, I love it.' He straightened up and trailed his fingers over her head. 'I think it's a fetish I never knew I had.'

'Half your team mates are bald,' Jools told him. 'No training for you today.'

He kissed her again, on the temple this time, and asked if he should get the wig.

Jools hadn't looked at it since she'd bought it with Eve. She'd been happy with it in the store, but once home, she'd reverted to her usual denial and put it away in her dressing room, tucked into the back of a cupboard where she knew the girls wouldn't find it. All she needed was to come home one day and find them using her ridiculously expensive human hair wig as a Girls' World.

'Do you know how to put it on?' Matt asked her, standing behind her again.

Jools held her fingers up to her forehead. 'If you lower it over the front, I can grab it and pull it down.'

It took a bit of arranging and wiggling and Jools's head felt weird – hot and itchy – but when she looked in the mirror, she couldn't quite believe it wasn't real hair.

'You know what you look like?' Matt said, his hands massaging her shoulders. 'You look like you did when we first met. Remember when we went on that boat?'

'The Duck Boat?' Jools said. 'On the Thames.'

Matt nodded. And I took a photo of you and you were embarrassed cos you weren't posing and you thought it was a bad angle or some bollocks.

'It was a bad angle.'

'But you looked amazing. The wind was blowing your hair back and your cheeks were pink.' He stroked his thumb over her jaw. 'I was already falling in love with you then.'

'You were not,' Jools said. 'And it's the fringe. I had a fringe back then. Briefly.'

She hadn't had a fringe for years, but she'd chosen a fringed wig because she thought the hairline would be less obvious. And it did actually make her look younger.

Matt kissed the back of her neck. 'Remember what we did after the boat?'

Jools laughed. They'd gone for dinner. And then to a bar with a huge screen on one wall and a singer who'd murdered Snow Patrol's 'Chasing Cars.' And then they'd gone back to Matt's place and slept together for the first time.

Matt ran his hands through the wig, lifting the hair into a ponytail and dropping it down Jools's back.

'I'm starting to worry this might actually be a fetish,' Jools said. First the shaved head, now the wig. All these years and I had no idea.'

'Have you got a spare I can take to training?' Matt joked, resting his chin on the top of her head.

Jools stared at him in the mirror, smiling at him around the sudden lump in her throat.

'Thank you. I couldn't do this without you.'

'Lucky you don't have to then, eh?' Matt said.

'It was actually OK,' Emma said, fiddling with the tiny biscuit that had come with the coffee. She didn't actually like them much, but god knows she needed the sugar. 'Hang on,' she said, standing. 'I'm going to get a pastry as big as my face. Want one?'

'I'll have a croissant,' Hanan said, reaching for her bag.

'Don't worry,' Emma said. 'I'll get it. Beth?'

Beth shook her head. 'I'm back at Slimming World. Again.'

As Emma waited in the queue for her pastry, she wondered what they thought of Beth at Slimming World since she looked like she was probably a size eight. She remembered Jools, picking at her sad bit of fish. Must be rubbish to live like that, so joyless. When Emma returned to the table with a croissant and butter for Hanan and a pain aux raisin so enormous that it didn't quite fit on the plate, Beth was explaining 'green days' and 'syns' to a horrified-looking Hanan.

'It's dead easy really,' Beth said.

'It doesn't sound it,' Hanan told her.

'No, it is,' Beth said. 'Emma's tormenting me with that pastry though.'

'Want a bit?' Emma said, although she didn't really want to share.

'Nah,' Beth said. 'Thanks though. So . . . go on!'

'Yeah,' Emma said, covering her mouth since it was full of pain aux raisin. 'It was OK. Bit awkward, but these things often are. It wasn't as bad as I thought it would be. And the restaurant was nice.'

'I don't want to know about the restaurant!' Beth said. 'What about Jools? And Matt Jackson?'

Every time Beth had mentioned Matt she'd used his full name. It made Emma laugh.

'They were fine! He was a lot nicer than her. But . . .' Emma paused and took a gulp of her coffee. 'She invited me to book club.'

'Oh my god!' Beth shrieked. 'She did not!'

'She didn't want to,' Emma said. 'Matt suggested it. And either she didn't know how to say no or she thought she shouldn't? I don't know. But she texted and asked for my email and then she sent me the rules. Hang on . . .'

'I can't believe Jools is texting you,' Beth said, as Emma tapped open her phone. 'That's it now. You'll go to book club and you'll be friends with them and you'll stop speaking to us.'

'I would never do that!' Emma said, scrolling through her messages. 'I'm just going to go once so she doesn't feel like I'm snubbing her or something, but I'm not interested in being friends with her, I promise you. We've got nothing in common.'

'What's the big deal with her anyway?' Hanan asked. 'Why is everyone so obsessed with her?'

'She's just so full of herself,' Beth said. 'She looks down on me cos me and my fella aren't married. I did the sweet stall with her once at the Summer Fair and she was really weird. Cold. And rude.'

Hanan shrugged. 'I just try not to let things like that bother me, you know? Like, I'm not interested in being friends with her so I just sort of tune her out. I'm not even sure which one she is. They all look the same to me.'

Emma laughed. 'She's the one with the amazing long blonde hair.'

She held up her phone. 'Listen to this, "Firstly, punctuality is important",' Emma read. '"Yes, Book Club is a social event, but we're all busy and none of us has time to waste waiting for other people to turn up." It starts at seven,' she told Beth and Hanan. 'But she also says we're to be mindful not to get there earlier than seven because she'll be putting the children to bed and won't be able to entertain us.'

'So what are you meant to do?' Beth asked. 'Stand outside until dead on seven?'

'I think that's exactly what we're meant to do, yeah,' Emma said.

She carried on reading. '"The person who chooses the book also prepares a short presentation about the book and writes the discussion questions."'

'Wow,' Hanan said. She leaned over and pulled a sippy cup out of the bottom of the buggy and gave it to Mohammed, who was sitting placidly tearing a napkin to bits.

'This is like bloody school!' Beth said.

'Yep,' Emma agreed. '"Following book discussion, we will take suggestions for next month's book. Please think of a book you would like to suggest we read together with a short list of reasons we might enjoy it."'

'What are you going to suggest?' Hanan asked. 'Dare you to say something filthy.'

'What's that one my sister got me for Christmas?' Beth said, scrunching her face as she tried to remember. '*My Dad Wrote a Porno*!'

'Oh my god,' Emma said. 'Can you imagine? Not that it matters since I'm not going to go back.'

'I bet you do,' Beth said. 'Once they've got their hooks in you . . .'

'It's not a cult,' Hanan said, laughing.

'Might as well be,' Beth said. 'I can't even remember the last time I read a book. I can barely get through a magazine these days.'

'Did you know they've got a nanny?' Emma asked Beth and Hanan, putting her phone back in her bag.

'Course,' Beth said. 'She's picked the kids up a few times. I think she's Polish?'

'She was telling me I should get one,' Emma said. 'Or an au pair anyway.'

'She's in a different world,' Beth said. 'She's got a cleaner as well, I bet.'

'I'd love a cleaner,' Emma said, pulling her pain aux raisin apart and folding some into her mouth.

Beth pulled a face. 'I'd hate it. Someone coming in my house? Seeing all my stuff?'

'What stuff have you got?' Emma asked, grinning.

'Just . . . you know. Personal stuff. Nothing dodgy.'

'Can I have a bit of that, actually?' Beth said, pointing at Emma's pain aux raisin. Emma passed her the plate.

'So when's the book club meeting?' Hanan asked Emma.

'End of the month,' Emma said. 'So I've got about ten days to read *Jude the Obscure*.'

'Ugh,' Beth said, spraying pastry crumbs. 'Good luck.'

Chapter Twenty-One

Jools was wearing a floaty blue dress that Emma knew would look like a tablecloth on her, but looked deeply stylish on the other woman. Her hair was pulled back into a low ponytail and Emma could see diamonds twinkling in her earlobes.

'Sorry I'm late,' Emma said. 'The kids were—'

'It's fine,' Jools interrupted, already walking away from Emma. 'Maggie's not here yet either.'

The kids were not keen on her going out, is what Emma had been about to say. But it wasn't entirely true. She hadn't been keen on going either, not least because she hadn't actually read the book. She'd tried, but it was so dark. She'd read a few pages and realised she hadn't taken anything in at all. For the past ten days she'd had a 'not done your homework' feeling hanging over her and it made her wonder why she was bothering with the book club at all. But Paul. And friends. And mental stimulation. That's what had finally propelled her out of the house.

Emma followed Jools through to a room with bi-fold doors opening out onto what looked like a beautiful garden – Emma could see a treehouse tucked away in the branches of an enormous oak. The wall above the fireplace was covered in framed photographs of Jools, Matt and their kids. It was bright and stylish, but comfortable and welcoming and Emma – who'd left her own house in disarray: Lego and clothes and dog hair and school books covering pretty much every surface – felt so envious she almost swooned.

Eve and Flic were sitting opposite each other on two sofas, and Emma found herself wishing that Maggie was there. She had been hoping to at least see one friendly face.

'Would you like a drink?' Jools asked. 'We've got vodka, gin, Pimms, wine . . .'

'Wine's good, thanks. Red, if you've got it.'

She was actually more nervous than she'd anticipated, so Dutch courage seemed like a good idea. It had been a while since she'd been around such intimidating women. She tried to channel London Emma, pre-kids Emma, but she felt very far away.

Jools disappeared into what Emma assumed would be an equally – if not more – covetable kitchen and Emma perched at the end of the nearest sofa, next to Eve.

Eve was possibly even more glamorous than Jools in a pristine white shirt and tight, ripped jeans, five inch stilettos on her feet.

'This house is beautiful,' Emma said.

The other two women hummed in agreement and then Jools was back with an enormous wine glass and a bottle of red. She put them on the coffee table in front of Emma and Emma immediately poured herself a glass. Jools sat on an armchair between the two sofas, crossing her legs, a glass of something with orange juice dangling from her fingers. While the other women talked – about their children, their husbands, Eve's job at a theatre in Liverpool – Emma looked around the room and wondered if Matt was home – upstairs with the kids maybe? And if so, would he come down and say hello?

'How are you all settling in, Emma?' Jools asked. 'You've been here, what? Three months now?'

'Yep, just about,' Emma said. She sipped at her drink, realising a second too late that she'd emptied her glass while everyone else was talking. She leaned forward and poured herself another.

She'd just taken a sip when she heard the front door open and Maggie came in and joined the other women in the lounge.

Maggie greeted Emma and Flic, but didn't acknowledge Eve, Emma noticed. Interesting.

'So?' Jools prompted Emma. 'You were about to tell us how you're finding living here.'

'It's great,' Emma said. 'It's so lovely. I love the beach.'

'Have you been to Hilbre yet?' Maggie asked, leaning forward on the sofa.

Emma shook her head. 'Not yet. I've been promising the kids every weekend. Ruby said we have to go cos they're doing a project on it? I just haven't got round to sorting it yet. You know how time gets away from you?'

By the expressions on their faces, Eve and Jools didn't seem to identify, so Emma looked at Maggie and Flic on the other sofa. Flic was smiling at her with a look of eager encouragement, while Maggie was staring at Eve with an unreadable expression on her face. Well, not entirely unreadable; Emma wouldn't want to be on the receiving end of it.

'You know you need to be careful of the tides?' Eve interjected. 'You can look them up online. You don't want to get stranded. There's nothing there.'

'Oh I don't know,' Emma said. 'I fantasise about being alone on an island. No kids nagging me. No husband who can't find his wallet. No washing. Or cooking. Or cleaning.'

Emma had expected the other women to laugh. Or agree. Or sympathise. Instead Eve said, 'You don't have a cleaner?' She sounded appalled.

Emma barked out a laugh. 'God no. Do you?'

As it turned out, they all did, apart from Flic. (Emma was unreasonably disappointed to find Maggie on the opposing side.) And Jools sent her husband's shirts out to a laundry service who collected them and returned them to the house. Emma had never even heard of such a thing.

Emma finished her second glass of wine and sneaked the glass onto the floor by the sofa. She wanted a third, but she knew that really wouldn't be a good idea. And she assumed the evening would be over soon anyway. It was, Jools announced, time to talk about the book.

It turned out that Eve had been the one to choose *Jude the Obscure*. She talked about how she'd studied it at university and adored it and how she'd been involved in an inspiring theatre production. She'd written her discussion questions in a Moleskine notebook and each woman commented in turn, although Maggie didn't seem to have much to say. It was all very civilised. But not much fun. Emma hadn't contributed anything at all, since she hadn't read the book and following the comments from the others, she never planned to.

'Does anyone have any suggestions for the next book?' Jools asked.

'Do you only ever read classics?' Emma said.

'That's not a rule,' Jools said. 'But that is what we've mostly chosen so far.

'OK, so I was just reading about this book,' Emma started. She'd read about it on one of the lifestyle blogs she seemed to now be addicted to. 'It was made into a TV show with Sheridan Smith? I don't know if you saw it. Anyway. It's a memoir by this woman who got breast cancer young and—'

'No,' Jools said.

Emma looked over at her, startled at her tone. 'OK, um, I just thought it might be—'

'I think we need to stick with novels,' Jools said. Her cheeks were flushed and her eyes looked bright with tears.

'I'm sorry,' Emma said. 'I didn't . . . It's funny, not sad. Well, it's a bit sad, but—'

'I said no,' Jools said, standing up and glancing around as if she was looking for someone to rescue her. 'Does anyone have any other ideas? I'm going to the bathroom.'

Jools left and the remaining women were silent for a moment before Emma said, 'Did I . . . I'm sorry I didn't . . .'

'It's fine,' Eve said. 'She just . . . she has a thing about depressing books. And strong opinions on what we should read in this group. You know?'

'Right,' Emma said. As if Jude the Obscure wasn't depressing.. 'I didn't . . . I thought it might make a change?'

Eve narrowed her eyes slightly and Emma immediately regretted opening her big mouth. 'We've had this book club for a while. This is your first time here. I think we're the ones who decide whether it needs to change or not, yeah?'

'Yes,' Emma said. 'Of course. I'm sorry. I didn't mean to . . .' She was babbling. And over-apologising. And she didn't even really know why. It wasn't that big a deal, surely. She'd just suggested a book that Jools didn't like the sound of, why was Eve acting like she'd come in and shit on the rug?

She poured herself another glass of wine. Her third, so it had to be her last. At her book club in London they'd kept pouring until none of them could see straight to pour any more, but clearly that wasn't how things worked here. She missed the girls in London. She should phone them. No, not phone. No one answered their phone any more. She should revive the group chat. Maybe when Paul wasn't so busy she could pop back down for the weekend and they could all go out and catch up. She wondered if they were still doing book club without her. If they'd replaced her with one of the other mums. The thought of it made her stomach twist painfully. If she'd thought she would make friends tonight, she'd clearly been mistaken.

Emma wished it was as easy for adults to make friends as it was for children. Just telling Ruby that she was arranging a play date with Amy, Flora and Violet seemed to have inspired the girls to form a solid gang of besties. But Emma found the politics of adult female friendships confounding. Beth and Hanan were great. And Maggie had seemed nice at school, but was completely different here. And she couldn't get a handle on Flic or Eve or Jools at all. She was pretty confident she wouldn't be coming to book club again.

Chapter Twenty-Two

'So?' Beth said, the following morning after the school run. 'Tell all. Did you meet the nanny? Did you take photos of the house? Did you get drunk and flash them?'

'Almost,' Emma said. 'I only noticed on the way home that the pin had come out of my top and my bra was showing.'

Hanan winced. 'And no one told you?'

The three of them had gone straight from school to Saucer and commandeered the big table in front of the window. Mohammed was asleep and Beth's twins were engrossed in an episode of *Peppa Pig* on a shared iPad.

'Right?' Emma said. 'But maybe they were embarrassed?' Or she'd wondered if maybe they hadn't noticed. But they had to have noticed, it was really showing.

'We would absolutely tell you,' Beth said. 'Me and Hanan. Your real friends.'

Emma laughed. 'I can promise I am not dumping you two for them. They weren't even really friendly.'

'Were they mean?' Beth asked.

Emma shook her head. 'No, not mean. Just . . . not friendly. They were fine. It was fine. But no I didn't meet the nanny – I saw her when she came in, but Jools didn't introduce her – and I didn't take any photos, sorry.'

'Well you're rubbish,' Beth said. 'If you go again, you need to sneak some pics. What's the house like?'

'Actually gorgeous,' Emma said. She told them about the house, about what Jools had been wearing, about Eve and Flic and Maggie.

'You know what?' Emma said. 'The thing I don't understand is all the maintenance it must take to look that good all the time. Like I expected her to be in jeans and a jumper at home, you know? But she wasn't – everything was perfect. The others were all dressed up too. When I get home, I get into my pyjamas.'

'She always looks perfect,' Beth said. 'She has lip fillers and botox and eyelash extensions.'

'She doesn't!' Emma said. 'Does she?'

Beth nodded. 'I know a girl who works in the salon she goes to. And she had her make-up and hair done professionally before the nativity. Because the paper came.'

'Oh my god,' Emma said. 'I can't even imagine. I put lipstick on the night we went out for dinner and that was the first time since we left London. I just . . . Who could be bothered?'

'I guess she's got an image to maintain? With her husband being a footballer?' Hanan said.

'That's true,' Emma said. 'But like I could imagine that if she was going to events and stuff with him. But just day to day? Or for the nativity?! It must be exhausting.'

Jools hadn't been able to get out of bed. She felt like she was suffering from the world's worst hangover, even though she wasn't drinking, had only drunk orange juice the night before, but every part of her body ached and her temples were beating like a steel drum. It seemed to take her longer to recover after each bout of chemo. The nurse had explained that chemo sometimes works like repeatedly punching a bruise – it might seem OK at first, but it becomes more and more tender over time. Jools certainly felt tender.

Matt had argued again that Jools should give book club up, but she refused to even consider it. If she had the strength to get out bed and look in the mirror, she would see someone she didn't even recognise. Someone small and frail, with no hair and pasty-looking skin. But if she had a reason to become the Jools Jackson people expected to see, then she wanted to do that. Because if she didn't, who even was she?

'Matt said the book club went well,' Paul said, over dinner. He'd picked up a Chinese takeaway on the way home and Sam and Ruby were beside themselves with excitement.

'Did he?' Emma said. 'It was OK. Better than I thought it was going to be.'

'He said Jools is going to email you about the next one.'

He reached for a sesame prawn toast and popped it in his mouth. He'd changed into sweats and a hoodie when he got home and looked more relaxed than he had for a while. Emma liked it. It made her want to snuggle up to him. Maybe later. Once the kids were in bed. So many things had to be put off until the kids were in bed.

'Wow,' Emma said, reaching for the seaweed before Sam inhaled the lot. 'I didn't think it went well enough for them to want me to go again.'

Paul shrugged. 'That's what he said.'

'Do you think it's just because of you?' Emma asked.

Paul shrugged. 'Maybe?' He had some sweet and sour sauce on his chin. Emma reached over and wiped it off with her thumb. 'This is a big move for him. But, you know, he's the talent. I need to keep in with him, not the other way around. Maybe she just likes you.'

'She's got a funny way of showing it.'

'You know it's hard though. When they're well-known. They don't know who they can trust. You remember what happened to Holly Lyons.'

Holly Lyons was the fiancée of one of the footballers Paul looked after in London. She met a woman at a club who became her new best friend. They went out one night and got drunk – at least, Holly did – and the woman took pictures of her passed out with her dress half-off, some random guy sucking on her neck, and sold them to the papers. Jack, Holly's fiancé, dumped her and she lost a few high-profile promo contracts she'd had too.

'I suppose so,' Emma said. 'But she's got other friends. I don't think I'll go again. It just wasn't my kind of thing.'

'Oh you need to go again,' Paul said. He was looking at his phone now and said it completely casually. Emma bristled.

'Why?'

'Just until the deal's done. I don't want to do anything to piss Matt off.'

Emma stared at him. The assumption that Emma would just go along, that she didn't have anything better to do. That it didn't matter if she liked these women or if the women liked her. The assumption that because it was related to Paul's job, Emma would just go along with it. It made her feel itchy. And it kind of made her want to tell Paul where to stick it. She didn't really fancy snuggling any more.

After dinner, after she'd cleared away the dishes, and put Ruby and Sam to bed, Emma checked her phone and sure enough there was an email from Jools. The next meeting was in a month. The book was *The End of the Affair* by Graham Greene. Flic had chosen it and was preparing the questions and perhaps Emma would like to think of a book to suggest next time?

Emma glanced around the room. The only book she could see was the Next Directory.

Chapter Twenty-Three

'Did I tell you I'm going to be late tonight?' Jim asked Maggie, as he swung his legs out of bed and stretched his arms overhead. 'Got to go and do an estimate on that new estate.'

Maggie knew that was a lie. If it had been true, he wouldn't have told her where he was going, what he was doing. The extra detail proved it was a lie.

'No problem,' Maggie said. 'Amy's got a friend coming round after school anyway.'

'Is it Matt Jackson's kid?'

Maggie tried not to sigh. 'Kids. Yes.'

Originally Flora and Ruby were meant to be coming too, but Flora had a party and Emma had a child psychologist coming round to talk to Sam, so they'd both cancelled. Maggie felt a bit nervous about spending the afternoon just with Sofia – she really didn't know her well at all – but she was sure it would be fine. She hoped it would be fine.

'And his missus?' Jim asked.

'No. The nanny.'

'Fucking hell, the nanny.' He stood up and pulled down the shorts he slept in. Even though it was dark – it didn't get light until almost eight now – Maggie could see his nakedness out of the corner of her eye. She wanted to pull the duvet over her face.

'Is she as hot as the wife?' Jim asked.

'She's pretty,' Maggie said.

'Out of my league anyway,' Jim said, heading for the door. 'The wife. I could probably do the nanny.'

Maggie flinched as the door bumped against the wall. Jim usually would never admit that someone was out of his league.

She'd always been a bit like that. When he'd hurt her in the past, she'd cried, maybe talked to a friend, and then pushed it to the back of her mind because there was nothing she could do about it was there, unless she was prepared to leave him. And nothing had been quite bad enough to end their marriage over. Until now. Now people would understand. In fact, people would judge her for staying with him. The fact that he had had an affair was a rock solid reason for leaving. Or for making him leave. But she still couldn't seem to do it.

The girls had wanted to go to Victoria Park, so Maggie and Sofia walked along the prom behind them as they careered about on their scooters. It was a dull day, the sky constantly threatening rain, not that the girls cared. Halfway along Marine Lake, they stopped to watch the seagulls swooping, so Maggie and Sofia sat down on a bench and looked over towards Wales.

'What's Jools up to this afternoon?' Maggie asked. Sofia had been doing the school run more than Jools lately and while Maggie was always happy to see her, she wondered why Jools had disappeared.

'She's in Liverpool,' Sofia said. 'I don't know what for.'

'What's it like working for her?' Maggie said, glancing over at the girls to make sure no one was listening. 'She can be quite . . . particular.'

'She's not,' Sofia said. 'Not really. There's a lot you don't know . . .'

Maggie instantly felt guilty. 'I'm sure. I'm sorry. She just . . . I thought she might be quite difficult.'

Sofia shook her head. 'I can't say anything. But she's got a lot on her plate. Is that the right expression?'

Maggie nodded. She wanted to ask more. She wanted to ask if something was wrong with Jools and Matt's marriage. If something was wrong with Matt. Maggie loved and hated Jools and Matt's relationship equally. She believed they were madly in love. And she envied them. But they seemed so perfect that she half-suspected it was all an act. And she also knew herself well enough to know that if Matt left, if they weren't so perfect after all, Maggie would be secretly at least a little happy.

'We should change the subject,' Sofia said. 'How are you?'

Maggie shrugged. 'I'm fine.'

She was always fine. Or at least, she always told herself – and other people – she was fine.

'Nothing interesting about me.'

'Don't say that,' Sofia said. 'I think you're interesting.' She bumped Maggie with her shoulder and Maggie's stomach fluttered. She turned to look at her, squinting into the sun.

Sofia was staring at her with this gentle expression that made Maggie feel self-conscious, like Sofia knew Maggie's insides. Maggie didn't even know Maggie's insides. Maggie tried to look back, but she had to look away. Because Sofia was beautiful. Not in a shiny, startling way like Jools. She wasn't someone you'd see and instantly exclaim, but the more Maggie looked at her, the more beautiful she seemed. The sprinkle of freckles on her cheekbone, her wide hazel eyes, even her perfectly-shaped eyebrows. Maggie had to draw her own eyebrows in with a pencil every morning – she envied Sofia her eyebrows. But it wasn't just that Sofia was beautiful, she was also kind. She gave Maggie her full attention. She was gentle and tender with Jools's daughters, always stopping whatever she was doing if they needed her. Maggie constantly felt as if she was too distracted around Amy – sometimes she was too distracted *by* Amy to actually focus on what Amy needed from her – Amy was kinetic. She reminded Maggie of Jim.

'Do you ever go out for a drink?' Sofia asked. 'In the evenings?'

Maggie nodded, even though she hadn't, for ages. 'Sometimes.'

'We could do that one day maybe?'

'Yes. Definitely. I'd love that.'

Chapter Twenty-Four

'It's nothing to worry about,' the child psychologist, whose name was Wendi, said from Emma's kitchen table. 'This kind of thing is very common.'

She'd already seen Sam at school and had told Emma that it had gone 'very well', but without giving any further details. Emma had asked Sam about it too, but apart from the fact that Wendi had shown him a 'bag of shapes' and some photos of dogs, she hadn't got anything out of him.

'How many words would you say he has?' Wendi asked now, as Emma made them both a cup of tea.

'Like . . . lots?' Emma said, feebly. 'Too many to count, certainly.'

'Was he a late talker?'

Emma nodded. 'He was almost three before he said anything at all. But then he started talking in almost full sentences, so . . .'

'Mama,' Ruby interrupted. 'Can you help me with my reading book?'

'Not right now, pickle,' Emma said, ushering her daughter back out of the room. 'Mama's a bit busy right now. I can help later.'

'Can you give me an example?' Wendi asked once Ruby had gone. 'Of Sam's speech.' She wrote something down in her notebook.

'Um, well, his first sentence was "more 'am"', Emma said. 'Ham.' She smiled at the memory. Sam had been so bloody proud when he'd first started talking and Emma and Paul and even Ruby had got so used to him not talking that it was like hearing a cat speak. For ages, whenever Sam said anything, Ruby would say 'Did Sam just talk?!' It took a long time for the novelty to wear off.

'Have you had his hearing tested?' Wendi asked now, as Emma brought the teas over to the table and sat down opposite.

'Um . . . only the standard tests. At the health centre. Do you think that's necessary?'

Wendi smiled over her glasses. 'Just something to consider.'

Ruby appeared again. She was still wearing her full uniform and looked as pristine as she had that morning.

'Mama? Have you seen my pencils? I've got to—'

'I'm busy right now, sweetheart,' Emma said again. 'And all I would do is look for them so I'm sure you can go and look for them yourself. They're probably in your bedroom.'

Ruby stood in the doorway, twisting the hem of her school cardigan in her hand. 'OK. It's just that we have to—'

'Rubes,' Emma interrupted. 'I know. I'm just talking to Wendi at the minute.'

'Won't be much longer,' Wendi said, smiling at Ruby.

Ruby nodded, a little frown line appearing between her eyebrows, before she headed off to her bedroom.

'Sorry,' Emma said. 'She gets quite wound up about her homework. Has to do it as soon as she gets in.'

Wendi nodded and glanced down at her notebook. 'Have you had any concerns about Sam's hearing?'

'No,' Emma said. 'Not at all. I mean, if I opened a packet of biscuits in here now, he'd come running down from his room, I'm pretty sure.' She pushed her chair back. 'Actually, would you like a biscuit? I—'

'No, I'm good thank you,' Wendi said.

Emma shuffled her chair back in again.

'I'll just ask you a few more questions and then if we can bring Sam in?'

Wendi's questions lasted as long as it took Emma to finish her tea, but she felt guiltier and like a worse parent with every single one. She couldn't remember when Sam had first had jabs. When he'd had chicken pox – she thought it was the first couple of months of preschool, but she couldn't be sure. She had no idea where his red medical book had got to and even struggled to remember his birth weight, which seemed ridiculous, since it was one of the things everyone asked about when you had a baby, even though it was basically meaningless.

'I'm sorry,' she said, eventually. 'I don't know what's happened to my memory lately.'

'Baby brain,' Wendi said. Emma hated that expression. And Sam wasn't even a baby. He was five. 'Happens to the best of us. Do you want to go and get Sam?'

It took Sam three trips from his room to the kitchen before he was satisfied he had enough to divert him while Wendi questioned and assessed him. Emma had told him it was just a chat, but he wasn't daft, he knew Wendi was watching him. He'd brought a Fireman Sam truck, helicopter and drill tower with accompanying figures; an enormous one-eyed Minion that Paul had won in the work's raffle last Christmas; and a Play-Doh cupcake maker. He started on the cupcakes as Wendi asked him about school and his friends.

Emma was enormously relieved when he answered. He didn't look up at Wendi and most of his responses were mumbled into his chest, but he was talking at least. When Wendi asked him about the drill tower he got quite animated and subjected her to a gruesome story of someone being burned at the top of a multi-storey car park because a helicopter couldn't land.

'Where have you heard that?' Emma asked him, appalled.

'On the news,' Sam said, shrugging. 'In the morning.'

'When in the morning?' Emma asked. As far as she knew, neither Sam nor Ruby ever watched the news. Why would they when they had Disney and Pixar's entire output on DVD?

'I don't know,' Sam said. 'But firefighters fought back the flames.'

Wendi made a note in her book. Emma hoped it was about the unintentional assonance of Sam's last sentence and not her neglect in letting him watch inappropriate television shows.

For about twenty minutes, Wendi chatted with Sam while he played. Ruby also visited a few more times, once on the verge of tears because she hadn't been able to find her pencils. Sam seemed happy enough so Emma went up to Ruby's room and found her pencils immediately on the window ledge.

When she got back downstairs, Wendi had closed her notebook and was smiling down at Sam. She pushed her chair back.

'I think we're done,' she told Emma, unhooking her jacket from the back of the chair. 'Lovely to see you again, Sam.'

Sam glanced up at her from under his fringe and smiled. 'Bye.'

As they walked down the hall, Wendi lowered her voice and said, 'Clearly there's nothing wrong with his speech. And I don't think with his hearing either.'

'Right,' Emma said. 'Good.'

'Which means that the issue is with school.'

'Yes,' Emma said.

'I'll report to Mrs Walker. And then I'm sure she'll want you to go in for a chat. School refusal is common too,' she said. 'So no need to worry.'

Emma had just opened the front door when Sam shouted something from the kitchen.

'What was that?' Wendi said. 'Did he say 'abundance'? His vocabulary is actually very good.'

'No,' Emma said, wincing.

Before she could explain, Sam appeared in the hallway, skidding a little on the wood floor in his socks, bent over and wiggled his hips from side to side.

'A bum dance,' Emma explained.

Wendi laughed, covering her mouth with her hand. 'He's a little sweetheart.'

Emma felt immensely relieved. Sam absolutely was a little sweetheart and she hated the idea that the school thought there was something wrong with him.

'Could I just mention something?' Wendi said, from the front path. 'It's not really my place since I came to see Sam, but I'd feel remiss if I didn't at least mention it.'

'Of course,' Emma said, her stomach clenching.

'Ruby is clearly a very dedicated student.'

Emma nodded.

'But she's much too stressed for a child her age. I think it would be a good idea to help her to relax, explain that homework isn't the be all and end all, no matter what the school will try to tell her – and you.'

Emma closed the door and rested her forehead against it. There was always something. She never seemed to be able to keep track of everything at the same time. While she'd been worrying about Sam, she'd somehow failed to notice that Ruby needed help. Her smart, perfect, highly strung Ruby. She banged her head gently against the wood. She didn't think she'd put any pressure on Ruby, but maybe she had. Or maybe it was hereditary. Emma had been so dedicated and determined at school, afraid to make mistakes, scared of getting told off, perhaps she'd somehow communicated that to Ruby, totally unintentionally.

Back in the kitchen, Ruby had set herself up at the dining table, an exercise book and a row of printed papers in front of her.

'Wow!' Emma said, standing behind her and kissing the top of her head. Her hair smelled like strawberries. 'What are you doing?'

'I asked Mrs Button for some more work,' Ruby said, glancing up briefly, before turning back to the pages.

'Why?'

'I like it.' She shrugged. 'And I thought that lady might talk to me.'

'Oh!' Emma said. 'No. She was just—' Buddy was pressed almost flat against the glass of the back door.

'Let me just let Buddy out . . .' Emma said.

She opened the back door for Buddy, who hared to the bottom of the garden, and then stood still, staring up a tree at a squirrel or pigeon or perhaps a particularly animated leaf. Emma pulled out a chair and sat down next to her daughter.

'Wendi came to talk to Sam because he doesn't talk at school.'

'I know,' Ruby said. 'I just thought she might . . . ask me some things.'

'OK,' Emma said gently. 'You know you don't have to do extra work, right?'

'I know,' Ruby said. 'I like it.'

Emma reached over and stilled Ruby's hand as it moved over the paper. 'Look at me.'

With an exasperated groan, Ruby dropped her pencil and turned to look at her mother.

'Rubes,' Emma said. 'Is this about the SATs? I don't want you to feel like you're under pressure.'

'I don't,' Ruby said. 'I like it. Really. It makes me feel . . .' She frowned and glanced down at the papers again. 'You know when you do a jigsaw and you find the right piece and you get that feeling when you put it in the right place?'

Emma nodded. She hated jigsaws. She got frustrated when she couldn't find the right piece and just found the entire endeavour boring.

'It's like that. Or like when Sam builds a wall with Lego and it's just perfect. Like that.'

'OK,' Emma said, curling an arm around Ruby's shoulders. 'I get that.'

Ruby picked up her pencil again. 'Can you make some fruit toast?'

Emma laughed. 'Yes. But promise me you'll tell me if it gets too much.'

'Promise,' Ruby said. But she was already writing again.

'We need to go to Hilbre Island,' Ruby said through a mouthful of toothpaste.

Emma was sitting on the loo, lid down, waiting for her daughter to finish her endless before bed routine.

'How come?' Emma said.

'For our project!' Ruby replied, exasperated. 'I've been telling you.'

'You have, darling, I'm sorry.' Emma wanted to close her eyes. Maybe she could. On the loo. Just lean back against the cistern and close her eyes until Ruby was done.

'Mama!' Ruby said.

Emma opened her eyes, reached a hand under the cold running tap and splashed water on her own face.

Ruby laughed, spraying foam onto the mirror.

'I'm tired, Rubes,' Emma said.

'I'm not.' Ruby rinsed her toothbrush and poked it back into the tumbler. 'Can I have another story.'

'You're joking, right?' Emma said. 'I can hardly keep my eyes open.'

She stood up, steadying herself against the tiled wall.

'I could read it to you?' Ruby suggested.

Emma took her daughter's face in both hands and kissed her on the forehead. 'That is a very sweet idea. But you need to go to sleep. And so do I.'

Emma needed to take Buddy out, but she physically couldn't face it. He'd be fine. She'd just let him out into the garden for a pee and then take him for a big beach walk in the morning.

'Can we have a cuddle chat?' Ruby asked, clambering into her bed and looking up at Emma with huge, hopeful eyes.

'A little one,' Emma said.

Chapter Twenty-Five

'So,' Emma said, twirling in her new dress. 'How do I look?'

Paul had loosened his tie, but was still wearing his work suit. Emma assumed he was going to leave it on for their evening out. She'd read about a new restaurant online and Paul had come home from work early especially. But now he had his phone up to his ear and a frown on his face. That was fine. She could deal with that. Get some food and wine in him, maybe run her foot up his inside leg in the restaurant. And then when they got back and the kids were fast asleep he could show her how he used that lube she'd been pretending to forget about. She couldn't wait.

The children were in the living room with Sage, and Emma's stomach had been rumbling for at least the last forty-five minutes. She was going to get a burger. And chips. And onion rings. And maybe also garlic bread.

'I'm sorry, Em,' Paul said, ending his call, dropping his phone back in his pocket. 'I can't go out tonight. I've got to go and have dinner with Matt Jackson.'

'Are you joking?' she said. He had to be joking.

He shook his head. 'It's something . . . I need to go and deal with this. It's delicate at this stage. I wouldn't if it wasn't important, you know that.'

Emma stared at him. She had known that, in the past, in London, but she wasn't even sure any more.

'Fine,' she said. 'Go.'

'It might not take long. Maybe we can still go when I get back, I—'

Emma shook her head. 'Just go if you're going.'

Fuck Paul and fuck work and fuck everything, Emma muttered to herself, once Paul had gone and she'd paid Sage and put the kids to bed. It was very much not the evening she'd had planned. She opened a bag of crisps and ate a couple but they tasted off. She threw them away, still muttering 'fuck' to herself.

In London, if she'd felt like this she would have called one of her friends, complained about Paul, listened to them complain about their partner, and then ended up laughing 'til she cried. But she'd hardly spoken to any of them since she'd been in West Kirby. At first because she was too busy sorting the house, and then because she missed London, she missed her friends, she missed her old life, and she didn't want to talk to anyone and be reminded of it. But she wanted to talk to someone now. And while Beth and Hanan were great, it was too soon to phone them like this.

She scrolled through her contacts. Gemma was probably out with her perfect husband, having a perfect meal before going home to have perfect sex. Steph might be home, but Steph could sometimes be a bit of a snore, if she was honest Emma didn't really want to talk to her. She scrolled until she found Amanda and pressed call before she could change her mind. It rang for a while and she was just about to hang up when she heard Amanda answer.

'I can't talk,' she said straight away. 'I'm at a thing.'

Emma wanted to ask her why she'd answered her phone

then, but instead she said, 'I was just checking in. Wondering how everyone's doing.'

'Aw,' Amanda said. 'You missing us?'

'Madly,' Emma joked. But it was entirely true. She missed the ease of her London friendships, where she'd known all the politics: who hated whom, who had previous with someone else's husband, who could keep a confidence and who should never be told anything, ever. She hadn't got to grips with that here yet. At all.

'You haven't replaced me yet then?' Amanda asked.

Emma laughed. 'You're irreplaceable.'

'You got that right. Listen, I really do have to go. I'm at the theatre and people are giving me daggers.'

'Oh my god, Mand!' Emma had laughed. But then she'd ended the call and she was alone and the house suddenly seemed very quiet. She needed to make more of an effort with the West Kirby women. Not just Hanan and Beth, but Maggie too. And even Jools and Eve and almost-silent Flic. They obviously had something, the four of them, and there was no reason Emma couldn't be part of it. She needed friends. She really needed more friends.

Emma was about to take her dress off when she heard the front door open. She thought about clambering into her pyjamas and getting under the duvet, waiting to see what kind of mood Paul was in. But . . . it had been so long since they'd had sex. And she missed it. She sat on the edge of the bed and tugged the hem of her dress up to mid-thigh. She hoped Paul was tired enough to come straight up. If she smelled toast or heard the TV go on, she was going to be pissed off.

But then she heard his tread on the stairs and immediately felt self-conscious, tugging at the hem and the waist of her dress. It was clingier than she'd expected it to be when she'd ordered it and she wasn't sure if it was too clingy. She stood up and looked at herself in the full-length mirror in the corner of the room. No, it was good. She looked good. She saw the door open in the reflection.

'Hey,' Paul said.

Emma smiled at him in the mirror. 'Hey.'

'I'm sorry about earlier.'

He walked up behind her and wrapped his arms around her waist, resting his chin on her shoulder, looking at the two of them in the mirror.

'I wouldn't have gone if it hadn't been important.'

'That's OK,' Emma said. 'I just hate it when it's last minute. Or if we've got plans.'

'I know,' Paul said. 'I'm sorry. I really like this dress.'

His hands slid down and he started edging the hem up her thighs. 'It makes your boobs look bigger.'

Emma laughed and then tipped her head back to give him better access to her neck. She was still a bit pissed off with him. But she was also horny. And he'd pushed her dress up so far that she could feel his erection pressing into her bum.

'What's got into you?' she said, laughing.

'It's just been a while since I saw you in a dress,' he said. 'I'd forgotten how sexy you are.'

Emma snorted as Paul's hand sneaked down the front of her knickers.

'This OK?' he murmured.

Emma dropped her head back against his shoulder, closing her eyes. 'Yeah. S'good.' Her legs were starting to feel wobbly and she was about to clamber onto the bed when Paul shifted slightly and bent Emma over face down onto the mattress. 'I'm so hard.'

'Shit,' Emma said into the duvet, as Paul slid her knickers down her thighs and pushed his own trousers off, kicking them to one side.

'Shit,' she said again, turning her face to the side where her neck was aching. Paul was holding her hips up and pushing into her with little grunts. God, they hadn't done it like this for so long, she'd forgotten how exhausting it was. Her thighs were burning. She pushed up on her arms and back against Paul who groaned and curled over her, pressing her down into the bed.

'Missed this,' he murmured into the back of her neck.

Emma slipped one hand down under herself and pressed it between her legs, moaning as she hit just the right spot.

'Too loud,' Paul murmured, his mouth right against her ear. Even though his grunts were almost certainly louder. 'You'll wake the kids.' But then he curled his hand over her mouth, his thumb pushing up against her cheekbone and she found herself coming, her feet pressing into the floor, hips jerking back against Paul's. And then he was coming too before collapsing on top of her.

'Fuck,' she whispered into his palm, then poked her tongue out to lick between his fingers.

'We should do that again,' he said, his forehead resting between her shoulder blades. He kissed the back of her neck and then stood up, smoothing one hand over her hip.

'I'll go and check on the kids,' he said.

Once he was gone, Emma pulled the dress off and headed into the bathroom for a wee. She didn't know what had got into Paul. Even when they'd been having sex more regularly he hadn't really been one to ambush her – they'd almost always done it in bed, late, after the kids were asleep. It had become predictable, yes, but Emma assumed that was the same for pretty much all married couples. She certainly didn't know any who were regularly shagging during the day or doing it anywhere other than bed. That stuff seemed to be reserved for the very early days of a relationship.

She looked at herself in the mirror as she washed her hands. And he'd never put his hand over her mouth before. She would never have thought she'd have liked it, but she really had. She wouldn't have thought Paul would have been into that either. But obviously he was. It had got both of them there really quickly.

Maybe they should be mixing things up a bit more? Maybe she should suggest something. She'd just always thought it would be weird if she brought something new up after so long together. Like, why had she never mentioned it before? Where had she learned about it? But maybe she should do some googling and they could talk about it. Paul didn't have to be the only one of them who had new moves. She smiled at herself in the mirror. Tonight had worked out pretty well after all.

Chapter Twenty-Six

The children had insisted they were fine to play out, even though it was cold, so Maggie, Emma, Beth and Sofia sat in the conservatory to keep an eye on them. They'd all been keen to finally make the playdate happen and it seemed to be going well so far.

'It's because of the playhouse,' Beth said. 'It was the first thing Flora said when she woke up this morning: 'Can we play in Amy's playhouse?''

'Ah, yeah,' Maggie said. 'It's always a bit of a draw.'

'It's amazing,' Beth told Emma and Sofia. 'Almost as big as my house.'

'It's not,' Maggie said. 'It is great though. Jim built it when Amy was tiny.'

'I love this,' Sofia said, pointing at the pebble picture on a side table. The box frame held three figures – clearly a dad, mum, and child – made of pebbles.

'I made that,' Maggie said. 'Amy asked me to.'

'Really?' Emma said. 'That's amazing.'

'Oh it's easy really,' Maggie told her. 'The hardest part is finding the right pebbles.'

The four women talked while the children played and Maggie found she was enjoying herself. Beth was hilarious, Emma seemed nice, and the children seemed to be getting on well. Maggie went through to the kitchen to make more tea. She was taking the milk out of the fridge when Sofia came through.

'Is it really OK to make me the pebble picture?' she asked, leaning back against one of the cupboards.

Maggie glanced over as she took the sugar out of the cupboard. 'Of course. I love making them. And it does sound like a nice thing to take home. Do you know what you'd want it to be?'

'I think two figures, maybe? Me and my mama. I think she'd like that. Because I'm far away.'

'You must miss her,' Maggie said.

Sofia nodded. 'When I was little, she worked in London. I stayed in Poland with my aunt. Mama would come to work for nearly all year and just come home for Christmas. So we are used to being apart. But it's still hard.'

'That sounds really hard,' Maggie said. 'I can't imagine being away from Amy for that long.'

Sofia shrugged. 'She had to make money, you know.'

'Of course.' Maggie had arranged everything on a tray and picked it up to carry through.

'How much would it be?' Sofia asked, as she passed.

Maggie stopped. 'How much?'

'The picture.'

'Oh! Oh no, you don't have to pay. It's just pebbles.'

'And your time. And a frame.'

Maggie shook her head. 'You don't have to pay.'

'Thank you. I will think of another way to pay you.' She smiled. 'We still have to go for that drink.'

'Oh!' Maggie said. 'Yes. Sorry, I've been snowed under, I haven't had time to even think about it.'

'No problem,' Sofia said. 'There's no hurry.'

'Soon,' Maggie said.

'Good.' Sofia smiled.

Chapter Twenty-Seven

'Mama, can you help me with my project?' Ruby called over from the dining table that afternoon. They'd stayed for lunch at Maggie's and the kids had seemed to have the best time, with Ruby, Flora and Violet declaring themselves 'treble best friends.'

'Not right now, angel,' Emma said, without looking up. 'I'm trying to make a special dinner for Daddy.'

'Is it his birthday?' Ruby said and Emma could hear the edge of panic in her voice.

'No, darling.' She looked up from the bowl of cherries to see Ruby, as expected, wide-eyed with worry. 'His birthday was just after Halloween, remember? I just wanted to make him something nice.'

'Because he's been working so hard?'

'Exactly that.'

'It smells good,' Ruby said. 'Is it for me and Sam too?'

'Nope,' Emma said. 'You've got chicken tenders and chips. This is just for me and Daddy. But I'll save you some cherries.'

She would too. Because she was sick to death of stoning them. She'd made the mustard dressing, the ham was in the oven along with the chicken tenders and oven chips. The new potatoes were on the hob par-boiling, and she'd opened a bottle of wine to breathe because last time they'd bought it, Paul had said it tasted better when it had been open for a while. (When they were in London, they never would have had an unfinished bottle of wine long enough to notice a difference.)

'Can you help with my project tomorrow?' Ruby asked.

'I should think so,' Emma said, pouring some frozen peas into a bowl and sliding them into the microwave. 'What do you have to do?'

While Ruby talked about her project, Emma looked around the kitchen to make sure everything looked neat and tidy. Paul had a thing about unfinished jobs, so sometimes when she was ready to relax, he had to take out the recycling and wash out Buddy's food bowl, change a lightbulb, fix a leaking tap. Emma didn't want any of that tonight. She wanted the kids in bed, meal on the table, and her husband to herself for at least a couple of hours.

'Mama!' Ruby almost shouted. 'You're not listening!'

'Sorry, darling, you're right,' Emma said. 'Tell me again.'

As Ruby started to talk, the oven buzzer rang.

'Gah, sorry,' Emma said. 'Tell me while you and Sam are eating.'

'It doesn't matter now,' Ruby said.

'It does, baby. I'm sorry. I've just got a few things to do right now.'

'I'll go and get Sam,' Ruby said, and left the room, looking dejected.

'Fuck a duck,' Emma muttered, as she slid the baking tray out of the oven with a tea towel, catching her knuckle on the metal. She was holding her hand under the cold tap when the microwave pinged. And then the doorbell rang.

'Left my keys at work,' Paul said when she opened it.

'Could you go get the kids?' she asked, heading back to the kitchen. Chicken tenders and oven chips on plates. Peas drained and poured into a bowl cos neither of the kids liked them on their plates. Ketchup on the table. Juice in cups: Paw Patrol for Sam, a hideous E.T. mug Ruby had found in a charity shop for Ruby.

She'd intended to get changed and put some make-up on before Paul got home. Typical of him to be early on the one night she wanted— No, that wasn't fair. She'd been complaining about his late nights for ages now, she couldn't also complain when he got home in good time. But she was aware that she was wearing baggy leggings and a shapeless top, flip-flops on her feet. She wished she'd thought to get a manicure and maybe a wax. Not that Paul cared. At all. But it would have made her feel better. She'd read in a novel once about a woman thinking it was important for her to make herself look presentable before her husband came home and, as she read it, Emma realised that wasn't something that had ever occurred to her. She liked to look nice, of course, but she'd never felt like it was dutiful.

One day she'd been hanging Paul's ancient saggy underwear on the radiator and thought about how for years she'd worn matching bra and pants, nice ones. Would have felt like if she hadn't, she'd be letting the side down, letting herself down. But how that wasn't something that would ever have occurred to Paul. Did men's magazines write about how men should buy nice new undies to keep their women interested? Did they fuck. She'd felt a flash of anger at the sight of Paul's pants ever since. But that was hardly his fault.

'What's for dinner?' he said from the doorway. 'I'm starving.'

Emma pushed one hand back through her hair. 'We're not having ours now. This is just for the kids. We'll have ours when they're in bed.'

'Fuck, really?' He'd taken his suit jacket off and was holding it over one arm, his briefcase still in his hand. 'I didn't get any lunch.'

'You can eat, like, one chip,' Emma said, squeezing past him and out into the hall. 'But don't eat anything else. I've been fucking about with cherries for bloody ages.'

'Do I like cherries?' Paul said, following her down the hall.

'Sam! Ruby!' Emma shouted up the stairs. She felt Paul's hands on her waist and turned to look at him. 'And yes. You like cherries. It's cranberries you don't like.'

Paul was looking at her mouth.

'What?' she said, smiling.

'Hi.'

'Hi.' He was still staring. It made her feel squirmy. 'What?'

'I've just had a good day, that's all.' He inclined his head and pressed his mouth to hers. He tasted like coffee.

'No kissing!' Sam shouted from the stairs.

'So tell me about your good day,' Emma said once the kids were in bed and she and Paul were at the dining table with the meal Emma had made, and wine in their glasses.

'The Matt Jackson deal is all signed.'

'Wow,' Emma said. 'That's great.'

The thought of Jools, of book club, made her stomach clench with nerves, but that wasn't Paul's problem.

'Photo call and announcement in the next couple of weeks.'

'Brilliant,' Emma said. 'Well done. I'm proud of you.'

Paul stabbed a piece of ham with his fork and popped it in his mouth. 'Holy shit, this is good. You should cook more.'

'Jesus,' Emma said.

Paul looked up from his plate. 'I didn't mean 'get back to the kitchen, wench' I just meant you're good at it.'

'Good save,' Emma said.

'Well I have spent the day at a football club.'

Emma shuffled her feet under the table and hooked her foot around Paul's. They always used to do that too. And in bed. They'd stopped doing that as well.

'Are you happy here?' Emma asked her husband. 'So far?'

Paul nodded through a mouthful of ham and then said, 'Yeah. It's great. You are too, right?'

Emma tipped her head to one side. 'Yeah. I mean . . . I don't really feel settled yet. I thought I would, faster, you know? I'd like more friends. And I'd like you to be home more. That was meant to be part of the reason—'

'I know,' Paul said. 'I'm sorry. It's unfortunate that this came up so soon. But once it's all done it should die down a little. And we can have the beach picnics and sunset walks.'

'Good,' Emma said.

'And I'll be getting a bonus so we can take the kids away at half term maybe? Disneyland Paris?'

'Oh god,' Emma said. 'They'll explode.'

Paul grinned at her. 'We could surprise them. Like on the adverts. It'd be great.'

Emma had finished her ham so she pushed her plate away and drank some more wine. She was only halfway down the glass, but Paul lifted the bottle and raised an eyebrow at her. OK. Sure. Good.

Chapter Twenty-Eight

Maggie couldn't sleep. Jim was snoring and the radiator under the window was ticking, but she'd been lying there for a long time now. Maybe hours. She'd been trying to work out where it had gone wrong, which specific decision had led her here, to this moment, these circumstances. She'd started with Jim asking her out for a drink, but there was a reason she'd said yes. Her father maybe. Her father telling her no one would be interested in her, making her think she needed to be grateful for anyone's interest and attention. Because she hadn't stopped to wonder if she was interested in Jim, attracted to him, even liked him. He'd asked her out and that had been enough.

Her mind kept returning to a thing her dad had said about her hair. She'd had it cut and blown straight – the hairdresser had suggested it – Maggie had been fifteen maybe. She'd loved it. It had felt smooth and sleek and it swung slowly when she turned her head. She couldn't stop stroking it. At home, her mum had raved about it, going so far as to go and find the camera to snap a quick pic. And then her dad had come home from work. Her mum had called him into the kitchen where Maggie had been sitting at the dining table doing her homework. She'd said, 'Mike?

Look at Maggie's hair! Isn't it lovely?' And her dad had given a short bark of laughter and said, 'It's something. I don't know about lovely.' Maggie had experienced a brief moment of breathlessness, like the time she'd fallen flat on the ground from the monkey bars. And then she'd felt . . . fine. What had she expected? Nothing? Something worse? She'd looked at her mum and watched something similar play out over her face: surprise, shock, pain, disappointment and finally resignation. She'd turned back to the oven, her dad had left the room. Done.

'Are you seeing someone else?' Maggie asked the darkness.

Jim didn't speak for so long that she'd almost convinced herself he was asleep and hadn't heard her, but then he said, 'Who told you that?'

Wrong answer.

'No one.'

Jim was already rolling over, away from Maggie, swinging his legs out of the bed.

'Was it Jools? That stuck-up bitch, I knew she couldn't—'

'It wasn't Jools,' Maggie said, while thinking *Jools knows*?

'So who then?' He'd pulled his sweatpants on and was halfway round the bed, heading for the door.

'I saw a text.'

He stopped. 'You looked at my phone?'

'It was on the table. The message popped up. I wasn't looking, but I saw it anyway.'

'I've told you about looking at my phone.'

Maggie felt the familiar fear start to rise. Her heart racing, her mouth drying. She told herself to breathe, to stay where she was, let him tire himself out.

'I can't believe you looked at my phone,' he said.

'I can't believe you're seeing someone else.' Except she could. It wasn't hard to believe at all. In fact, she realised now that he'd probably been seeing other women all along, for as long as they'd been together. She was an idiot.

'Who is she?' Maggie asked, rolling onto her side and pulling her legs up towards her stomach. Even though she already knew. She wanted to hear it from him.

'Why do you care?' Jim asked. He was in the doorway now, almost out of the room, and Maggie wanted to shush him so Amy didn't hear.

'Why *wouldn't* I care?' Maggie asked. 'Do I know her?' She wanted to sit up, get out of bed, but she also wanted to stay exactly where she was, possibly for ever.

'I'll stop seeing her,' Jim said. 'I'll tell her now.'

'You don't have to,' Maggie said, closing her eyes.

'What's that supposed to mean?'

Maggie opened her eyes again and stared at the shape of her husband in the low light at the foot of the bed.

'What are we even doing? I'm not happy. You're clearly not happy if you're shagging someone else—'

'It's just sex,' Jim said. 'Fuck knows you don't want to—'

'It's not just sex to me,' Maggie said. 'It's lying and sneaking around and other people knowing. I don't want to be the kind of wife who wonders where her husband is whenever he's not home. I don't want to be afraid to put my hands in your pockets when I'm putting your clothes in the wash. I never wanted any of that.'

But beyond that she didn't, couldn't, trust him any more, she'd realised that she didn't even like him any more. She'd been happier in the summer when he wasn't around. She was happy when Amy interrupted them when he wanted sex. She was happy when he went out in the evening, even though she knew he was going to Eve. She deserved better than that. And she had to set a better example for Amy. She absolutely had to.

'So what are you saying?' Jim sat down at the foot of the bed and half-turned towards her.

'I think you should move out,' Maggie said.

Jim stood up. Stretched his arms behind his back. Stared at Maggie in the dark. And said, simply, 'No.'

Chapter Twenty-Nine

Emma woke suddenly. She'd heard a bang, downstairs, she was sure.

She pushed her foot against Paul's calf and whispered his name. Nothing. She listened, half-sitting up in bed, but she didn't hear anything else. Maybe it had been in her dream. But she was sure it had been real. She felt as if she could almost still hear it, echoing around the room. She swung her legs out of bed and opened the door.

Ruby's bedroom door was open and she could see faint light coming from downstairs. Her heart racing, she headed down the stairs and into the kitchen, where she found Ruby at the dining table, homework spread out in front of her.

'Rubes!' Emma said, coming up behind her daughter and wrapping her arms around her. 'What are you doing?'

'I couldn't get back to sleep,' Ruby said, without turning. 'So I came to finish my homework.'

Emma rested her chin on her daughter's head. 'What was the bang?'

'I got a chair to put the light on . . .'

It was only then that Emma noticed Ruby had switched on the light in the oven's extractor hood.

'And then I knocked it over. Sorry.'

'That's OK,' Emma said. She moved around the table and pulled out her own chair, sitting down and looking over at her daughter.

'But you know you don't need to get up in the night to do homework, right?'

'I know,' Ruby said. 'But I wanted to. I like it.'

Emma frowned. 'Did you have a bad dream?'

Ruby shook her head. 'I don't *think* so.'

Emma wasn't sure what to do. This didn't seem healthy. But Ruby seemed happy. And if she couldn't sleep, Emma couldn't force her. She remembered a time in her own childhood when she'd wake in the night and struggle to get back to sleep and how much easier it would have been if she'd been able to get out of bed and just do something, rather than lying there for hours getting more and more annoyed about not being able to drop off again.

'Would you like some hot chocolate?'

'Please,' Ruby said. She was idly tracing a pencil over a page of one of the books.

'What homework are you doing?' Emma asked, as she crossed the kitchen to the fridge for the milk.

'It's about plants,' Ruby said. 'The life cycle of a plant.'

Emma leaned back against the countertop as she looked back at her daughter. 'Seriously? I don't think I learned about that until high school!'

Ruby smiled then and shrugged. 'It's interesting.'

'Want to tell me about it?'

While Emma made the hot chocolate, Ruby told her everything she'd learned so far about osmosis and chlorophyll (which she couldn't actually pronounce) and the water table. It made Emma feel oddly nostalgic for school.

'There's an experiment,' Emma said. 'Something with food colouring and celery, I think?'

'We did that at preschool,' Ruby said.

'Oh.'

'But could I get a plant for my room? Like a real one? That's growing?'

'Course,' Emma said. 'I'll get one tomorrow after I drop you off.'

Ruby smiled and then yawned so widely it almost looked painful.

'Hey,' Emma said. 'I think you might be tired.'

Her daughter smiled, bashfully.

'Want to come and drink the hot chocolate in my bed?'

Ruby's eyes lit up.

'Em.'

Emma groaned. She could already feel that her back was tense, her shoulders tight, and she wasn't even close to being awake.

'Em,' Paul said again.

She forced one eye open and winced against the morning light. Paul was sitting on the edge of the bed, staring down at her. He looked happy and handsome and she almost wanted to pull him down on top of her, but he was already in his suit and the kids would be awake in a minute and—

'Look at her,' Paul said, his voice reverential.

Emma turned to find Ruby fast asleep in bed next to her. She looked impossibly younger and more beautiful when she was asleep. Her cheeks pink, bottom lip pouting out, long eyelashes fanning over her cheeks. Emma wanted to kiss her and kiss her and kiss her, but also just to stare at her perfect face.

'Did she have a bad dream?' Paul asked.

Emma shook her head. 'Went downstairs to do her homework. At two a.m.'

'Christ,' Paul said. 'That's not good. You going to have a word with the teacher?'

Emma hadn't really thought about it during the night, it hadn't seemed quite real, but yes, yes she was.

She nodded.

''kay,' Paul said. 'Text me.'

'Will do,' Emma said.

She suddenly remembered a time when they'd not long been together. Emma had the day off. Paul had got up to go to work, dressed in his suit and tie, and come back to the bedroom to kiss Emma goodbye. She'd pulled him back to bed with the tie and kissed him until he gave up any suggestion of going into work. Then he'd taken the tie off and used it to fasten Emma to the bed. That had been a good day. She curled one finger around the end of his tie now and tugged lightly.

'Remember that time—'

'Sorry,' Paul said. 'Got to go.'

He dipped his head and kissed her quickly on the mouth before leaning over and brushing his lips over Ruby's forehead.

'Have a good day, angel.'

'You too,' Emma said.

'I was talking to . . .' he started to say and then he smiled. 'Have a good day, Em.'

'You too. Love you.'

'Love you too.' But he was already almost out of the door.

Emma rolled over and cuddled up against her sleeping daughter.

'Did Daddy go?' Ruby mumbled.

'Yeah,' Emma said. 'He did.'

Chapter Thirty

Maggie was dreading book club. Actually dreading it. It had never exactly been fun, but she'd always been OK with going, even if just to get out of the house, but since she'd found out Eve was fucking her husband, she was dreading it. It had been awful last time and she couldn't believe she was going to put herself through it again. But what was the alternative? Unless she was willing to explode everything and she just wasn't. She wasn't brave enough.

She'd asked Jim if he'd told Eve that she knew, but he wouldn't even talk to her about it. He wouldn't talk about moving out either. He was acting like none of it had happened. Which was how he'd always dealt with disagreements and Maggie had always let him get away with it, but she wasn't going to this time, she was sure. Almost sure.

She thought about not going to Jools's, but she didn't want to stay at home with Jim either, and Nick had fully moved out now, to a small flat in the Georgian Quarter in Liverpool. Maybe she should get dressed and head out as usual and just go to the pub. The Viking. Or the place Amy had her birthday that Maggie could never remember the name of – they roasted marshmallows at the table and had a cinema room for the kids. Maggie wondered if she could buy a jug of margarita and take it into the cinema room by herself. Probably not.

Maybe she should go over to Liverpool. See a film. Or go to the theatre. Or just sit in a coffee shop or bar by herself and have some time to think. She wasn't sure she was ready to think yet. Because if Jim did move out, she didn't know how she would manage.

She knew she'd end up going to book club as always, knew she wasn't brave enough to do anything else yet. But she felt something stirring, could imagine that one day she could have a different life. Just not today.

She decided to walk so she could have a drink and on the way stopped off at Morrisons to pick up a bottle of her favourite wine to take with her. The image of her throwing the wine over Eve flashed into her head and she almost laughed – she hoped Eve was wearing one of her crisp white shirts – but she knew she'd never do it. At least she didn't think she'd ever do it, but then she wouldn't have thought she'd punch a stranger in a car either.

She grabbed the wine and headed towards the checkout, stopping to glance at the cover of one of the weekly magazines on the stand at the end of the queue. Someone bumped into her from behind and a woman's voice said 'Oops!'

Maggie turned to find Sofia with an enormous bag of Kettle Chips in her arms.

'Hi,' Maggie said, her stomach fluttering again. 'Stocking up for the apocalypse?'

Sofia laughed. 'Jools sent me out for them and they only have these giant bags. I'm not sure if it's better to go back with this or nothing at all.'

'Tricky one,' Maggie said. 'I'm trying to think if there's anywhere else, but . . .'

'I don't think anywhere else is open,' Sofia said. She hoiked the bag up in her arms. 'Ah well. I'll take a chance.'

Maggie paid for her wine and then Sofia the toddler-sized bag of crisps and they both headed outside into the car park.

'Did you drive?' Maggie asked.

Sofia shook her head.

'Me neither. It's such a nice night, I wanted to walk.' She didn't mention how she also wanted to get drunk. Or how she'd been fantasising about not going at all.

'Do you walk on the main road or the prom?' Sofia asked.

'Prom?' Maggie said. They were already heading that way anyway. It was clearly so much nicer, particularly at this time in the evening when the sun was setting and turning the sky pink and orange and red and the seagulls were gliding over marine lake and the river.

They didn't even talk. They just walked, looking out over the water at the colours painting the sky. Every time Maggie looked at Sofia, Sofia was looking back at her, a small smile on her lips. The setting sun edged her outline in rose gold and Maggie wanted to take a photo she could keep for ever.

Chapter Thirty-One

Emma felt much more confident in her new dress and boots. She didn't expect to be quite as glamorous as the other women – she wasn't sure she'd ever be as glamorous as Jools or Eve – but she'd got a lot closer than last time. The only problem was that she hadn't read the book. Again. She didn't know what was wrong with her, she just couldn't seem to concentrate for long enough. She'd watched the film though. And looked up discussion questions online, so she didn't think it would be a huge problem. And she'd decided to walk so she could maybe have one extra drink and loosen up enough to perhaps make friends of these women. One or two of them, at least. Maybe just Maggie.

She'd seen them at the school gates since the last book group, of course, but not one of them had spoken to her, not properly, not even Maggie. They'd all acknowledged her – a nod or a smile or even just a look where they would have looked away before – but that was it. No hellos. No chats. No invitations for coffee. It was weird. But she had to remind herself that they probably all had stuff going on too.

The manicured hedge that bordered Jools's garden was strung with twinkly white lights. Emma stopped for a moment, wondering if they could possibly be Christmas decorations, but no. It was only early November.

'We put them up for Halloween and the girls insisted we leave them,' a voice said.

Emma turned and saw Jools's husband, Matt, climbing out of his silver sports car.

'Oh hey,' she said. She nodded at the hedge. 'They look good.'

'How are you?' he asked, crossing the gravel driveway. 'Nice to see you again. How's Paul?'

'He's good,' Emma said, even though she'd only seen him for a few minutes before she had to leave to get to book club on time. 'But you know that. You've seen him more than I have lately.'

'Hey, not me,' Matt said, laughing as he opened the front door. 'I haven't seen him since we went out for dinner.'

'Yeah, that's what I'm saying,' Emma said. 'Last week. Paul and I were meant to be going out and then you stole him away from me.'

Matt shrugged. 'Nope. Not guilty. I haven't seen him since the four of us had dinner: me and you and Paul and Jools.'

Emma frowned. Paul had definitely said Matt Jackson, she knew he had.

'Ah,' she said. 'I must have got the wrong end of the stick.'

'No worries,' he said, pushing open the front door.

Matt called out to Jools as soon as they were inside the house and she appeared almost instantly. She was wearing a velvet jumpsuit the colour of red wine with leopard print trainers. Emma immediately felt both over-dressed and frumpy.

'You look amazing,' she told Jools.

Jools looked down at herself, smiling. 'Thank you!' She looked Emma up and down and said, 'You look nice too.'

Nice. Great.

'Hey, babe,' Matt said, pulling Jools towards him and kissing her on the mouth. Jools grinned at him, nuzzling into the side of his neck before smacking his arse as he headed for the stairs.

Emma followed Jools through to the back room. Only Maggie and Flic were there so far, sitting on opposite sofas just like last time. Emma assumed they all sat in the same positions each time. Like school. They were both much more casually dressed than last time too. Was there a dress code memo she wasn't getting?

'Gin?' Jools asked Emma and she nodded, even though she hadn't actually been listening. She'd been thinking about what Matt had said; he hadn't been with Paul. Paul had gone out and come home and fucked her like they'd never fucked before. So where had he been? Who had he been with? Emma swallowed hard, blinking back tears. She couldn't think about it now. She had to get through book club. And once again she hadn't read the book.

'Amy was asking when Ruby can come over again,' Maggie said.

'Any time,' Emma said. 'They seem to really like each other.'

Maggie nodded. 'It's worked out well.'

'Violet too,' Emma said, as Jools came back into the room.

'What about her?' Jools asked.

'In a little gang with Ruby, Amy and Flora.'

'They just need one more and they can be the Spice Girls,' Maggie said.

Jools laughed and Emma stared at her. She wasn't sure she'd actually seen her laugh before.

Emma suspected she'd drunk the first gin a bit too quickly. Jools seemed to be topping her up before the other women had even started on their drinks. She couldn't stop thinking about Paul. About where he might have been if he hadn't been with Matt Jackson. They could hear Matt and the children playing upstairs. The girls giggling wildly. Matt laughing and occasionally shouting encouragement.

'I hope they're not jumping on the bed,' Jools said. She looked fond, Emma noticed. She'd never really paid much attention to how Jools interacted with her daughters at school, but her face looked much softer now, as she talked about them.

'I'm always telling him they'll break it,' Jools said. 'But he doesn't care. He's worse than they are.'

She smiled at Emma and Emma squinted back at her. Was she wearing false eyelashes? Emma was pretty sure she was. Who wore false eyelashes in their own home? For book club?! Or what had Beth said? Extensions?

'So what's new with you?' Jools asked.

'My boots!' Emma said, swinging one foot in the air. Unfortunately, it connected with Jools's glass, knocking it into the hearth, where it both smashed and soaked the dove grey carpet with the orange contents.

'Oh my god!' Emma said. 'I'm so sorry!'

'Don't worry about it,' Jools said, standing, but her mouth was set in a straight line. 'Accidents happen.'

'I'll get it,' Eve said, dropping her hand on Jools's shoulder and then heading out of the room. Jools sat down and for a second looked, to Emma, weary, like she was only just holding it together. Then she blinked and smiled and was back to her usual self.

When Eve came back, Matt was with her, carrying a dustpan and brush and a hand-held vacuum, a cloth over his shoulder. Emma noticed every single other woman in the room sit up straighter at the sight of him. But she couldn't judge, since she'd sucked her stomach in too.

'You didn't need to come down, babe,' Jools said. 'It's just a broken glass.'

'I was down anyway,' Matt said. 'Violet wanted a glass of milk.'

Eve sat back on the sofa as Matt crouched down – Emma tried not to look at the way his grey joggers stretched over his perfectly-shaped arse – and brushed up the glass, sucked up the spilled drink with the vacuum, and dropped the cloth over the whole area. When he stood up again, he quickly pressed a kiss to Jools's forehead before smiling at everyone and disappearing again.

What, Emma thought to herself, *the fuck*?

Was Jools incapable of brushing up a bit of glass herself? Had Eve called him as if he was a member of staff? And why hadn't he just told her to do it herself, like Paul would have done? Emma wasn't sure she'd ever met anyone quite as spoiled as Jools.

Flic had chosen the book and so Flic led the discussion. Her first question was why had Bendrix and Sarah fallen in love? Was it because something was missing in their lives? And what was the purpose of the affair? Was it sex? Or were they looking for love? Understanding? As the other women talked, Emma tried to formulate some sort of argument, but her mind was blank. *Did that explain the lube*? *Had Paul bought lube to use with someone new*? She felt sick. Actually she really did feel sick. She probably shouldn't drink anything else.

'Emma?' Jools said.

Emma blinked at her. Something about what they got from the affair. Right. She swigged some gin.

'I think that she – Sarah – I think she's looking for something. But she's not entirely sure what. Or she doesn't want to admit it to herself even. The part where Julianne Moore—' Shit.

'Sorry?' Jools said.

Shit.

'Julianne Moore?' Jools said.

Emma felt like she was back at school. Everyone else in the room was silent. They could still hear the children giggling upstairs and Emma suddenly wanted to giggle herself. She'd definitely had too much gin.

'Sorry,' she said. 'I mean Sarah. The part where Sarah—'

'You didn't read the book?' Jools asked.

'Um,' Emma said. This wasn't school, she reminded herself, she was a grown woman. She didn't have to read the book. 'No. Sorry. I mean, I started it. But I just didn't get a chance—'

'OK!' Jools said, brightly. 'Maggie! What did you think of the book?'

Emma opened her mouth and closed it again. She wanted to argue. To explain why she hadn't read it. But what difference did it make? She hadn't read it. And Jools had moved on. So she thought Emma was useless? So what? Jools was the one who'd invited her to this group. It wasn't as if Emma was particularly invested.

She realised she was shrugging her shoulders and she forced herself to relax and listen to Maggie, who didn't seem to have much to say about the book either, but at least she'd actually read it.

'It made me think about affairs a bit . . .' Maggie said, hesitantly. 'About how easily they can happen. And about how sometimes people tolerate them because they don't see an alternative.'

'I've been thinking about that too,' Emma said. Her mouth felt dry from the gin. 'Do you ever wonder? If your . . . partner . . .' She wasn't sure all the women had husbands.

'I don't,' Jools said, confidently. 'We talk about it a lot. Because it's so common with footballers. Women throw themselves at Matt all the time. But I trust him.'

Emma rolled her eyes before she could stop herself.

'I don't think they have to be a big deal,' Eve said. 'It's just sex. It's different if you fall in love with someone.'

'Are you in love with my husband?' Maggie asked.

Emma looked from Maggie to Eve, whose mouth was set in a straight line.

'Mags—' Jools said.

'Oh don't Mags me,' Maggie said. 'You knew about it. You're supposed to be my friend. And you're cool with this bitch fucking my husband.'

'Look,' Eve said, shuffling to the edge of her seat and leaning on her knees to get closer to Maggie. 'I'm sorry. I didn't know who he was to begin with.'

'To begin with?' Maggie let out an inappropriate bark of laughter. 'Oh that's fine then. I apologise. Carry on.'

Emma glanced at the other women, who were looking back at Maggie. No one spoke.

'You can have him,' Maggie said, her voice tight. 'I don't want him. I asked him to go, but he won't. So come and take him. Help yourself.'

Emma pictured Paul bending her over the bed. Bending someone else over a bed. And bile rose in her throat.

'Can I use your loo?' Emma managed to croak out.

Jools frowned. 'Let me just—' she said, gesturing for Emma to follow her into the kitchen.

The kitchen was just as impressive as Emma had expected. Glossy white units, black and white tiled floor, huge window overlooking the garden. One wall was covered with kids' drawings, which Emma was surprised by. And then she rolled her eyes at herself, as if Jools was so glossy she didn't love her own children. Jools had disappeared down a corridor at the corner of the kitchen, but she came back and said, 'All good. You know what kids are like for flushing.'

'Oh god, yeah,' Emma said, heading for the bathroom. 'My loo's always disgusting.'

Why had she felt the need to say that? she asked herself, as she locked the bathroom door behind her. It was true that Sam rarely flushed, but their bathroom was still generally clean. Ish. Most of the time. Jools's bathroom, however, was spotless. Emma couldn't imagine what Jools had been checking on since she wouldn't have been surprised if she was the first person ever to use it. The white towels were folded and hanging neatly on a heating rack, even the soap on the side of the basin looked brand new. Emma peed, washed her hands, checked and double-checked that her skirt wasn't tucked into her tights and then reapplied her lipstick, looking in the huge ornate-framed mirror.

She shouldn't have any more gin. Her vision was blurring slightly so she knew she'd definitely had enough already. She'd realised years ago that going to the loo was always a good barometer of how drunk she was – she couldn't seem to tell when she was in the thick of things, but once she was alone . . . Although she didn't think she'd had that much. Had she? She was probably dehydrated. And she hadn't eaten much all day.

Dropping her lipstick back into her bag, she tried to turn the door handle, but it wouldn't budge. She took a step back and stared at the door as if there was another way to open it that she'd forgotten about in the last two minutes. No. Still just the handle. She tried it again, but it didn't turn at all. She tried it clockwise in case there was some trick to it, but no. It was definitely stuck.

'Fucknuggets,' she said, resting her forehead on the wood.

She waited to see if someone would notice she'd been a while and come and get her, but when no one did she knocked and shouted. 'I'm stuck in the bathroom!' It was horribly embarrassing. And then she remembered her phone. She could text Jools and tell her.

She rummaged through her bag, but her phone wasn't there. She remembered taking out out when she'd first arrived – to let Paul know she'd got there – and she must've left it on the chair.

She stared at the door. 'Shit. Shit shit shit.'

Her mouth filled with saliva and she swung around, staggering again, and only just made it to the loo before throwing up. Jesus, what was the matter with her? Or what was up with the gin? She wanted to lie down on Jools's bathroom floor and have a little nap. Instead she washed her hands, patted her face with water, and looked around for air freshener to cover the vomit smell. She couldn't see any. She opened the cupboard under the sink and found, to her relief, mouthwash, but still no air freshener. The cupboard was crammed with stuff though. It wasn't quite Emma's Tupperware and crap cupboard, but it was a relief to know that not every bit of Jools's home was as pristine as it seemed. She rummaged a bit, moving cleaning products and various other canisters out of the way, before eventually finding a bottle of Dolce & Gabbana perfume. She spritzed it lightly, hoping it would cover the smell of sick in the room and then sprayed a little on the back of her neck in case she smelled too.

She tried the handle again, but it was still stuck. It seemed completely outrageous to Emma that it wouldn't open. She tried hammering on it. But nothing.

She grabbed the handle with both hands, bracing her feet against the door, leaning back with her full weight. It didn't budge. And then her hand slipped and she staggered backwards across the bathroom, banging her head on the wall unit.

'Shitting FUCK.'

Near tears, she crossed the room again, and kicked the bottom of the door hard. The wood splintered at the same time someone opened the door from the outside.

Jools stared at her. 'What are you doing?'

'The door,' Emma said. 'Sorry. I couldn't get out. I did knock. And I shouted. My phone—'

'It's fine,' Jools said. But she was staring at Emma like she didn't recognise her.

'My bag,' Emma said, turning back to the sink. She saw herself in the mirror. Her hair was a mess, her face red, her lipstick smeared. She grabbed a tissue and wiped it off.

'Sorry,' she said again. 'I'll pay for the door.'

As she followed Jools through the kitchen she could hear the other women talking – Eve's voice cold and Maggie's sounding on the verge of tears – but as soon as she appeared in the doorway they fell silent, staring at her.

How had they not heard her shouting? Emma wondered. Surely they must have done. But if they had, they would have come and let her out. Wouldn't they?

Emma sat down and fumbled down the side of the sofa for her phone.

'Mummy?' One of Jools's daughters had appeared in the doorway, blinking into the light, her face scrunched from sleep.

'Did you have a nightmare?' Jools asked.

'No,' the little girl said. 'I just wanted to know . . . what's a fucknugget?'

'Where did you—' Jools started, frowning.

'Shit,' Emma said. 'I mean . . . oops.'

'Please leave,' Jools said, pink patches appearing high on her cheeks. 'Now.'

'Seriously?' Emma said.

'This really isn't working out,' Jools said, wincing as she bent down to pick up her daughter.

'Right,' Emma said. She couldn't bear to look at the other women. She stood up, the backs of her thighs making a ripping sound as she peeled them off the leather sofa. She turned back for her coat, before remembering she hadn't brought one, and then followed Jools down the hall to the front door.

'I'll see you at school, I guess—' Emma said, but the door slammed behind her.

Chapter Thirty-Two

It was dark when Emma woke up. It was dark and she was too hot and her tongue was stuck to the back of her teeth. She reached for her phone, but it wasn't on the bedside table where she usually left it. Shit. When did she last have it? She couldn't even think. She pushed herself half up to sitting, leaning back against the pillows, and looked over at Paul. He was on his back, face crumpled, snoring gently.

Emma's eyes felt dry and scratchy and her neck was stiff as hell. She carefully swung her legs out of the bed and pushed herself to standing. She staggered a little and her hand slapped against the wall as she steadied herself. Paul rolled over but didn't wake up. Emma had no clue what time it was. That was the problem with phones – everything was on there. She had no music, no camera, no alarm clock, nothing outside of her phone. Where the fuck was her phone?

In the bathroom, she stared at herself in the mirror. She looked pale and wan, her hair sticking flat to her head – her hair had been doing a weird floppy thing lately, she really needed to find a hairdresser – a few strands caught in some drool dried on her cheek. She splashed her face with cold water and then wiped her make-up off with a baby wipe.

Paul.

Paul might be having an affair.

Gin.

Gin and she'd kicked Jools's bathroom door open.

And sworn in front of her kid.

And then Jools had thrown her out.

She gagged and lurched over the loo, bracing herself against the wall, but she wasn't sick. Instead she coughed, spat, and then wiped her face again. Shit.

On the way downstairs, she checked on Sam – fast asleep, one arm thrown across his face, breath smelling like chocolate milk – and on Ruby, who murmured 'You home, Mummy?' with her eyes tightly closed, the cuddly monkey she'd had since she was a toddler gripped firmly under her arm.

Emma felt like shit. Physically and emotionally. She knew all about The Fear, had experienced it many times over the years, but not lately. And rarely with people she barely knew. What must the other women think of her? What must Jools think of her? And that little girl? She'd probably scared the crap out of her, kicking through that door.

Downstairs, she flicked the kettle on and greeted Buddy, who was beside himself at a surprise middle of the night visit. Emma's phone was on the dining table and so she was finally able to establish it was four a.m. The worst possible time to be awake, hungover, full of regret and feeling like shit.

Emma was still sitting at the table with her third – or fourth? – tea when Paul came down. He flicked the kettle on and came to sit at the table opposite her.

'So you were a bit of a mess last night.' He grinned.

Emma stared at him across the table. He couldn't be having an affair. It must be something else. He just wouldn't do that. He wouldn't.

'I don't even remember getting home,' she said.

'Fresh air,' Paul said. 'Well, that and the gin.'

'Fucking gin,' Emma said, massaging her temples with the tips of her fingers.

'So did you really get thrown out?' Paul asked, getting up to make the teas.

'Well,' Emma said. 'Not thrown out exactly. She just asked me to leave.'

'Cos you kicked a door in. And spilled something? And swore at a kid?'

'I told you all that?' Emma asked.

Paul opened the back door for Buddy and let in a blast of cold air. Emma shivered.

'Yep,' Paul said. 'You were very chatty. And then you went upstairs for a wee and didn't come back down. When I went up to check on you, you'd passed out.'

'Ugh god. I'm sorry.'

'S'all right,' Paul said. 'It was funny.'

'No, I mean about all of it. Like, she invited me to book club because—'

'Because of Matt? We signed the contracts yesterday. So he can't get out of it now.' He grinned at her.

'Well,' she said. 'That's something, I guess.'

'Are you OK to take the kids to school?' Paul asked.

'Yeah, I'm fine. I've had a lot of tea. I feel OK.'

'Thought you might want to avoid the other mums too.'

'Ugh,' Emma groaned. 'I hadn't even thought about that. God. But better to get that out of the way too.' She rested her head on her folded arms on the table. 'Why did I have to get so drunk? I don't even know how it happened!'

'You got drunk?' Ruby was standing in the kitchen doorway. She was still in her pyjamas, her monkey tucked under her arm, but she'd brushed her hair.

'Little bit,' Emma said. 'But I'm fine.'

'I can't find my uniform,' Ruby said, joining Emma and Paul at the table.

'I put yesterday's in the wash,' Paul said. 'It had glue on it.'

'From the crafting table,' Ruby confirmed. 'I made a bottle whale.'

'What's a bottle whale?' Emma asked.

'A whale made out of bottles,' Ruby said witheringly. She started to tell Emma how it was to do with recycling and conservation, but Emma was remembering that she'd put Ruby's other uniform in the wash too and she couldn't remember actually putting the washing on . . .

'Hang on a minute, sweetie,' she said. 'I just need to go and check something.'

By the time Emma had realised Ruby didn't have a clean uniform at all, Sam was up. Paul gave them both breakfast while Emma fished various bits of uniform out of the washing machine, spot cleaned and Febrezed them and threw them in the dryer.

'I need to get going,' Paul said, coming up behind her and sliding his arms around her waist, kissing the back of her neck.

'What's got into you?' she asked, half-turning. A little voice in the back of her mind said 'guilt?' but she pushed it away.

'Oh I don't know. Deal's done. Feeling much less stressed. And you were funny last night.'

'Oh god,' Emma said.

'Reminded me of when we first started going out.'

'When I was a drunken mess?'

'Yep,' he said, kissing her neck again. 'I'll pick up a bottle of gin on the way home from work, hey?'

'Definitely do not do that!' Emma said. But she was smiling.

*

Emma saw Eve before she saw Jools. She was intending to head straight over and apologise – had been practicing exactly what she was going to say all the way there – but Eve didn't give her a chance.

'You owe Jools an apology,' she said immediately, standing directly in front of Emma, blocking her path.

'I'm about to apologise to her,' Emma said. Eve was about a head taller than Emma in her heeled knee high boots. Plus she was standing way too close. Emma took a step back.

'You turn up here, thinking you're all that because your husband . . .' She waved her hand, shook her head. 'You don't know anything about anyone. We've had that book club for years and no one's ever behaved like that. Jools puts a lot of work into it and—'

'I apologised,' Emma said. 'Last night. I offered to pay for the door. I'm going to talk to Jools this morning, as soon as I see her. I don't know what it's got to do with you.'

'No,' Eve said. 'You wouldn't.'

'Mama?' Sam said.

'Can I take my kids to school?' Emma said.

Eve shrugged and stepped out of the way.

'Jesus,' Emma muttered under her breath as the three of them carried on up the path.

'Why do you have to apologise?' Ruby asked. 'What did you do?'

'I broke the bathroom door,' Emma said, tugging the children through the gate.

Beth was standing near the classroom door, looking over at Emma, her eyes wide. Surely she couldn't have heard about it already, Emma thought.

Ruby ran off to the playground to play with Flora.

'Did you fix it?' Sam asked Emma.

'What?'

'The door.'

'Oh. No. But I said I'd pay for it. It's OK, don't worry about it. Why don't you go and see if you can find Yahya?'

'OK,' Sam said, and ran after Flora. Emma couldn't actually see Hanan so Yahya probably wasn't there yet, but she assumed Sam would find someone else to play with.

'Was she having a go at you?' Beth asked, as soon as Sam had gone.

'Yep,' Emma said. 'Last night was an absolute disaster, I can't even tell you.'

'Don't tell me,' Beth said. 'Wait for Hanan.' She nodded and Emma turned to see Hanan coming up the path to school. Yahya ran off, presumably to find Sam, and Hanan joined Beth and Emma by the door.

'How did it go?' Hanan asked.

Emma hadn't even got halfway through the story by the time first whistle went. The kids came back to say bye. Emma kissed Ruby – trying to ignore the smell of Febreze wafting up from her sweatshirt – and leaned down to cuddle Sam.

'See you later, sweetest of peas,' she said into his hair.

Yahya already had his arm around Sam's shoulder and when the two of them walked in together, Sam didn't even look back.

Jools was getting out of her car as Emma, Beth, and Hanan walked down the hill.

Despite the dull day, she was wearing sunglasses and her hair was pulled back into a messy bun.

'I don't think I've ever seen Jools late before,' Beth whispered in the vicinity of Emma's ear.

'Do you think it's cos of me?' Emma said, her stomach flickering with guilt.

'Nah,' Beth said. 'They probably got pissed after you left and she overslept.'

'Jools,' Emma said, once they were close enough. 'I—'

'No,' Jools said without looking at her. She actually held up her hand as if she were a celebrity fending off the paparazzi. She kept walking – past Emma, Beth and Hanan – up the hill towards school.

'What the fuck?' Emma said, stunned.

'She's so stuck-up, I told you!' Beth said. 'You're well out of it.'

'I can't believe her,' Emma said, turning round to watch Jools walk up towards school. One of her daughters – the one who said 'fucknugget', Emma suspected – had turned round to look back, but Jools tugged on her arm to make her face forward as they headed through the gate.

'Fuck her,' Beth said, passionately, once they were all ensconced in Saucer. 'Fuck them all. You don't need them!'

'I know,' Emma said. 'I know it doesn't matter. But . . .' She shrugged. She knew she was too old to care this much about what people – people she didn't even particularly like! – thought about her. But . . .

'I don't like upsetting people. But I apologised! I don't get what her problem is. Hers or Eve's.'

'Eve's a bitch,' Beth said.

Emma smiled. She didn't think Eve was a bitch though. Not really. Or Jools. And she knew she'd behaved really badly, but you should be able to do that with your friends, shouldn't you? You should be able to get drunk and a bit messy and have a laugh and not be judged – and definitely not ostracised for it – shouldn't you?

Emma sat straight up in her chair. 'We should start our own.'

'What?' Beth said.

'Our own book club,' Emma said, picking up her coffee and taking a tentative sip. Too hot. But god she needed some caffeine. 'A no pressure, no judgement book club. With no discussion questions or presentations.'

'And no classics,' Hanan said. 'Fun books only.'

'We should do this!' Emma said. 'Shouldn't we? For real. Would you want to?'

'Course!' Beth said. 'But, like, I might not always get a chance to read the books. But I'll watch the film – if there's a film. And if not we can just get together and talk and have a drink.'

'Like we're doing now?' Hanan said, the corner of her mouth twitching with a smile.

'Yeah,' Beth said. 'But. Without the kids.' She glanced at the twins, asleep in their buggy. 'And with alcohol.'

'I don't drink,' Hanan said. 'But a night out without kids sounds good.'

'Yeah?' Emma said. 'Just us three?'

'It could be,' Beth said. 'To begin with. But if we keep it going, we could suggest more people. I wouldn't want it to be, like, exclusive. Like Jools's thing.'

'Yeah.' Emma said. 'I really want to do this. Are we really going to do this?'

'Why not?' Hanan said.

'Can I pick the first book?' Beth asked.

'Is it going to be the new Marian Keyes?' Emma said, sipping her coffee again.

Beth grinned. 'I love her books.'

'Perfect,' Emma said. 'OK, so what will we say? Like . . . one month from today?'

'A month?' Beth said. 'I can't wait that long. I haven't had a night out for ages. Can we have a first meeting without a book to read?'

Beth and Hanan picked up their phones to check their calendars. While they both tapped at their screens, Emma said, 'Do we need a name? Or should we just call it book club?'

'Oh we def need a name!' Beth said. 'The Not Bitches Book Club.'

Emma and Hanan both laughed.

'The You Don't Have to Read the Book Club,' Hanan suggested.

One of Beth's twins stretched in his seat, his eyes blinking open, mouth widening into a yowl.

'Oh bollocks,' Beth muttered under her breath, picking up a slice of toast and ripping it in half, before holding half out to her toddler, whose face was already bright red with fury and disappointment at being awake again and still in his buggy.

'I probably should go,' Beth said. 'He'll go back to sleep if I walk along the prom for a bit. He closes his eyes against the wind and then drops off.' She unhooked her coat from the back of her chair and started pulling it on. 'I'm such a bad mum.'

'You're not at all,' Emma said.

'That could work . . .' Hanan said, smiling up at Beth.

'What?' Emma asked.

'The Bad Mums' Book Club?'

Emma laughed and when she looked at Beth, half-worried she might be offended, Beth was grinning back at them, the other half of her toddler's toast in her mouth.

'I love it,' Emma said.

'Yours don't call you mum though, do they?' Beth said.

'Mama,' Emma clarified. 'That doesn't matter though. Still works.' Her coffee now cooled a little, she took a huge gulp.

'Or,' Hanan said. 'How about The Bad Mothers' Book Club?'

Emma grinned at her two friends. 'Perfect!'

Chapter Thirty-Three

'This is really nice,' Sofia said, looking around the bar. It was the definition of modern rustic – untreated wood everywhere, metal framed seats, industrial lights hanging from fruit crates attached to the ceiling.

'You haven't been here before?' Maggie asked her.

'I usually go out in Liverpool,' Sofia said. 'With friends.'

'Right.' Maggie wondered what Sofia's friends were like. Were they young? Was one of them more than a friend? What would they think of Maggie, if they ever met her? What were the chances that they ever would?

Maggie cleared her throat and took a breath. 'Why did you suggest going out for a drink that time? By Marine Lake?'

'I think you were lonely,' Sofia said, shrugging a little. 'It made me sad.'

Maggie nodded, her eyes prickling. 'Things haven't been good. At home. So . . . thank you.'

Sofia touched the back of Maggie's hand with her index finger, gently. 'You're welcome.'

As they drank their wine, they talked – about their childhoods, about Poland, about films and kids and the beach and Sofia asked about Maggie's pebble art – why she'd started making it, how she did it. Maggie admitted that she wanted to try making more, maybe even sell it in one of the local shops. It was the kind of thing that might go down well with both locals and day-trippers, but Maggie wasn't sure she had the confidence to even try.

'You should do it,' Sofia said. 'If it doesn't work, what have you got to lose?' She smiled. 'Just pebbles?'

Maggie laughed. 'You're right. I just feel like . . . I've been Amy's mum for so long and I can't remember what it's like to do things just for me.'

'Ok,' Sofia said. 'I have an idea.'

She took out her phone and started tapping. 'There's a craft fair in Sefton Park next month. You could go there.'

'Oh I don't have time to make enough for that,' Maggie said.

'You don't need to make many,' Sofia said. 'Just go and see. Research. You could take some for . . . I can't think of the word. To show people?'

'Samples?'

'Yes! I think so!' She beamed. 'And I can come with you, if you wanted. For support?'

'That sounds really good,' Maggie said. 'I hadn't even thought about craft fairs. Thank you.'

Sofia shrugged. 'I like your pictures.'

I like you, Maggie thought, but didn't say.

Maggie was on her third glass of wine when she started thinking about kissing Sofia.

She couldn't really – do it or want it – but she kept thinking about it. She watched Sofia's mouth as she talked – she'd had lipstick on at the start of the evening – a deep pink – but most of it had worn away now, just a fine line under her bottom lip and a little more in the V of her top lip remained.

Maggie wanted to reach over and wipe it away with her thumb. Maybe she could. She could claim she'd spaced out and done it on instinct, like she would with Amy. She pushed her left hand under her thigh and picked up her wine with the other hand.

She wanted to tell Sofia she'd been thinking about her, that she'd dreamt about her (Sofia in her kitchen saying 'I will think of another way to pay you' and then taking off her clothes, the sunlight through the back window turning her skin gold until she shone so brightly that Maggie couldn't even see her any more), that she'd been counting the days until this evening. But all of that would make it weird.

She didn't want to make it weird.

'Sorry I'm late.' Hanan hung her coat on the back of a chair next to Emma. 'Bet you thought I wasn't coming, didn't you?'

'Nah,' Emma said. 'I've not been here long anyway. Can I get you a drink?'

While Emma was at the bar, Beth arrived and by the time Emma got back to the table with the drinks, they were both in fits of laughter. Beth was flicking through a book, her eyes zipping across the pages.

'What book is it?' Emma asked.

'*Lace.*' Beth held it up to show Emma.

The cover was garish and looked like something from the eighties: glossy red lips and nails, ribbons, a gold chain, even some shocking pink leopardskin.

'I haven't read it,' Emma said. 'But I've heard about it. There's a bit with a—'

'Goldfish,' Hanan said. 'Yeah, Beth just showed me.'

'My mum had it when I was a kid,' Beth said. 'It was on her bedside table – it wasn't this cover, it had four women on it, I think? Like a portrait maybe? – anyway, I used to sneak away and read it. Mostly just the dirty bits. And then I forgot to put it back one day and Mum found it in my room and hit the roof.' She laughed. 'It disappeared after that. Still haven't read the whole thing.'

'I never saw my mum read a book,' Hanan said. 'My dad read all the time – huge thick non-fiction mostly – but my mum was always cooking or rushing around after all of us. She read magazines sometimes, but never a book.'

'Mine's always reading,' Emma said. 'When I was little, we'd go to the library and spend ages choosing books for me and then she used to just grab a few for herself from the returned trolley, you know? Didn't even read the back, she'd just take them home and read them, whatever they were.'

'Did you bring a book?' Beth asked Emma. 'Hanan didn't.'

'The one I'm reading's on my phone,' Hanan said. 'So I actually did.'

'I didn't,' Emma said. 'I thought this time we were going to decide on rules or whatever. And pick a book for next time.'

Hanan laughed. 'I would actually like to read something though. Maybe we don't need to have read something every time.'

'We can work our way up to it,' Beth said. 'What rules were you thinking of?' She poured herself and Emma some more wine.

'Not like you-know-who's,' Emma said. 'Just, like . . . Actually, I don't know. I was going to say to make sure we read the books? But I didn't manage that with Jools's, so . . .'

'What about no boring talk about our kids?' Beth said. 'Since I'm dead happy to be away from them. And what if we pick our favourite books to begin with? But it's OK if we don't like them. We have to promise not to get upset.'

'Are we always going to meet in the pub?' Hanan said. 'Because I was going to suggest meeting at each other's houses. Bit more relaxed. And cheaper.'

'God,' Beth said. 'If you're going to come to ours I'll have to get a cleaner. One of the ones that blitzes the whole place. Deep clean.'

'No,' Emma said. 'It's meant to be fun, not stressful. We won't judge.'

Beth laughed. 'Put that in the rules then: no judging Beth's messy house, particularly the big hole in the ceiling where the bath leaked, and the cat sick stain on the carpet.'

'Done,' Emma said.

'So are your husbands home with the kids?' Beth asked Emma and Hanan.

Hanan nodded. 'He was reading to Mo when I left. Him and Yahya are going to watch a film. Probably *Star Wars* again, cos I won't watch it with Yahya cos he's seen it so many times.'

'Is Paul working better hours now?' Hanan asked Emma.

Emma pulled a face. 'Not really, no. He got back on time tonight cos I told him I was going out, but he's still late a lot. It's part of his job though. He takes clients to dinner and shows and stuff. And he's doing more at the minute cos he's new and trying to establish himself, you know? Can't really say no yet.'

'Don't you worry he's shagging around?' Beth asked. 'That's what I always think when Gaz works late.' She didn't wait for Emma to reply. Emma was glad. She drank some wine to attempt to loosen the sudden tightness in her chest. 'I sometimes think I'd quite like Gaz to have a bit on the side,' Beth continued. 'When he's doing my head in. I think it'd be quite nice for him to just . . . go away. And, you know, get some. And then he could come home and we could cuddle without him wanting sex.'

Hanan laughed. 'Not really though?'

'I don't know,' Beth said. 'For a while it was like I was always saying no to him. I've got people crawling over me all day, you know? I haven't had a poo on my own for about four years.'

'Why do they go in the bathroom with you?' Hanan asked. She looked genuinely confused.

'They just do, Hanan,' Beth said, picking up her wine. 'I can't keep them out.'

'Doesn't your bathroom have a lock?' Hanan looked appalled.

Beth shook her head. 'Flora locked herself in there when she was a toddler, so we took it off.'

'Oh I wouldn't like that,' Hanan said.

Beth laughed. 'I don't like it either. Every time I try to have a bath, one of them gets in with me. And then quite often poos.'

'Oh god!' Hanan covered her face with both hands.

'Once,' Emma said. 'When Ruby was little, we went to a wedding in this, like, country house hotel. In Kent. There was a jacuzzi in the room. So as soon as we got there, we all stripped off and got in and after about five minutes, Ruby, you know, went. And we all had to get out.'

'Obviously,' Beth said, pouring herself more wine.

'And I said . . .' Emma started to laugh. '"Can't we even have a jacuzzi without someone shitting in it?"'

The other two women joined her laughter.

'We'd never even tried a jacuzzi before,' Emma said. 'Where would we? But I was outraged. Paul still says it sometimes. If I'm freaking out about something ridiculous.'

'It's hard, isn't it, when they're small,' Beth said. 'Particularly with your first. Everything feels so dramatic. I remember crying once cos Gaz picked up Flora's dummy with his fingers. I was sobbing, I'd told him so many times about sterilising stuff. I was dead paranoid. I told the health visitor and asked what would have happened if I hadn't seen him. And she said, oh, she'd probably just have a dicky tummy. A dicky tummy! I thought all this shit was going to kill her! No, a dicky tummy. Which she had all the bloody time anyway cos she was a baby!'

Hanan phoned home to check on Mohammed, so Emma took the opportunity to get another bottle of wine and Beth nipped to the loo.

'Guess who's round the corner by the fire,' Beth said when she got back.

'Not Jools?' Emma whispered.

She'd managed to avoid her at school – standing with Beth or Hanan at the opposite end of the playground, hanging back if she saw Jools and Eve walking to their cars. Once, she'd been about to go into the coffee shop opposite Morrisons, but she spotted Jools through the window and so detoured to Saucer instead. It made her feel ridiculous. But she really didn't want another confrontation. And she just didn't know how to talk to Jools after what had happened.

'Nope,' Beth said. 'Close though. Sofia. With Maggie.'

'Ooh,' Hanan said, leaning closer. 'You don't think she's trying to poach her?'

'She wouldn't dare,' Beth said. 'Jools would flip her shit. Maggie would be ostracised.'

'Well,' Emma said. 'I shouldn't tell you this . . .'

'Oh my god, you've got gossip!' Beth shrieked. 'I knew you did! I can't believe you haven't told us!'

'Go on,' Hanan said.

'Maggie's husband is having an affair with Eve.' Her stomach churned again just at the word 'affair' but she pushed it down with more wine. 'Maggie had a go at her at book club.'

'Holy shit,' Beth breathed.

'You can't tell anyone!'

'I wouldn't!' Beth said, affronted.

'I don't even talk to anyone else,' Hanan said.

'You don't, do you?' Beth said.

Her eyes were starting to look unfocused and Emma squinted at the wine to see how much was left. There was probably another glass each in it.

'I'm sorry I never talked to you before Emma came,' Beth told Hanan. 'It wasn't cos you're, like, Muslim or anything, honest. You just never looked like you wanted to talk to anyone!'

'That's OK,' Hanan said. 'It's because I tried talking to people when Yahya first started and it was just . . . weird. They'd talk to me like I didn't speak English or get me to repeat my name over and over.' She said 'Ha-na-n' in an exaggerated manner. 'I mean, it's not that hard, is it? So then I just stopped bothering.'

'People are dicks,' Emma said. Her mouth felt a bit weird. She probably shouldn't have the last glass of wine. She picked up the bottle.

'They really are,' Beth agreed.

'But I am very glad you talked to me that day,' Emma told Hanan.

'Oh well we both got called in to see the teacher!' Hanan said. 'So I had to.'

'And I'm very glad,' Emma started and then stopped. Her lips felt too big for her face. That was weird. 'I'm very glad you talked to me too. Beth.'

Beth laughed. 'We're all glad. I think we can all agree on that. And I think it's probably time to get you home.'

When Maggie and Sofia left the pub, the sun was just starting to set, the sky was already a deeper blue and Maggie could see the golden glow of the sun at the bottom of the hill.

'Are you walking back?' Maggie asked Sofia.

'I think so,' Sofia said. 'Maybe along the promenade. I like to see the sunset.'

'Me too.' Maggie had to get home, but she really didn't want the evening to end. They walked down the hill, Sofia talking about a weekend she'd had in Rome before she'd started working for Jools. Maggie pictured herself there with Sofia. Sitting in a square, drinking coffee and eating pastries. Or with wine and pizza. Holding hands under the table and trying to speak a little Italian. The kind of thing she'd never do with Jim. Her belly fluttered at the idea.

By the time they reached the prom the sky had darkened to almost purple, the sun shining gold across the ridged sand.

'Do you have to be home now?' Sofia asked.

'I've got a little time,' Maggie said, even though she really should have been getting back. 'Why?'

'I like to walk on the sand.' Sofia was already kicking her shoes off so Maggie sat on a rock to pull off her Converse. The sand was cold and Maggie stood for a second, letting her skin adjust.

Sofia took a few steps towards Hilbre Island and then turned in a slow circle, her arms spread out to the sides, her face turned up to the sky.

Maggie wanted to kiss her. She really wanted to kiss her.

Sofia turned to look at Maggie and said, 'I want to run! Do you want to run?'

'Always,' Maggie thought.

She glanced up from Sofia's lips to find Sofia looking back at her, eyes wide and bright and crinkling at the corners as she smiled.

'I think,' Sofia said, her voice low. 'You're thinking about kissing me.'

'Oh my god,' Maggie breathed. She felt like her breath was trapped behind her breastbone, like she was underwater and needed to struggle to the surface. 'I was,' she said. 'I am.'

'So?' Sofia tilted her head to one side.

Maggie frowned. 'Are you serious?'

'Of course. That would be a terrible joke.' She reached out and touched Maggie's arm, so quickly that Maggie wasn't certain she hadn't imagined it.

Maggie stared at her. The freckles on her cheekbone, the tiny turn up at the end of her nose, the V of her top lip.

'I want to,' Maggie said. 'But I don't think I can.'

Sofia smiled again. 'Why not?'

'I'm scared. And I'm married.'

Sofia nodded. 'But you're not happy. And I think sometimes you have to jump.'

Maggie pictured herself on a boat on holiday a few years ago looking down into the clear water where some other tourists were already swimming, having leapt with a shout from the top of the ladder, screaming as they hit the chilly water. Maggie had considered it and then lowered herself down the ladder.

'Not today,' Maggie said, her voice small.

Sophia nodded. 'OK. But one day.'

Maggie tipped her head back and looked up at the sky. There was a sliver of moon she hadn't noticed earlier. 'One day,' she agreed.

Chapter Thirty-Four

'Do you want me to come with you?' Eve asked, leaning into Jools's side.

The two women were sitting on the swing at the bottom of Jools's garden, looking back towards the house. Jools stared at the balcony off her and Matt's bedroom and thought about how it was what had sold the house to her. She'd already been most of the way there, but when she saw the balcony, that was it, she had to have it. She'd pictured herself drinking coffee there in the morning or wine in the evening, her legs stretched out, feet up on Matt's lap. (She'd also thought about sex out there, but that hadn't happened as often as she'd hoped – Matt was worried about being overlooked.)

'No. Thanks. Matt's coming.'

'I would hope so. But I thought you might want me too.'

Jools laughed, dipping her head onto her friend's shoulder. 'Are you worried he'll be too nice?'

'Yep. I want to be there in case there's some ass that needs kicking.'

'It'll be fine. It's all really straightforward. I'll be home the next day.'

'That's ridiculous,' Eve said. 'They chuck your tit in the bin and send you on your way?'

'Lovely way with words,' Jools said, laughing. 'But yeah, basically. I'll have a drain in a little bag and then I just go back to get the dressing changed.'

'Little bag? Do they have Marc Jacobs?'

Jools giggled. 'No. But I did think about trying to find something on eBay. It might get ruined though. With boob juice.'

'Right, you're knocking me sick now, princess,' Eve said. 'I don't mean to be unsympathetic, but let's never speak of your boob-drain again.'

'Noted.' Jools tipped her head back and closed her eyes, the autumn sun warming her face. 'Did I tell you what they're using for the reconstruction?'

'I don't think so?'

Jools opened her eyes so she could see her friend's face when she told her. 'Pigskin.'

Eve's eyes widened and she laughed out loud. 'Seriously? Will it smell like bacon when you sunbathe?'

'Oh my GOD,' Jools said. 'That's what I said!'

'Of course you did,' Eve said. 'It's the obvious question.'

'But the surgeon said no one's ever asked it before.'

'God, really?' Eve said. 'I guess that's why we're friends.'

Jools dropped her head down on Eve's shoulder. 'I guess so.'

Maggie opened an incognito window and typed 'how do you know if you're gay' then backspaced it all and closed her eyes, massaging her forehead with the tips of her fingers.

She would know if she was gay, of course she would, she was thirty-two years old.

She opened her eyes and typed 'straight woman crush on woman' and hit enter before she could change her mind. The first result was an agony aunt column entitled 'I'm a Straight Woman with a Crush on a Straight Woman' which wasn't entirely appropriate since Sofia was gay – she'd mentioned a girlfriend last night and Maggie had to try really hard not to show any sort of reaction – but Maggie scanned it anyway. She got to a bit about how straight people have crushes on people of the same sex all the time and it doesn't mean anything and she exhaled, her shoulders dropping. It was a girl crush. Girl crushes were perfectly normal. Frequently when she was out with friends and they'd had a few glasses of wine the conversation would turn to girl crushes and everyone had one. Holly Willoughby. Beyoncé. Davina McCall. Even Jools had admitted to one once, although Maggie couldn't remember who it was. She could remember that she'd added exactly what she'd like to do to whoever it was and Jools had given her an odd look, so she'd shut up. She kept reading. About how sexuality is fluid and just because lots of straight people got crushes, it doesn't mean you're not gay. Because you could be.

Maggie closed the page and opened settings to delete her history. She remembered reading a similar thing in a magazine years ago. About how if you fantasise about other women it doesn't mean you're gay. She'd been relieved then too. But that article hadn't said 'but it might' like this one did. She wasn't gay though. She couldn't be gay. She'd always liked men, had always been turned on by them. If she was ever a bit bored having sex with Jim, it was other men she'd think about. Tom Hiddleston. Or Matt LeBlanc on *Top Gear* (Jim had always watched it and Maggie had always hated it, but Matt LeBlanc had improved it dramatically). But as she tried to think of more examples, different examples slid into her head. The woman on the train that time when everyone had to stand and Maggie had bumped her with her bag and the woman had smiled and Maggie had felt . . . something. Every time she'd glanced over at her, she'd been looking back. Maggie had wondered if she had lipstick on her chin or if the woman recognised her from somewhere, but that night, with Jim, she'd constructed a fantasy in which the toilets on trains were roomier and significantly less disgusting.

Chapter Thirty-Six

The kids were in bed and Emma and Paul had been watching TV. Well, Paul had been watching and Emma had been going over and over things in her head. The lube, the sex, the dinner with Matt. She was exhausted with it.

'What?' Paul was looking at her in that odd way again, as if he wasn't quite sure who she was. He never used to look at her like that. She didn't like it.

Emma downed some of her wine, feeling it burn behind her sternum. She knew what footballers were like. And she knew what men were like for encouraging each other to do things they wouldn't otherwise do.

Emma swallowed. She stared at the edge of the coffee table. There was a chip in the wood she hadn't noticed before. Had that been there a while or had it happened during the move?

'Are you having an affair?' she made herself say. She wanted to take it back immediately. Both because she couldn't believe she'd asked the question and because she wasn't as sure of the answer as she would have liked to be, as she would have been in the past, before they'd moved.

'What?' Paul said. He sounded properly incredulous and Emma felt something loosen in her chest. Maybe it was going to be OK.

She forced herself to look at him. She was fairly confident she'd be able to tell if he was lying or not, but he looked genuinely shocked. And confused.

Her throat felt tight and for a second she was sure the wine she'd just drunk, along with the dinner she'd eaten (which had actually only been the bits of the dinner that Sam and Ruby hadn't eaten) was going to reappear. She pressed a hand to her stomach and swallowed.

'Are you having an affair?'

'Are you serious?' Paul said.

She scrunched her eyes closed and then opened them again. 'Yes. I'm sorry.' She shook her head. 'But yes.'

'Em,' Paul said, his voice soft. His face had changed now. He no longer had that confused, unreadable expression. He almost looked like he was going to cry. Paul didn't cry. Was this it? Was he about to tell her he'd fallen in love with someone else? He was sorry, he'd still see the kids, obviously, but—

'Of fucking course not,' he said. 'Why would you even think that?'

Emma blinked. The things that had seemed fairly conclusive in her head felt flimsy now. Lube? How they stopped having sex and then the sex had been . . . new? His long hours. The dinner that didn't happen.

'You told me you had dinner with him – with Matt Jackson – the night before book club. But he said you didn't.'

Paul's eyebrows pulled together and he closed his eyes briefly. 'Jack Jackson. He's another agent. I had dinner with him.'

Emma picked up her wine again. Her fingers were trembling. When she'd thought about this before – about asking Paul – she'd pictured herself strong, accusing. She'd pictured herself throwing him out of the house, sliding to the floor, weeping, and then picking herself up and kicking arse. But she didn't feel like that at all now. Now she felt like curling into Paul and asking him to never ever leave.

'I love you,' Paul said. 'I love you so much. And the kids—I would never—'

Emma put her wine back down without drinking any. 'I'm sorry. I don't know— I found that lube. And then we had that amazing sex. And you've been coming home so late—'

'I've got a new job, Em. And you knew it involved entertaining. And late nights. You knew. Didn't you? And the lube was in the mini bar in a hotel. I brought it home thinking it was shower gel.'

Emma shook her head. 'I just . . . once I started thinking about it, I just—'

Paul reached for her hand and slid his fingers between hers, brushing his thumb over her wedding ring.

'I love you. I don't want anyone else but you. And I would never do anything to hurt you.'

'I'm sorry,' Emma said. She was crying. She wasn't sure when she'd started.

Paul slid across the sofa and wrapped his arms around her. She pressed her wet face into his neck and inhaled. She'd always loved the way he smelled, but now there was something wrong. She felt his lips on her temple and his hand sliding into the back of her hair.

'Are you wearing aftershave?' she asked him. 'Or maybe it's shaving foam.'

'What is?'

'You smell weird.'

'Probably pheromones.'

Emma snorted. 'Yeah, that'll be it.'

'I'll try to get home from work earlier,' Paul said into her hair. 'At least a couple of times a week.'

Emma laughed, sniffling. 'That's OK. I know you have to work long hours sometimes.'

'And I'll be nicer. When I'm home. I know I've been snapping at you. I'm just tired.'

'Me too,' Emma said.

Paul kissed the top of her head. 'I forget sometimes – because I'm at work – I forget that you're dealing with shit at home too. You know? Like I hate leaving in the morning because the kids are being cute and you've made breakfast and it all seems really cosy and I have to go and sit in traffic and get through the tunnel and I forget that you have to get them off to school and walk the dog and do all the house . . . stuff.'

'I don't do that much house stuff,' Emma said. 'I could do more house stuff.'

She slid her fingers across Paul's stomach, towards his navel. He sucked in a breath and she kept her hand moving up under his shirt.

'I'll try harder,' Paul said.

'I think you're pretty hard already,' Emma said, sliding her lips along the side of his neck.

He laughed. 'Upstairs?'

'Yeah,' Emma said, swinging her legs off the sofa. 'You can show me what to do with that lube.'

Chapter Thirty-Six

Maggie had loved the idea of the Book Club when Jools had first suggested it. She thought it would be fun. She couldn't have been more wrong. From everything she'd heard, book clubs were an excuse for a night in with friends, drinking wine and gossiping – the book was an afterthought. Jools's Book Club turned out not to be like that. At all. Jools's book club was like school.

The first time Maggie had to choose a book, she'd almost been sick with nerves. She'd worried about what the others would think of her book, she'd worried about having to introduce it to them and tell them why she'd picked it. She'd worried about everything. She'd come so close to pretending to be ill – actually she was going to make herself sick so that it didn't feel like a lie – but then Jim had come home in a mood and she'd wanted to get out of the house anyway, so she'd gone. And it had been fine. Not fun – far from fun – but fine.

So she'd kept going. Because it was a night out of the house. A night just for her. Even if she hated it.

When Emma came, Maggie knew she'd thought the same thing as she had – she'd been expecting everyone to have a couple of drinks and loosen up. But Emma had been the only one to loosen up, and too much. And she'd been much looser than the rest of them to begin with.

Maggie had spent most of the meeting daydreaming about being brave enough to say 'Why don't we just get out of here?' and the two of them would leave and walk to The Viking and get burgers. Maybe sit out in the beer garden under the fairy lights and talk about books that they actually loved, not that they only read because Jools made them. She thought Emma was a laugh and Maggie didn't seem to laugh much lately.

Instead she'd stayed put on the sofa and watched Emma get more and more flustered by Jools. Because Jools didn't get flustered. Jools was always in control. She'd been together when Maggie had first met her – that was one of the things Maggie liked about her: Jools always knew what to do. And Maggie had been completely bewildered by early motherhood, never knowing if she was doing the right thing – in fact, often convinced she was doing entirely the wrong thing. Terrified that every mistake she made, every wrong decision, would harm Amy irreparably. Jools had been the one to tell her that if breastfeeding was such a living nightmare, she could just stop. Maggie had thought about it – in the middle of the night when her boobs were so painful she had to press her face into her pillow so she didn't scream, when Amy sucked a blister into her nipple and then preferred that breast to feed and every tiny suck felt like a hot needle drilling right through the centre of her body. But that had been eight years ago. And she and Jools hadn't been friends for a while now, she didn't owe her anything.

She set off to drive to the next book club meeting and instead found herself driving to The Viking. She'd never gone to a pub on her own before, but she didn't want to go to Jools's house and she didn't want to go home. Maybe Nick could come and join her.

But when she walked into the pub, the first person she saw was Emma. With Beth and the Asian woman whose name, Maggie was embarrassed to realise, she didn't know.

'Hey,' Emma said and waved half-heartedly.

Maggie wasn't surprised. She'd hardly been friendly towards her. She couldn't even think why now. It was almost as if Jools had cast a spell over the other women and they only ever did what she did and said what she said. Emma came to book club because Matt was signing for Liverpool and her husband was involved in the deal. Even though over the years, they'd all suggested inviting other people and Jools had refused to consider it.

Maggie made herself walk across the room with 'What Would Nick Do?' beating a rhythm in her head. Nick wouldn't be intimidated. Nick made friends everywhere he went. Nick would not have put up with Jools's shit – or Jim's for that matter – even for months, never mind years.

'Is it OK if I join you?' Maggie asked as she stood at the end of the table.

'Of course,' Emma said.

Maggie went to the bar and bought a bottle of wine.

'Do you ever just feel like you're failing at everything?' Emma asked the other women, once they'd all (apart from Hanan) had some wine.

'God yeah,' Beth said. 'I don't think I ever actually feel like I'm succeeding at everything. Or anything.'

'Really?' Emma asked. 'I snapped at Ruby. And then when I apologised for hurting her feelings she said, "My feelings get hurt very easily" in a tiny voice.' Emma welled up remembering it.

Beth snorted. 'She's got you wrapped around her little finger.'

Emma smiled. 'Maybe. But still.'

Hanan nodded. 'I try not to be hard on myself. When Yahya was a baby I lost it completely. I thought everything had to be perfect all the time. I'd read so many books when I was pregnant and I told myself I could do it all as long as I was organised and had a system.'

'Oh god,' Beth said.

'Yeah. That didn't last. But I made myself ill trying to do it. I could barely sleep. I didn't let Hashim do anything. I wouldn't even let him cook for me because I'd put myself on this special diet. It was ridiculous.'

'And what happened?' Emma asked.

'He came home from work one day and the baby was crying and I was crying and neither of us could stop. He called my sister and she fed Yahya, made me some soup, put us both to bed, and I slept for something like sixteen hours.'

Beth leaned forward. 'I don't think I've slept for more than four hours at once for eight years.'

'I just feel like . . . once one thing goes wrong – or not even goes wrong, once I even forget about something – everything falls apart. It's like I've got all my plates spinning – up on the poles, perfectly balanced – but then when one falls, they all fall. And I haven't got the energy to get them back up again.'

'Bloody hell,' Beth said. 'Exactly that.'

'I've got so many smashed plates I've made a mosaic,' Hanan said.

Maggie smiled. 'We should all start buying paper plates. Go to Costco and get them in bulk.'

'God. I'm so glad you all feel the same.' She drank some wine. 'Remember before you had kids? I remember lying down to go to sleep and then it would be like . . .' She blinked. 'And it was morning! Like magic. And now I toss and turn and I can't get comfy. I hear a noise or one of the kids comes in. I wake up at four and start thinking about death . . .'

The other women all laughed.

'Someone told me once that more deaths – natural deaths – happen at three a.m. than any other time,' Hanan said.

'I can believe that,' Emma said. 'I got out of bed once – I thought I heard something in the street, this was when we were still in London – and I opened the curtains and everything just seemed overwhelming and terrifying.'

'It looks so creepy, doesn't it?' Beth said. 'I've thought that. And do you know what? I didn't even notice you can't see colour at night until Flora said! They learned it at school!'

'Right! So I looked out and it was kind of film noir-ish with puddles of light from the streetlamps, the sound of car tyres on the road. And I just thought *fucking hell, I can't do this!*'

'But we have to,' Hanan said. 'That's the thing that weirds me out.'

'There's no escape!' Beth said in a dramatic voice.

'That's it though!' Emma said. 'Like, I worry about the kids all the time. And that's never going to go away. Never! I could live to be ninety and still be worrying about them. That's if they're still even alive. Shit.' She wiped her eyes with the back of her hand as Hanan leaned over and squeezed her knee. 'And I did this to myself, that's the mad thing! I don't regret having them, honestly I don't. But I did a thing that means I'm going to worry every single day for the rest of my life.'

'Twice,' Hanan agreed.

'Three fucking times,' Beth said and they all laughed.

'What you need to do,' Beth said. 'Is set them up with a game. One they can play on their own, like Pop-up Pirate or something. And then lock the bathroom door and . . . bingo.'

Emma, Maggie and Beth were most of the way down another bottle of wine. Hanan had left a little earlier, kissing each of them on the cheek and telling them to make sure they got taxis at closing time. Emma had no idea how they'd got onto the topic of masturbation, but she was glad they had.

'Oh my god,' Emma said, wiping her eyes. 'That is brilliant. That's what I'm going to call it from now on. "You OK, love? Just nipping off for a Pop-up".'

'You talk to your husbands about it?' Maggie asked.

'Sometimes,' Emma said. 'Not as much as we used to before kids, but he's into it.'

'I do!' Beth said. 'He loves it. Gets him all worked up. I text him sometimes when he's at work and I've nipped off for a sneaky one. Comes home and puts the kids to bed at like half five.'

They all laughed.

'God,' Emma said. 'We used to be a bit like that. But not any more.'

'Do you miss it?' Beth asked.

Emma frowned, trying to think. 'Yeah. I do. I miss the closeness of it more than the actual . . . you know. I haven't got the energy for much of that these days. It just feels like one more thing I've got to do, you know?'

'It's important though,' Beth said. 'I think. Like I don't want to be his friend or his sister. I'm his wife. And that means we need to have sex.'

'You know what I realised?' Maggie said. 'We never did it cos I wanted to. I didn't even think about it. We did it cos he wanted to and cos I felt bad if we hadn't for a while.'

'Oh we can be like that too sometimes,' Emma said. 'But then I enjoy it when we do.' She wasn't sure if Maggie wanted the others to know about Jim and Eve. Even though she was dying to ask herself.

'You said you don't want to with Jim,' Beth asked Maggie. 'Who do you want to do it with? Who's your dream shag?'

Maggie laughed, dipping her head. She ran her hands back through her hair and pressed her fingers into the back of her neck. Her head already felt heavy. She shouldn't have had more wine.

'There's a woman,' she said from under her hair.

'Oh wow,' Emma said. 'Really?'

'It's not Jools, is it?' Beth asked, laughing.

Maggie straightened up. 'God. No. I shouldn't have said.'

'No, this is good,' Beth said. 'You should sort yourself out. It's someone you know, yeah? It's not like . . . Beyoncé?'

Maggie grinned. 'No. It's not Beyoncé. It's . . . I'll show you.'

She reached for her phone and tapped open Sofia's Instagram. She'd spent so much time looking at it lately, she knew the order of the photographs. A selfie on the beach with her hair blowing over her face. Birds flying over Marine Lake. Her hand holding a takeaway coffee, her nails blue, her name spelled wrong.

'Look at your face!' Beth said, reaching over and taking the phone. 'Oh my god. I know her!' She turned the phone to show Emma.

'Sofia,' Emma said. 'She seems lovely.'

Maggie nodded as she drank some more wine. 'I don't know what I'm doing. I like her and I'm pretty sure she likes me, but I don't know how to go from, like, hanging out to . . . stuff.'

'You should message her,' Beth said.

Maggie snorted. 'And say what?'

'What would you want to say?' Emma asked.

'Just . . . that I like her. And I'd like to know her better. Maybe. I don't know.' Maggie felt suddenly exhausted. They'd talked about a kiss, but Maggie wasn't sure she'd ever be able to make it happen.

'You could just say you're thinking about her,' Beth said.

Maggie sighed. 'No. I don't know. I don't know if you know that my husband's having an affair? I just—'

'There,' Beth said and handed Maggie her phone.

Maggie blinked at it. 'What?'

'You didn't!' Maggie heard Emma say, but her voice sounded like it was coming from very far away.

Maggie looked at her phone, but her eyes weren't focusing properly. It definitely looked like Beth had sent the message. And then underneath it, three dots appeared.

'She's typing,' Maggie said.

'Told you!' Beth said. 'You have to put yourself out there! What's the worst that could happen?'

Maggie could think of so many worsts she couldn't even articulate them. Instead she typed. 'Sorry. Drunk.' And closed her eyes. When she opened them, there was a reply from Sofia: 'Talk tomorrow? Drink lots of water.' And a smiley face.

'You're in there,' Beth said.

'I'm absolutely hopeless,' Maggie said. They'd got more wine. And a few bags of crisps. Emma felt a bit dizzy. She was scared to go to the loo in case she fell over. She really needed to stop drinking.

'Every single month it's a surprise,' Maggie was saying. 'I wonder why I'm tearful or bloated or . . . I get sort of restless, like I want to run away?'

'I always feel like that,' Beth said.

Maggie laughed. 'Seriously though. Like I want to chuck everything and start my life over. I wish I could pick my house up and shake everything out and sort through it all. I always feel like I've got so much stuff. And then I'm fine for three weeks and then it's the same again.'

'I use a apper track,' Emma said, before laughing and correcting herself, 'a *tracker app*, and it's still a surprise. And I always forget to buy tampons. Like I need them every month, have done for almost twenty years, why not buy in bulk? But no. I buy one pack and then I come on and there's one tampon in the box.'

As Beth started telling them how she'd been using a Mooncup for a while, Emma became aware of something nagging at her. She reached for her phone, but there were no messages from home. She texted anyway 'All OK?' and took another sip of her drink.

'Do any of you get any ovulation pain?' Maggie was asking.

'God, yeah,' Beth said. 'Sometimes it doubles me over. My mum used to get it too. There's a word for it.'

'Mittelschmertz,' Maggie said. 'I get PMS before it too. I've got PMS more than I haven't.'

'I only realised I got that when I was shouting at the kids one day,' Emma said. 'I think I mustn't have had it when I was on the pill, so I never thought about it. But I remember I was yelling at Ruby and she had this expression on her face like . . .' Emma shook her head. 'Like she was scared of me. And I thought *I can't do this. I can't cope with this* and I realised I'd thought that before, but maybe it was a month before? That's when I started keeping track.'

'Gaz has mine in his diary,' Beth said. 'Which fucks me off cos it's so, like "are you on the rag, love?" but also . . . I'm different when I am. I don't think I'm unreasonable though,' Beth continued, 'I think maybe I let things go usually but at that time I don't.'

'I once read that the way you feel before your period is your real self,' Maggie said. 'The rest of the time you're who you allow yourself to be.'

They all stared at each other as they took it in.

'Wow,' Beth said. 'The real me is a total bitch.'

They laughed.

'I do think there's something in it though,' Maggie said. 'I spend a lot of time telling myself I should feel the way I feel. That's why I hit that guy in the car, you know? It wasn't about him. It was so much other stuff coming to the surface right at that moment. Stuff with Jim. And Jools. And even my mother.'

'Right at the moment you felt your child was threatened,' Beth said. 'Primal.'

Emma tried to picture herself in the bathroom of the new house with tampons and she couldn't. Did she even have any? Where would they be? She thought there were maybe some in her washbag, but she couldn't think of using them in the new house. But she must've done.

'You OK?' Beth asked her.

'Yeah, thanks. I think. I'm just . . . I can't remember when I last had a period.'

'You said you use a tracker app?' Maggie said.

'Yeah, but I'm not great at updating it.' Emma picked her phone up again and opened the app. She hadn't updated it for three months, since before they'd left London.

'Are you usually regular?' Beth asked.

Emma ran a hand through her hair. 'Yeah. I think so. Yeah.'

'Do you think you could be . . .'

Emma shook her head. 'I've got a coil.'

'I'm not being funny,' Beth said. 'But my mate's a midwife and she once delivered a baby holding the coil in its hand.'

'That's not true!' Emma said. 'Is it?'

Beth shrugged. 'None of them are one hundred per cent, are they? Not even the snip.'

'Fuck,' Emma muttered. She picked up her wine, but then put it down again. What if she actually was pregnant. She'd been drinking all this time. The baby could have horns.

'You could go to Morrisons now,' Maggie said. 'It's open 'til ten.'

It was nine. How was it still only nine? She felt like they'd been drinking and talking for hours.

'It's OK,' Emma said. 'I'll go in the morning. After school. I probably have had one and just don't remember. I don't feel pregnant.'

'Did you fee pregnant last time?' Maggie asked.

Emma sighed. 'No.'

Chapter Thirty-Seven

Maggie leaned closer. She was going to kiss her. Sofia. She couldn't believe she was, but she was. But she couldn't do it yet. She couldn't move from wanting to kiss her to actually kissing her. The anticipation was incredible. She was still leaning in, looking at her lips, and then Sofia moved just a little but enough to press her mouth to Maggie's. Maggie felt like her veins were fizzing with champagne. She lifted her hand and ran her index finger along Sofia's cheekbone, and pulled back a little, gasping.

'Yeah?' Sofia said, breathlessly.

Beth's message had worked. Sofia had called Maggie first thing and asked if she could come round as soon as Jools's girls were in bed that evening. Jim was working – or with Eve, Maggie didn't know or care – and Amy was staying overnight with Nick, so the timing was perfect.

'Please.' She kissed her, letting her tongue run along Sofia's bottom lip. Sofia tangled one hand in the side of Maggie's top and Maggie shifted forward on the sofa. She slid her hand around the back of Sofia's neck. Her skin was so soft, her hair, Maggie wanted to tangle her hands in it.

'I shouldn't be doing this,' she said against Sofia's lips.

Sofia smiled and Maggie cupped her cheek, pressing her thumb into the dimple at the corner of her mouth.

'I'm married,' Maggie said.

'I don't need anything from you,' Sofia said now. 'Not yet. I want you to be happy. I want to make you happy. I don't want to put any pressure . . .'

Her hands fluttered and Maggie stared at her fingers. She wanted to kiss them. Turn Sofia's hands over and press her lips to her palm.

Emma had no idea what time it was when she woke up still in Sam's bed. One arm had been bent under her head and her shoulder was stiff and aching. Her mouth felt like carpet. She lowered herself to the floor and used the bedframe to push herself up to standing.

She forced herself to go downstairs and open the back door for Buddy, who had peed – just a little – on the doormat.

'I'm sorry,' Emma told him. 'I'm just very, very tired.'

The dishes from dinner were still on the table. In fact the dishes from lunch were still in the sink – she'd meant to put them in the dishwasher, but it had just seemed overwhelming. She wasn't sure if either of the kids had clean uniforms for the next day. Or where their reading books were. Or if they'd done their reading.

She found her handbag where she'd dropped it in the hall and pulled out the pregnancy test she'd bought that morning, intending to do it straight away. Instead she'd ignored it all day while it sang to her from her bag like Poe's Tell-Tale Heart. Except the Tell-Tale Heart didn't sing a medley of 'Baby Love,' 'Ooo Baby Baby,' and 'Baby' by Justin Bieber.

She sat on the loo, peed on the stick, waited two minutes, and then found out she was pregnant.

*

'Babe,' Paul said, his mouth against her ear. 'Em.'

Emma groaned and tried to raise her head, but found she couldn't, it felt like lead.

'Why are you asleep on the table?'

Emma shuffled her arms underneath her head and slid the pregnancy test across the table.

'Holy shit,' Paul said. 'Seriously?'

'S'why you smell weird,' Emma said. 'And I kept thinking the crisps were off. And got sick at book club. But that might've been the wine. I've drunk so much wine. This baby's going to come out hammered.'

Emma felt Paul's lips against her temple. 'Nah. It'll be fine. We'll be fine.'

'I need to puke,' Emma said, pushing back from the table.

And Paul helped her into the bathroom and held her hair back.

Chapter Thirty-Eight

'I want to know everything about you,' Maggie said, running her index finger along Sofia's arm. They were in bed in Maggie's house. But not Maggie's bed. She'd thought about it, but had instead steered Sofia into the spare room, the one Nick had slept in when he'd stayed. Maggie felt reckless having Sofia in the house, but to sleep with her in the bed she shared with Jim felt wrong.

Sofia laughed. 'That's a lot.'

Maggie dipped her head and kissed Sofia's shoulder. 'I know. Start at the beginning.'

Sofia turned her head and pressed her lips against Maggie's. 'We can talk anytime. I can email you the story of my life. I think we have other things to do now.'

'God,' Maggie said, hiding her smile against Sofia's neck. 'You're right.' She traced her lips along the other woman's collarbone. 'This is my favourite bit, I think.'

Sofia rolled onto her side and pressed her palm into the soft flesh above Maggie's hip. 'This is my favourite bit.'

Maggie shook her head. 'I hate that bit. Love handles.'

Sofia burrowed under the covers and kissed down Maggie's side, rubbing her face against her hip like a cat.

'No. It's the best bit. So soft. I love it.'

Sighing, Maggie rolled onto her back and Sofia moved back up the bed, settling her body between Maggie's thighs, smiling down at her.

'You're beautiful,' Sofia said. 'Don't argue.' And then she kissed her.

Emma was about to turn into the Majestic Wine car park to buy wine for Beth and Maggie for the next book club meeting when she did a double-take. Jools was on the opposite side of the road, leaning against the wall. She thought it was Jools anyway – she was wearing the black and white striped jump-suit she'd seen Jools wear, but she had a headscarf on and it couldn't be Jools surely.

Emma parked the car and immediately crossed the road. By halfway she realised it was Jools. In a headscarf. And no make-up. She looked awful.

'Jools?' Emma said and then gasped as the other woman looked up at her.

Jools's face was grey and Emma could see the pain in her eyes.

'Are you OK?' Of course she wasn't OK, god. 'What happened?'

'I'm just waiting for a taxi,' Jools said. 'Don't worry. It should be here in a min—' She winced and took a ragged breath.

'I think you need to go to the hospital,' Emma said.

'That's what the taxi's for,' Jools said sharply. And then, 'Sorry.'

'I'll take you,' Emma said. 'My car's just there. Come on.' She reached for Jools's arm and watched as Jools took another careful breath and pushed herself up from where she'd been leaning against the wall.

They were halfway down Black Horse Hill before Jools spoke.

'Matt's in a meeting. His phone's off. I tried calling everyone, but I couldn't get hold of anyone. I don't understand where—'

She shook her head. 'I was going to drive, but when I got in the car I couldn't put my seatbelt on.'

'There's no way you could drive yourself,' Emma said.

'Oh god!' Jools said, reaching down between her feet. 'I need to cancel the taxi, they'll—'

'Don't worry about it,' Emma said. 'Honestly they'll just turn up and when you're not there they'll go again.'

'No, it's on an account and I don't want them to . . .' She stopped and slumped back against the seat, letting her bag drop back down between her feet. 'Fuck it. It doesn't matter.'

Emma glanced over. 'It's fine. Honestly. Happens all the time.'

'I didn't just mean the taxi,' Jools said. 'All of it. Fuck it all.' She took a deep breath. 'I've got breast cancer.'

'Oh fuck,' Emma breathed, her hands tightening on the steering wheel. 'I'm sorry.'

'No one knows,' Jools said. 'Hardly anyone. I didn't want anyone to know. I was diagnosed this time last year. I've had chemo and a lumpectomy and now I think I've got an infection. They did warn me this might happen. They didn't warn me it would make me feel like this.'

'I'm sorry,' Emma said again. 'So are you— Did they—'

'They think it's all gone, yeah,' Jools said. 'So I thought that was it, you know? It was all over and I could go back to normal and no one would ever need to know.' She laughed. 'While I was waiting for that taxi all I could think was that I hoped no one would recognise me. How fucked up is that?'

Emma messed about on her phone until the charge was critically low and she needed to preserve it in case there was a call from the school. She put it in her bag – so she wasn't tempted – and picked up one of the slightly crispy magazines from the coffee table.

She was aware of the rhythms of the hospital moving around her as she read about celebrities she didn't even recognise and knew nothing about. She'd just finished a two page spread about a couple who had apparently met on Love Island – which Emma had never watched – when someone tapped her shoulder and she looked up.

'Hey,' Emma said. 'Are you OK?'

Jools nodded, but her eyes filled with tears. 'I just want to go home. Is that OK?'

'Of course,' Emma said, standing and dropping the magazine on the table. 'Do you need anything. Bottle of water? Coffee? Gin?'

Jools laughed weakly. 'No. Thanks. I'm OK. I've been drinking water. I feel a bit shaky.'

Emma hooked her arm through Jools's and said, 'Is this OK?'

Jools nodded. As was so often the case with hospitals, there was a long and winding walk to the car park and Emma didn't know whether she should try chatting or just be quiet. She compromised with occasional comments on things like the coffee shop in the foyer or the creepy hologram woman telling everyone to make sure to wash their hands. Her voice sounded bright and artificial, like she was talking to a toddler, and she wanted to kick herself.

'Sorry,' she said when they finally made it out through the main doors and into the surprisingly warm afternoon air. 'I'm rubbish at this. I don't know what to say.'

'I'm not dying,' Jools said, her voice stronger than Emma would have expected. 'It was just an infection.'

Emma guided Jools over to the parking machines.

'Are you OK to . . .?' Emma gestured at a bench next to the ticket machine.

'I can stand,' Jools said.

While Emma paid for the parking, Jools said, 'I found the lump this time last year. It took a bit of time to get a diagnosis.'

Emma took Jools's arm again.

'And then I had a lumpectomy. And that's what got infected.'

Emma couldn't remember where she'd parked the car. She'd been so desperate to get Jools into the hospital. She stopped at the end of one of the crossing places and looked around.

'It's on Row C,' Jools said.

'Fuck me,' Emma said. 'How did you know that?'

They walked towards the car.

'That's what I do,' Jools said. 'I have to know everything, control everything. Everything has to be perfect.' She blew out a breath. 'Fucking not though, is it.'

Emma almost laughed. 'No. I don't think anything ever is. Nothing works out how you expect. And sometimes when everything seems to be going along perfectly, some fucker like cancer comes along and shits all over everything.'

Jools did laugh then. 'I'm sorry I was a cow to you.'

Emma shook her head. 'You weren't. I—'

'Oh come on. Of course I was. I just . . . it's hard for me to make friends. Cos of Matt. Since he started playing I've been a bit weird about it. And it's worse with the girls – I've had women use their children to befriend the girls to get to Matt. It's awful.'

'Jesus.'

They were at the car now. Emma opened the passenger door for Jools and walked round to the driver's side.

'And then since this happened, I've got so much worse. I was so determined not to fall apart, you know? Even when the doctor first told us – as she was talking – I was making plans in my head. First I'll do this and then this will happen and as long as I can this then it'll all be OK. You know?'

'I think that's normal though,' Emma said, putting the key in the ignition. 'Trying to control the uncontrollable.'

'I thought I was doing so well,' Jools said. 'I was being really strong, not falling apart. Organising everything. I thought if I didn't tell anyone, no one would ever need to know. I got that stupid wig and I had my eyebrows done and I pay a fucking fortune for false eyelashes every couple of weeks and what's it all for? It's put so much more pressure on Matt cos he feels like he has to be strong for me.'

Emma eased out of the parking space and looked over at Jools. 'I think you're being really hard on yourself.'

'I had a go at him for crying. He was crying and scared and I told him it was making me feel worse and if he wanted to cry, he should go and do it somewhere else. And at the same time I was thinking, *Why's he even crying? I'm fine. I'm going to be fine.*'

'But you are, aren't you?' Emma said. 'I mean . . .'

'Yeah. Apparently. I mean, I haven't had the all-clear yet, but it's looking pretty positive. And the type that I had is unlikely to recur. So they tell me.'

'Jools,' Emma said. 'That's amazing.'

'I know. I'm lucky.'

And then she started to cry.

'Oh fuck!' Maggie heard Sofia say. She sounded panicked and Maggie's first thought was that Jim was home. Her stomach flipped over with fear. She knew he wouldn't even consider that she and Sofia were sleeping together unless he actually found them in bed, so as long as they could both get dressed before he—

'We fell asleep,' Sofia said, she was gathering her clothes from around the room, stumbling against the wall as she tried to clamber into her underwear. 'It's 3.45.'

'No,' Maggie said. The children finished school at 3.30. 'Oh my god.'

'I'm going to be fired,' Sofia said, pulling her dress over her head. 'Jools will kill me.'

'No, you phone the school and say you're held up somewhere so they know you're coming.'

'But if we both say that—'

'I won't. I'll wait 'til after you've gone and say I fell asleep. Or something. It doesn't matter. Amy'll be fine, she'll be playing. I don't want you to lose your job.'

Sofia stepped into her shoes and headed for the door. 'Thank you. I'll call now. I'll text you later.'

Maggie nodded, sitting back down on the bed.

Sofia reached the door and then turned back, quickly crossing the room to kiss Maggie on the mouth. 'Thank you.'

Maggie waited until she heard the front door close and picked up her phone. She had two missed calls from Jools. Why had Jools been calling her? She hadn't left a message. And the school hadn't texted yet, but she'd been late collecting Amy before and she knew they would. She thought about getting dressed and rushing to the school and seeing Sofia there. She couldn't do it. Instead, she texted Nick.

Emma drove them to the nearest Starbucks and Jools waited in the car while Emma got them both coffees. While she was waiting, she called Paul who offered to go and collect the children.

'I'm sorry,' Jools said, stirring sugar into her coffee, as the two of them sat in the car. 'You must think I'm an absolute wreck.'

Emma shook her head. 'Not at all. Or no more than the rest of us. I got hammered and puked at your house and you threw me out.'

'God,' Jools said. 'I really am sorry. I just . . . I don't do well with things being out of control and between you and Maggie—'

'I know,' Emma said. 'It's fine. I was rude anyway. I didn't read the books. And I drank too much. I was nervous. And I . . .' She didn't know if she could trust Jools, but surely after today she could give her the benefit of the doubt. 'I started thinking Paul might be having an affair and I wigged out.' She bit her lip. 'Fuck. Sorry.'

Jools smiled. 'It's OK. Today's the first time I've left the house without hair.'

'You still look beautiful,' Emma said.

'I can't imagine that can possibly be true. But thank you.'

'So when I got to book club, I wasn't in a great place.'

'I mean, I made it the least fun it could be, didn't I?' Jools snorted, which made Emma laugh. 'It's because I failed my exams. Matt says I'm overcompensating with the book club only reading classics, because up until a year ago I only read romance and then the *Metro* did a feature that was basically thick people made good. I was in there – along with my exam results – but I'd made good by marrying Matt, you know? I didn't do anything but fall in love.'

'That's such bullshit though,' Emma said. 'It's no one's business what you read. Read what you enjoy. Did you enjoy *Jude the Obscure*?' Her mouth twitched.

'God, no,' Jools said. 'It was so depressing.'

A tiny part of Emma wanted to suggest Jools come along to Bad Mothers' Book Club, but she knew that was a little hasty. And that Beth would kill her. But forcing yourself to read improving books – at the same time as possibly dying of cancer – seemed dreadful.

'Apparently our daughters have hatched a plan,' Jools told Emma.

'Yeah? For what?'

'For us to take them to Hilbre,' Jools said. 'They want to go together, apparently. With Amy too. And Flora. They got fed up of waiting for me to do it.'

'Ruby asked me too,' Emma admitted. 'More than once.'

'I think it could be nice,' Jools said.

'Me too.'

Chapter Thirty-Nine

'So,' Nick said, once he and Amy were home and Amy had gone up to her room to tidy it, which actually meant play on her DS. 'What happened to you?'

He was leaning back against the kitchen cupboards and Maggie wondered again how her brother managed to be so comfortable in his own skin.

'We should go and sit down,' Maggie said, heading for the conservatory.

'Oh god,' Nick said. 'Do I need a drink? Have you got wine?'

'It's four thirty!'

'So?'

Maggie stopped in the doorway. Actually a glass of wine sounded pretty good.

'And can I just say,' Nick continued, 'how lucky you were that I was over here anyway, cos if I'd been in Liverpool I never would have got over fast enough.'

'I knew you were,' Maggie said, pulling a bottle of red out of the wine rack. 'You told me you had a job in Heswall.'

'Oh,' Nick said. 'Yeah. Well. Good memory.'

'I'm just going to come out with it,' Maggie said, once they were both in the conservatory with their wine.

'Go for it.'

'OK.' She stared down into her glass and then up at her brother. 'I've been seeing someone. A woman.'

'Woah,' Nick said, his eyes widening. 'I did not expect that.'

He gulped his wine. 'Shit, Mags. I'm the gay one.'

Maggie laughed. 'I know. But there can be more than one gay one. And I'm not gay.'

He leaned towards her, glancing over his shoulder to make sure Amy was nowhere near. 'Hate to break it to you, but if you're having sex with a woman you're at least bi.'

'I know, god. I just haven't, I don't know, labelled it yet? I just like her. The one woman. Not, like, all women.'

'I don't like all men, Mags, that's not how it works.'

'I know, god. I'm freaking out, Nick! Stop being a smart-arse for five minutes.'

'I'm sorry.' He grinned, and then put his hand over his mouth. 'I am, really. I know I don't look it.'

'You're a dick.'

'So, who is she?'

Once Maggie had finished telling him everything she could think of about Sofia, he said, 'You are so smitten.'

'Shut up.'

'This is amazing. So is this the first time? Or have you been having lesbian affairs for years and never told me?' He drank some more wine. 'Mum's going to die, by the way. This will kill her.'

Maggie snorted with laughter. 'Can you even imagine. Yeah, that's not happening. Remember Vicky Morgan? At school?'

'Princess Di hair? Massive feet?'

Maggie rolled her eyes. 'That's the one. I used to stay over at her house every Friday and we did some stuff.'

'Bloody hell. I had no idea.'

'Why would you?'

'You knew when I was getting off with Stephen Shaw.'

'Everyone knew when you were getting off with Stephen Shaw. You practically hired a sky writer.'

'He was so hot though. He works in Sainsbury's now. I see him sometimes when I'm at Mum's. He pretends not to see me though.'

'Vicky tried to add me on Facebook a couple of years ago. I didn't accept.'

'Afraid all the old feelings would come flooding back?'

'No. I don't know. Maybe.'

Nick stared at her, his face serious for once. 'Why didn't you ever talk to me about it?'

She shook her head. 'I don't know. I never really admitted it to myself. It's really hard to explain.'

'I mean, I get it. Obviously.'

'It's not like I was having all these feelings and repressing them. I feel like I repressed them practically before I had them, you know?'

'Mum?' Amy said from the doorway.

Maggie felt blood rush to her face and she looked helplessly at Nick, before saying, 'What's up?'

'Can I stay at Nick's tonight?'

Maggie blinked at her daughter.

'If you like. Why?'

'We get pancakes for breakfast. And he said he'd take me on the ferry.' She grinned at her uncle.

'Well I can't compete with that,' Maggie said. 'Go and get your stuff together then?'

'Done it already!' Amy said, turning to show the small rucksack on her back, a puppy's head poking out of the top.

'Let's get going then, Miss,' Nick said. He turned to Maggie: 'Will you be OK?'

Maggie nodded. 'I'll have a bath. I'll be fine.'

'Yeah,' Nick said. 'You will.' He dropped a kiss on her forehead before picking Amy up in a fireman's lift and running through the house while she squealed.

When Emma dropped Jools at home, Jools was surprised to find the house empty, but the French doors from the lounge wide open. She could hear the girls talking and giggling from the treehouse at the foot of the garden and see light bleeding out from between the planks. She'd texted Matt to tell her she was out with Emma, but not that they'd been at the hospital, not what had happened. She hated worrying him.

She felt a sharp pain in the side of her breast when she pulled herself up the ladder to the treehouse, but once she was inside it faded away.

'Mummy!' the girls shouted, all trying to grab her at once.

'Wow,' she said, looking around. 'Who did this?'

One side of the treehouse was piled with pillows and cushions. The other side was covered with a white screen on which Frozen was playing. The rafters were twined with fairy lights.

'Daddy made a cimena!' Eden shouted, her eyes wide.

Jools curled her hand around the back of her youngest daughters neck and tugged her close to press a kiss on her forehead.

'I gave Sofia the night off,' Matt said. 'She had some bad news.' He glanced at the girls, indicating that he would tell Jools later. And then his eyes flickered up to the top of her head and she realised she wasn't wearing a wig, she still had on the headscarf Eve had bought her. She hadn't even thought about it for hours. Her hand flew up and brushed over it, while she tried to think of how to explain it to the girls.

'Did you forget your hair?' Violet said, frowning at her mum.

'I did,' Jools said. 'Silly me.'

'I've seen it in your bathroom,' Eloise said.

Jools smothered a gasp with her hand, looking over at Matt, who was smiling gently at her. She had no idea the girls had known she'd been wearing a wig. She'd tried so hard to protect them.

'I like it,' Eloise said without looking away from the make-shift screen. 'It's like Elsa's.'

Jools laughed. 'It is a bit, yeah.' She crawled across the treehouse and squashed in next to her husband.

'You OK?' Matt whispered against her temple.

'Perfect,' Jools said.

When Emma got home, Ruby and Sam were in the garden, shrieking with laughter. Paul was sitting on one of the outdoor beanbags, beer in one hand, phone in the other. He smiled up at her.

'Want a beer?'

'I'll get it,' Emma said.

'You'll have to,' Paul said. 'Don't think I can get out of this bloody thing.'

'Mama!' Sam yelled, sliding down the slide and running across the garden to wrap his arms around her waist. She kissed the top of his sweaty head, tears pricking her eyes at the thought of Jools and what she could have lost, how scared she must have been.

'Daddy picked us up at school!' Sam yelled against her stomach.

Emma laughed. 'I know!'

'It was so cool,' Sam said. 'He played football.'

'Did he now?' Emma said, raising an eyebrow at Paul.

'Look, the ball came my way, what was I meant to do? Ignore it?'

Emma rolled her eyes.

'Did you have a good day?' she asked Sam.

Sam looked up at her, his cheeks pink, sweaty hair stuck to his forehead, freckles sprinkled across his nose and cheekbones. She loved him so much she could hardly stand it.

'It was so fun,' he said.

'Yeah?'

'Yes!' As Sam ran through everything he'd done at school that day – from helping with the teachers' chairs at the end of assembly, to having chocolate cake for lunch, to football with daddy at pick-up, Emma smiled over the top of his head at Paul, glancing over to see Ruby lying on her back on the lawn.

'Rubes?' Emma called out when Sam had finally finished his litany of school fun. 'You OK there?'

'Just watching the clouds,' Ruby called back.

'She told me she was going to 'medintate',' Paul said, smiling. 'Apparently Violet told her it will help her relax.'

Sam ran back to join his sister and Emma got herself a Coke and a beer for Paul. Back in the garden, she held out her hands and hauled her husband up out of the beanbag and pulled him towards her, wrapping her arms around his waist and pressing her forehead into his chest.

'Jools has got breast cancer,' she said quietly, making sure the children couldn't hear.

'I know,' Paul said into her hair. 'Matt told me.'

Emma tipped her head back to look up at her husband. 'When?'

'First time I met him.'

Emma could tell he was slightly nervous about telling her this. His eyes were cautious.

'Why didn't you tell me? I was such a bitch about Jools!'

'That's a bad word, Mama!' Sam shouted from the lawn.

'It's not,' Ruby argued. 'It just means lady dog.'

'That's not very nice,' Sam said.

'Sorry,' Emma called. She still had her arms around Paul. 'I feel awful.'

Paul kissed her on the forehead. 'You weren't to know.'

'But I judged her so much. For her hair and everything else. And she was just trying to keep it all together.'

'What if she hadn't been though,' Paul said. 'What if she was fine and she just did all that shit cos she liked it. It made her happy. Like Holly. What did you say she'd had done?'

'Micro dermabrasion,' Emma said. 'Even though she looked about sixteen anyway. You're right. We were talking about this at book club too. About judging women. Women's choices. I'm such a dickhead.'

'Mama!' Ruby yelled.

Paul squeezed Emma and pushed her away slightly, taking his new beer from her. 'You helped her out today. When she really needed you. That's more important than stuff you said about her eyebrows. Stop worrying about it.'

Emma swigged her Coke. She hadn't realised how thirsty she was. She'd only had one sad plastic cup of coffee in the hospital and then her decaf Starbucks had gone cold.

'I can't believe you knew,' she said.

'I wanted to tell you,' Paul said. 'If that helps at all.'

Emma drank some more and then said, 'Eh.' But she was smiling.

Maggie had not long been out of the bath when she heard the doorbell. She was going to ignore it – she was wearing a dressing gown and no make-up, her hair curling damp around her shoulders – but she assumed it was Jim who'd forgotten his keys and so opened it.

It was Sofia.

'I'm sorry,' she said immediately. 'I shouldn't have come here.'

'What's wrong?' Maggie said, glancing out into the street. 'Has something happened?'

Sofia nodded. Her eyes were red and her hands were fluttering over each other as if she couldn't control them.

'Come in,' Maggie said. 'It's OK. Jim and Amy aren't here.'

Sofia nodded and stepped inside, following Maggie down the hall to the kitchen. Without asking, Maggie poured them both a glass of wine each. When Sofia took hers, Maggie could see her fingers were trembling.

'What's happened?' she asked. 'Are you OK?'

'My mother,' Sofia said. 'She was in an accident. Stupid. She was filling her lighter with . . . I don't know the word. Cigarette lighter. You put liquid . . .'

'I don't know,' Maggie said. 'Lighter fluid?'

Sofia shrugged. 'And she . . .' She made a flicking motion with her hand. 'And woof! On fire!'

'She set herself on fire?' Maggie said. 'Oh my god!'

Sofia nodded. 'So stupid. Always when she fills it up, we say it's dangerous and she say she knows not to . . .' She made the flicking motion again. 'And now see.'

'I'm so sorry,' Maggie said. 'Is she going to be OK?'

'Think yes. But she is burned. Her face and her hair. I have to go home.'

Maggie's stomach clenched, even as she said, 'Of course.'

She was being selfish. She knew she was infatuated and she knew she was embarrassing and she didn't even care. But she loved spending time with Sofia, had loved the afternoon they'd spent together, even the way it had ended. She knew she'd miss her.

'For how long?' Maggie asked.

'I don't know,' Sofia said. 'Maybe not long. But I have to go to see.'

'Of course you do,' Maggie said. 'You must be so worried.'

Sofia had drunk all of her wine and crossed the kitchen to put the glass down on the counter next to Maggie. Once her hands were empty, they started fluttering again.

'Hey,' Maggie said, reaching out for her hands. 'It's OK.'

'I'm sorry,' Sofia said again, slotting her fingers between Maggie's. 'I'll go. I know I shouldn't be here. I just wanted to see you.'

'It's OK,' Maggie said. 'Honestly. Jim's out. He's probably with Eve. I don't care.' She pulled on Sofia's hand, tugging her closer, and Sofia came easily, pressing up against Maggie and tucking her head into the side of her neck.

'This afternoon was so good,' Maggie said into her hair.

Sofia huffed out a laugh. 'I can't believe we fell asleep. I run to the school so fast I couldn't even breathe.'

'I told my brother about you,' Maggie said, pushing one hand up into the back of Sofia's hair and curling it around her fist.

Sofia tipped her head back and looked at her. 'Yeah?'

'He was fine about it. Surprised. But he wants me to be happy, so . . .'

'That's nice,' Sofia said. She glanced back towards the kitchen door, before pressing her mouth to Maggie's.

'Is this OK?'

Maggie shook her head. 'We probably shouldn't.'

'No,' Sofia agreed.

Maggie remembered the day Jim had pressed her up against the cabinets and she'd desperately tried to think of a way out of sleeping with him. It seemed like so long ago. So much had happened. She had to tell him about Sofia. She had to tell him their marriage was over. They couldn't carry on the way they had been doing. It wasn't fair to anyone, just because Maggie wasn't brave enough to—

Sofia slipped one hand inside Maggie's dressing gown, running her fingers along her ribs. Maggie moaned, pulling her closer.

'We really can't,' Maggie said. 'I don't know when he'll be back and—'

'I know. I'm sorry. You just look so—' She kissed the side of Maggie's neck, her hand sliding up her ribs to curl over her breast.

'God,' Maggie said. 'Sofia.'

She wanted to slide down to the floor and pull Sofia down with her. But Jim could be back at any time. And also the tiles were cold. Maybe the conservatory? Except that was very slightly overlooked by the neighbours and—

Sofia had pushed the robe off one of Maggie's shoulder and was kissing down her collarbone and chest, her hand moving round to the small of Maggie's back as her tongue curled around her nipple.

'Oh my god,' Maggie said, squeezing her eyes shut and her legs together. 'Oh my god.'

Maggie didn't hear the car pull up. She didn't even hear the front door open. The first thing she heard was a snort from Jim, followed by "I don't fucking believe this."

Maggie had been slumped against the kitchen units, one of Sofia's hands still on her breast, the other between her legs. She pushed at Sofia's shoulders a little and watched her stagger back, saw the fear on her face. She didn't know what to say. To either of them. She pulled her robe back up over her shoulder, held it tight across her torso.

'Where's Amy?' Jim said, his voice cold.

'Staying with Nick.' She forced herself to look at him and the expression on his face made Maggie's breath catch in her chest. He hated her. He'd spent years yelling at her, putting her down, shagging around, and now that she'd found happiness with someone else, he hated her.

'Well that's something, I suppose,' he said, crossing the room. Maggie and Sofia both flinched. 'I'd hate our daughter to know what you are.'

He picked up Amy's pebble picture and threw it against the wall. The frame cracked, the glass smashed, and the pebbles skittered across the tile floor.

Chapter Forty

Two weeks later

Ruby had been determined to get her Hilbre project done before Easter and luckily for her, there had been a prolonged period of warm, dry weather. Rain was forecast for the following week and so the women had arranged to finally get together to make the walk over to the islands, kids in tow.

'I think the tide's coming in,' Emma said, frowning.

As they walked towards the island, she could see water curling around it. It was only a narrow channel, but it was getting wider, and, she thought, running faster.

'It's just a channel, I think,' Maggie said. 'We can step over it. Or splash through it.'

Ruby and Sam had run on ahead with Yahya, Flora, Amy and Jools's daughters, all of them shrieking with laughter and splashing each other. Sam was still holding the bucket and spade he'd refused to put down since he'd got up that morning.

Emma looked back over her shoulder towards the beach. They'd been walking for about half an hour now and while it didn't look too far away, it certainly looked too far to turn back before the tide came in. The beach was still busy though – dogs and children running, people playing frisbee, and couples strolling, so it certainly didn't look like anyone was concerned. She was almost certainly worrying about nothing.

'Is there anything to do when we get there?' she asked Maggie, to distract herself.

'I don't think so?' Maggie said. 'I know there're seals. Otherwise I think it's just nature? And we've all brought food, right?'

'Yep,' Emma said. She had a cool bag stuffed with crisps, sandwiches, and other random crap the kids had insisted she bring.

Ruby and Sam came running back, skidding to a stop just in front of Emma, sand flying.

'Can we go in the water?' Ruby asked. Her hair was falling out of its ponytail and her eyes were bright, cheeks pink.

'No,' Emma said automatically, but immediately felt guilty when Ruby's face fell.

'Why not?' She stamped her foot, showering Emma legs with sand.

'Because I don't think it's safe,' Emma said. 'If you look you can see the water coming round and—'

'I think it's OK,' Jools interrupted. 'These channels run round all the time, they're pretty shallow. I was just about to suggest my girls go and have a bit of a splash.' She turned to her daughters. 'Looks like fun, right?'

'But then they'll be wet when they get there—' Emma started.

'But you brought a change of clothes, didn't you?' Beth said.

Emma remembered that, yes, she had. So it should be fine. It was only water. It didn't need to be a big deal.

'OK,' she told Ruby. 'But be careful! And look after your brother!' The last part was shouted since Ruby and Sam had already run away towards the channel.

'I don't even know why I said no,' Emma murmured to Hanan who was closest. 'It just came out. It's only water, right? What's the big deal?'

'It's hard,' Hanan said. 'I know. You want to keep them safe.'

'I just don't like the way the water's coming round,' Emma said. 'I wasn't expecting it. I thought it was just sand all the way.'

'It's always a bit wet,' Jools said. 'That's why we said to wear wellies.'

Jools was, of course, wearing a pair of Hunters which Emma knew – from seeing them in *Grazia* – cost a hundred quid. Emma's wellies were a tenner from Primark and her socks had wriggled down and bunched at her toes within thirty seconds of them setting off.

Ahead, the children were sitting in the channel, howling with laughter and splashing each other. Emma watched as Ruby scooped up a handful of mud and dumped it on Sam's head. Sam laughed so hard he fell over backwards.

'I don't know how we're even going to get them clean,' Emma said.

'It's only sand,' Beth said. 'It'll brush off. They'll scream, but still.'

Jools's two oldest girls were jumping in the water and shrieking with laughter. Emma gasped as Eden kicked an arc of water over Ruby's head, waiting for Ruby to wail or scream, but instead she laughed, turning to Flora and pulling her down in the water at her side.

'When we were back in London she would've flipped out about that,' Emma said to no one in particular.

'Getting soaked's a bit different in London though,' Hanan said, bumping Emma with her shoulder. 'She's a lovely girl.'

'It's done her so much good being friends with the girls,' Emma said. 'She's much more relaxed than she was at the start of school.' Emma shook her head. 'I feel awful even saying that. An eight-year-old shouldn't be anything other than relaxed!'

'There's a lot of pressure on them at school though,' Hanan said. 'Don't beat yourself up about it.'

'And Flora couldn't give a toss,' Beth said. 'So she might've passed some of that on. You'll be sorry when she fails her SATs.' She grinned.

'Oh she's not that relaxed,' Emma said.

It was only when the women reached the channel that Emma realised just how deep the water had got. Sam was still sitting down and it was up to his chest. The girls were standing now and letting the water ebb around them, sucking their feet down into the mud. Emma felt another flicker of fear.

'Should it be this deep? Really?'

'I don't—' Maggie started.

'It definitely wasn't this deep last time we came,' Jools interrupted. 'Are you sure you got the times right?'

Maggie nodded, 'I checked and double-checked.' She pulled her phone out of her pocket and then shrieked as it slipped through her fingers and splashed into the water.

'Fuck!'

All the children looked up, Amy's eyes were wide with something that looked, to Emma, like fear.

'It's OK,' Maggie reassured her daughter.

'Is it broken?' Amy asked, reaching for Maggie's free hand.

'It might be OK once it dries out,' Maggie said. 'Don't worry about it.' She dipped her head to drop a kiss on her daughter's wet and sandy hair. 'And we're nearly there!' she said brightly. 'Picnic soon.'

'I'm starving!' Sam yelled, rolling over in the water.

'Can you get out now, sweetheart?' Emma asked. 'We need to keep walking.'

Out of the corner of her eye, Emma could see more water curling around the island. The channel was probably four times wider than when Emma had first noticed it and also as deep.

'How much longer?' Emma asked.

'Fifteen minutes maybe?' Jools said.

Emma shuddered as freezing water washed over the top of her wellies. She looked over her shoulder at the beach which now looked very far away. People and dogs, she reassured herself. People walking like everything was fine. No one seemed to be panicking or setting off flares. Although she wasn't convinced she'd be able to tell if they were.

Just a few minutes later the water had reached knee-level on the women, who were speaking to the children in bright 'everything's going to be fine' voices.

'Sam, can you jump on my back?' Emma said, squatting slightly and shuddering as the cold water splashed over the backs of her thighs. Beth took the cool bag from Emma.

Ruby – eyes wide and face serious – said, 'Are we going to drown?'

'Don't be silly.' Emma forced herself to laugh. 'We're almost there. It's just a bit deeper than we were expecting, that's all.

Sam clambered onto Emma's back, cold and wet and covered with sand, he immediately wrapped both arms around her neck.

'Let go a little, sweetheart. You're strangling me.' She started walking again, looking over at Hanan, who had already been carrying Mo in a backpack carrier. The water was sloshing around his feet.

'Just keep putting one foot in front of the other,' Hanan said. 'We're almost there.'

Emma watched Jools wince as she picked Eden up, but she shifted her to her hip, reached for Violet's hand and kept walking, as she told Eloise to hold onto her sister.

'Do you want Beth to take her?' Emma asked Jools quietly.

Jools gave her a tight smile. 'Thanks. But I'm OK.'

'I'm sure I got the times right,' Maggie said again. She'd also picked Amy up and had her on her back, the rucksack she'd been carrying hanging from her front.

'It doesn't matter now,' Emma said. 'Just keep walking.'

They ploughed on and no one spoke. Even the children were quiet. When Emma looked over at Jools, her face looked pinched and pale but she kept walking, the water sloshing around her. They'd almost reached the rocks when Hanan slipped and shrieked, falling down onto her knees in the water. Emma reached her hand out and tried to plant her own feet more firmly while Hanan struggled back to standing. Mo had burst into tears the second the water hit him and was now howling.

'Almost there,' Emma told Hanan. 'You're OK.'

Hanan squeezed her hand, but then Emma had to let go to keep hold of Sam, who was sliding down her back with every couple of steps.

When Emma finally felt rock under her feet rather than sand, she could have cheered.

They all stayed silent until they got up to the rocks and were able to put their children down. Ruby immediately burst into tears and Emma hugged her while Sam said, 'Why are you crying? I didn't know we were going to swim. Do we have to do that when we go home too?'

Fifteen minutes later, the children were wrapped in towels and eating satsumas that Jools had brought, grinning at each other with orange segments in front of their teeth, and not giving any indication of being traumatised by the journey.

'How long before the tide goes out again?' Beth asked. She was only wearing a T-shirt and she shivered against the cool breeze.

'I think it's five hours,' Maggie said.

'So we're stuck here for five hours?'

'Does anyone have a working phone?' Jools said, dropping her own back into her soaked bag. 'I need to call Matt.'

'We need to call the lifeboat, more like,' Beth said. 'We can't stay here for five hours!'

'They won't come out for this,' Hanan told her. 'People do this all the time. You can either walk here and back at low tide or walk out at low and then wait out the high tide.'

'Mine should be OK,' Emma said. She'd put it in the top pocket of her jacket so it shouldn't have got wet. 'Shit,' she said, taking it out. 'It's on five per cent. How?'

As she opened her texts to message Paul, she noticed the percentage had dropped to two, and as soon as she started typing it died.

'Shit,' she said again. 'It's dead. Is that it? None of us has got a working phone?'

'You saw me drop mine,' Maggie said. 'I just can't believe I got the times wrong.'

'Stop saying that!' Jools said, her voice shrill. 'Obviously you did or we wouldn't be in this fucking mess.'

'Jesus, what is the matter with you?' Maggie hissed, glancing over to make sure the children were otherwise engaged and not listening. 'We're all stuck here, not just you. It's only five hours, I think you can spare that from your busy schedule. Or did you have an important hair or eyelash appointment this afternoon?'

'Maggie,' Emma said, a warning in her voice.

'No, I'm sick of this. She thinks she's better than all of us, just because she's married to a footballer? What an incredible achievement.'

'I'm sorry,' Jools said, her voice small. She slumped down to sit on the sand, putting her head in her hands. 'I didn't mean to be—' She looked up. 'I've got breast cancer. So I know Matt will be worried. I just wanted to let him know . . .'

'Oh my god,' Maggie said, dropping down next to her and curling an arm around her shoulder. 'I'm so sorry. I had no idea.'

'That's because I didn't want anyone to know.' Jools gave her a small smile. 'I was trying to control it like I try to control everything.'

Maggie shook her head. 'You don't. I'm sorry. I shouldn't have said any of those things.'

'It doesn't matter,' Jools said. 'Honestly.'

Hanan crouched down next to Jools and held out a cup of tea from a flask.

'Oh my god,' Jools said. 'You're an angel. Thank you!'

'That's the only cup I brought,' Hanan said. 'So we'll all have to share I'm afraid.'

'That's OK,' Jools said. 'Cancer's not contagious.'

'Oh my god!' Maggie said, laughing.

'Too soon?' Jools smiled.

The breeze died down and the children ran off to play in the grass, dropping the damp towels in the sand behind them. Emma picked them up, shook them as hard as she could, and handed them to the other women.

'They're a bit damp and gross, but they should help a bit.'

Beth had been rummaging through Emma's cool bag, checking what food they had for the next five hours, and she suddenly shouted, 'Emma, you beauty!'

'What?'

'There's matches in here!'

'Oh right. Last time we used it we had a disposable barbecue,' Emma said. 'Anyone know how to make a fire?'

'I do,' Jools said. 'I think. I mean, I used to. I was in the Guides.'

'I can't imagine you in the Guides,' Beth said. 'I never went, but I was a Brownie.'

'Me too,' Emma said. 'Pixie Seconder.'

'Pixie Sixer!' Jools said. And then added 'Sorry.'

'I was an Imp Seconder for about a week,' Maggie said. 'And then they did away with the Imps cos there weren't enough of us. Story of my life.'

'*I Was An Imp Seconder: the Maggie Marshall Story*,' Emma said and everyone laughed.

The women collected a good pile of sticks and Jools arranged them into a pyramid, poking smaller sticks in between. She curled her hands around the matchbox as she struck the match and dropped it into the centre, sheltering the whole thing with her body.

'Did it work?' Beth asked, leaning over to look.

'Give it a second,' Jools said.

They all watched, transfixed, as the flame caught and appeared to run along to the twigs, which started to smoke before suddenly flaring.

'Well done!' Emma said.

Jools smiled. 'I'm amazed that worked, actually. Haven't done it for years'

Later, when the children were back and everyone was gathered around the fire, eating crisps and passing Hanan's tea around like it was some sort of ceremony, Jools said, 'I can't believe I'm going to say this, but I'm almost happy we got stranded.'

Emma laughed. 'I wouldn't go that far. But this is nice.'

She watched the shadows cast by the fire playing over Ruby's face. Ruby's sand-encrusted, dirty face. Her hair, that Emma had fastened into two plaits that morning, had mostly come undone and was damp and curling, strands stuck to her cheeks. She wanted to squeeze her.

As the day went on, the wind died down and they were warm enough in the sun. The children investigated the island

– there was much excitement when they spotted seals lounging on the rocks on the far side – while the women took turns to watch the children, and the rest of them sat around talking or just soaking up the sun.

They talked about Jools's cancer, Emma's loneliness when she'd first moved up from London. They talked about their husbands and their children and how they all worried they drank too much wine. They talked about homework and their husband's jobs and how they felt guilty for not working, but guilty when they considered working. They talked about how almost all the parents at the school gates were women, how the shops and cafés and playgrounds were full of women.

'I sometimes look around and think *where are all the men*?' Emma said. 'You know?'

'They're at work,' Beth said.

'But you'd think some of them would want to be at home with the children, wouldn't you,' Emma said. 'Even for a little while. I wouldn't have felt bad about working if Paul had been home.'

'You probably would have done,' Jools said. 'Mums learn to feel bad about everything, really early. Before you're even pregnant. I couldn't choke down those massive folic acid tablets and got told off at every appointment.'

'The way I look at it,' Hanan said – she'd taken her hijab off and her hair hung down her back, shiny and smooth and then tangled and sandy at the ends – 'Is that people are going to judge you no matter what you do. So you might as well just do what you want.'

'God,' Beth said. 'I wish we had wine. Cos I would like to drink to that.'

'We should promise to try not to do it to each other,' Jools said. 'Any more.'

'Like, take a blood oath?' Maggie said, laughing.

The sun was lower in the pink-streaked sky and it was starting to get chilly again. The women had shuffled closer to the fire and each other.

'Maybe we should just remember this,' Emma said. 'All of it.'

And they would.

Epilogue

Emma wiggled her bare toes into the sand as she watched Ruby and Sam chase Buddy through the puddles left by last night's long hoped-for rain. The summer had been hot and oppressive, the constantly open windows filling the house with kamikaze flies and drowsy wasps, the children stripped down to their underwear, yet still clammy and complaining. And it had still been the best summer Emma could remember.

The school year had ended with both Ruby and Sam taking part in the assembly – Ruby presenting her project about Hilbre Island, which had started out as a study of the nature on the island and ended up as a much-needed demonstration of tidal safety and wilderness survival tips. Sam had sung one line in a song about friendship, his hand clutching Yahya's on one side and Miss McCarry's on the other. When Emma thought back to that first meeting with Sam's teacher, she was so proud she could burst. Instead she'd cried so much that a mum she didn't know had passed her a tissue from further down the row.

Paul's bonus for successfully completing the Matt Jackson signing had allowed them a long weekend at Disneyland Paris where the children had eaten too much candyfloss and popcorn and had their photos taken with every Disney Princess and animal character they could find. It had been exhausting, but joyful, and when they'd asked Sam what his favourite part was, he'd said the big fish in the river, so possibly also completely pointless. Perfect.

After Disneyland, when the weather was hot but still tolerable, they'd started meeting the other families on the beach each morning. The children played together, while the women sat on towels and talked and ministered to the smaller kids. Hanan and Jools had become particularly close when one of Hanan's oldest friends back in Wakefield was diagnosed with breast cancer. Flic had turned up once to tell them she was moving away and then she was gone.

They'd started bringing pot luck picnics and bottles of wine, a tent for the little ones to sleep in the shade, disposable barbecues. The women – even Jools – had soon stopped wearing make-up, showering, brushing their hair. Emma had joked that it must be what living in a commune was like. Beth had suggested they buy a chicken or burn incense.

'Hey,' Paul said, coming up behind Emma and handing her the ice cream she'd asked for, before calling the kids over to collect theirs. 'What are you thinking about?'

Emma watched Ruby and Sam laughing as they raced towards their parents, Buddy barking, sand flying through the air behind the three of them. She bit the top off her ice cream and rested her hand on her burgeoning belly. She turned to smile at Paul, tanned and stubbly, looking about ten years younger than he had in London.

'How lucky we are,' she said.

Maggie wrapped the picture in tissue paper and placed it in the box on top of the others, before stuffing the spaces with newspaper and sealing the box with tape.

'Have you finished now?' Amy shouted from the living room.

Maggie carried the box to the front door and then went to join her daughter on the balcony.

'Yep.' She kissed the top of her head. 'All done.'

'Can we go to the beach?' Amy pointed. 'Ruby and Sam are there.'

Maggie squinted into the sunshine. She could just about make out the two children and their dog, and maybe Emma and Paul standing nearby, but that could be any two people.

'How did you spot them?' Maggie asked her daughter.

'Ruby's red wellies. And Buddy. Can we go?'

'You can't, sorry,' Maggie said. 'You're going out with Daddy this afternoon.'

Amy's face – almost completely covered in freckles thanks to the long, hot summer – broke into an enormous smile. 'I forgot!'

'I thought so,' Maggie said. 'Even though I've told you – ooh – about twenty times.'

When she and Amy had moved out of the house and gone to stay with Maggie's parents, she'd worried about Amy's relationship with her dad, but they seemed happy enough. Amy was always happy to see him – she spent every other Saturday with him – but she didn't want to stay in their old house now that Eve lived there, and she was always happy to come home to Maggie. It helped that all but five of her collection of puppies had stayed in the old house and Jim brought a different one – or so he said – with him each time.

Jim seemed a lot happier too, which had been a difficult thing for Maggie to process. She'd spent a while thinking of herself as the victim – of his moods, his temper, obviously of his affair with Eve – but she'd come to realise that she'd never fully invested in the marriage, had never even really been in love with him, and how unfair that had been to him. And also to herself, of course, but she was working on forgiving herself for that. And creating a whole new life. Renting the flat overlooking the marina, the beach and Victoria Gardens had been the second step. The first step had been leaving.

Sofia had decided to stay in Poland, at least for a while. Her mum's injuries had been worse than they first thought and she seemed to have contracted repeated infections. They'd Skyped a little at first, but not for a while. Maggie missed her,but she'd also realised – with the help of a counsellor – that Sofia had been something like an escape hatch. She'd helped Maggie understand herself better, but she hadn't been the answer. Maggie was starting to understand that no one was the answer. No, that wasn't right. She herself was the answer. She just had to keep working on the question.

Matt squeezed Jools's fingers where their hands were joined in his lap. Jools glanced at him and smiled, but then focused back on the doctor, willing the woman to say what Jools and Matt were so desperate to hear. Or, at the very least, not say the thing they dreaded.

The doctor smiled and said it was good to see them both, that they looked well.

'I love your hair,' she told Jools.

Jools ran her hand back over her head. Her hair had started to grow back, but it was completely different. Where it had always been smooth and – despite what many people seemed to think – naturally blonde, now it was light brown and swirling in soft curls. Matt loved it, running his hands over it constantly, as if she were a cat. Jools wasn't sure what she was going to do with it yet. Apparently the curls were 'chemo curls' and might not stay, but the colour brought out the hazel in her eyes, so she was going to wait and see. Also it meant that every time she looked in the mirror she was reminded of what she'd gone through, what she'd survived. She hoped.

'So,' the doctor said and looked down at her notes.

Matt squeezed Jools's hand again and she felt like her heart was squeezing in her chest. She tried to breathe. Whatever happened, it would be OK. They would be OK.

When the doctor looked back up she was smiling. 'There's no sign of cancer. Your bloods are clear.'

Jools gasped out a breath, followed by 'Oh my god.'

The doctor blurred in front of her eyes and then she was being pulled into Matt's arms, one of his hands – as was often the case lately – cradling the back of her head, fondling her hair.

'I love you so much,' Matt murmured in her ear. 'I'm so proud of you.'

Tears dripped off Jools's jaw and soaked into the shoulder of her husband's shirt.

'Fuck,' she said, into the side of his neck and he laughed.

'Obviously you'll need regular check-ups,' the doctor said, once Jools was upright again, Matt leaning into her side. 'But for now everything looks really, really good.'

Jools shook her head. 'Thank you. For everything.'

'It's my job,' the doctor said, but she was smiling.

'I got two bottles to start,' Emma said, pushing glasses across the large table. 'And a jug of juice for me and Hanan.'

She was huge now, with just a few weeks to go. All along she'd been so much bigger than with either of the other kids, as if her body recognised what was happening and just relaxed right into it.

'I need to tell you all something,' Maggie said, pouring the first glass and taking a sip. 'I was going to ask you last time we met, but I chickened out and then I had to just make myself do it before . . .' She took another sip. 'I invited Eve.'

'Holy shit,' Beth said. 'Are you going to beat her up?'

Maggie laughed. 'God. No. And she'd totally batter me. I just . . . we need to get on really. If she and Jim are going to stay together. And I thought it made more sense for her to come to book club where she knows everyone, not just me.'

Emma squeezed Maggie's arm. 'That's really nice of you.'

'Also if I hate her I can just get hammered,' Maggie said.

'You won't hate her,' Jools said. 'She can be a right cow sometimes, but her heart's in the right place. She was an amazing help when I was ill.'

I could have helped, Maggie thought, not for the first time. Over the past few months, she and Jools had talked about how and why their friendship had fallen apart. Jools had felt guilty knowing about Jim's extra-marital behaviour, Maggie had been insecure in her relationship and capabilities as a mother and had put too much pressure on Jools. In trying to control her cancer, Jools had tried to push away everything she couldn't control. They weren't yet back to the ease of their old relationship, but they were getting there.

'I've got an announcement too,' Hanan said, pausing until everyone was looking at her. 'I'm going back to work. In the shop. Well, the office at the shop.'

'Wow,' Emma said. 'What brought that on?'

'Mo's at nursery three days and I just want something else to do. And Hashim's not that good at the admin side of things so I've helped out a couple of times and it's just . . . I like it. It's nice to have something to shower for, you know?'

The other women laughed.

'I showered for this, obviously,' Hanan said.

'It makes me laugh when I think about when we all first met,' Emma said. 'I'd worry about what to wear and do my make-up and everything. I bought new clothes for Jools's book club!'

'Sorry,' Jools said, cringing. They often teased her with stories about how controlling and un-fun her old book club had been. They all knew and understood her reasons, but it was still fun to take the piss a little.

'And now you've all seen me at my worst,' Emma said.

'Some of us saw you at your worst at my book club,' Jools said, grinning.

'I was pregnant and I didn't know it!' Emma said, as she had so many times before. 'Hormones are a bastard!' She smiled around the table at her friends. 'Anyway, my point is that now I'm like, have I washed? Am I wearing a bra?'

'I'm not,' Maggie said.

'Our washer's broken,' Beth said. 'I'm wearing a swimsuit under this.'

The women all laughed.

'Bloody hell,' Emma said. 'What I'm trying to say is that I love and appreciate you all. I know we've had a bumpy road to get here. But I'm glad we're here.'

'And I'm glad we're picking our own books and not Jools's classics,' Beth said. 'I vote for *Fifty Shades*.'

'We are not reading *Fifty Shades*,' Maggie said, laughing. 'How many times do we have to have this conversation?'

'If that's what Beth picks,' Emma said. 'That's what we have to read.'

'Maybe we could have a few rules . . .' Jools joked, and the other women shouted her down.

'To the Bad Mothers' Book Club,' Emma said, raising her glass.

'To the Bad Mothers' Book Club,' Maggie, Jools, Beth and Hanan echoed, clinking their glasses together.

'May we one day actually read a book.'

Acknowledgements

Thanks to: Sam for giving me the opportunity to write this book and for mentioning Harry Styles in her off letter; My agent Hannah Sheppard for talking me up and down; Laura Gerrard for patient editing; My sister, Leanne, for tolerating my questions about cancer and treatment (and for, you know, not dying); Fatima Patel for answering my nosy questions, letting me nick her children's names, and for being one of the school mums who made the school run fun; Heather Jargus for the 3am deaths conversations; and Lindsay (surname redacted!) for the 'Pop-up Pirate' tip. As always, thanks and love to Harry and Joe for inspiration and distraction.